Ian S. Maloney':

is a time capsule, a Whitmanian ode to writing and old Brooklyn, all the way down to how to properly pronounce the Kosciuszko Bridge. It is also a love letter to its protagonist Jonah's larger-than-life father, Jimmy Bugs Fennell, a character as compelling as he is unpredictable, an artist of extermination. In a fascinating move, *South Brooklyn Exterminating* interweaves Jonah's early efforts to become a writer with his adventures in pest control, culminating in his decision to write about being an exterminator's son for a college process essay, his dad helping him find the thread. Maloney deftly explores the parallels between squirrel trapping and termite work and writing to remind us that penning an essay is also a way of working with one's hands, and extermination, too, an act of shrewd intellect—a tough calculus of death, taught by the incomparable Jimmy, a veritable professor of battling rats and finding roaches in teapots.

Caroline Hagood, author of *Weird Girls*

Ian S. Maloney

taps into the poetry and pathos around the glue traps, aerosol bombs, and shadowy scurrying inside the homebase of *South Brooklyn Exterminating*. What cannot be eradicated is the love between a father and a son, the larger-than-life Jimmy "Bugs" Fennel and the up-to-the-challenge schoolboy Jonah, their relationship tested and contested through bouts of terror and violence—along with onslaughts of unspeakable kindness. Here Maloney's Brooklyn comes to life in startling ways, funny and sad in equal measure, and readers will be engrossed by illuminating excursions into the crevices and hiding places where all families, especially the Fennels, take shelter. For as Jonah, our tender-hearted and tough narrator, says about his dad and his company, "South Brooklyn Exterminating takes on the world." And to our everlasting wonder, that is precisely what this resonant, powerful novel does again and again.

Joseph Di Prisco, New Literary Project;
Subway to California, The Pope of Brooklyn,
My Last Resume

Ian Maloney has written a book that is at once steeped in tradition and wholly original. A young man and his father. The forgotten hours and corridors of New York City, airports at three am and the back corridors of the halls of power and splendor. There are hints of Joyce and Selby and Yates in this prose. There is the violent orchestra of the American dream in these pages. South Brooklym Exterminating is the graceful debut of a true American stylist.

Charles Bock, NYT bestselling author of
Beautiful Children and *I Will Do Better*

Ian Maloney's *South Brooklyn Exterminating* immediately takes its place among the plain-spoken, hilarious, and heartbreaking classics of American working-class fiction. It's a book about many things: fathers and sons, husbands and wives, and the ways in which the need to always makes ends meet supersedes so much else in our lives. Also, it's about rats. Lots and lots of rats. Jesus Mary and Joseph, all the rats.

Ron Currie, author of *The One-Eyed Man*

South Brooklyn Exterminating is working class fiction at its finest—at once highly relatable, and illuminating, full of pathos, humor, and authenticity, with characters who walk off the page and experiences that feel lived.

   Jonathan Evison, author of *Again and Again*

In *South Brooklyn Exterminating*, Ian Maloney documents, in spare, crystalline prose, the complications of growing up and navigating through a working class family and that family's business. This is a moving story of youth with all its contradictions of loyalty and rebellion, connection and estrangement, courting freedom and danger at every turn. A stellar debut novel.

   Robert Lopez, author of *A Better Class Of People*

South Brooklyn Exterminating

Ian S. Maloney

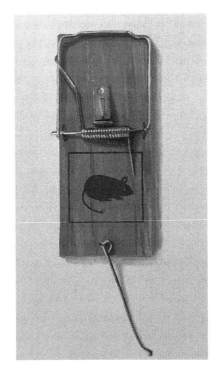

SPUYTEN DUYVIL

New York City

This is a work of fiction. Unless otherwise indicated, all the names, characters, businesses, places, events and incidents in this book are either the product of the author's imagination or used in a fictitious manner. Any resemblance to actual persons, living or dead, or actual events is purely coincidental.

© 2024 Ian S. Maloney
ISBN 978-1-959556-90-9
Cover art : Jen Maloney

Library of Congress Control Number: 2024936824

For Jim and Cathy Maloney.

With love, gratitude, and appreciation.

Night Plane

Dad woke me from a deep slumber. The call came in downstairs at 2:50 am. Never heard the phone ring. My head was covered in my Star Wars sheets, dreaming about playing baseball in space. I was seven years old, living in Marine Park, Brooklyn and tagging along as an exterminating assistant with my dad, Jimmy "Bugs" Fennell. His footsteps creaked across the parquet floors upstairs and a light tap followed on my bedroom door.

"Jonah, *Jonah*. Up for an adventure for a few bucks?"

"Now? What time is it? Where?"

"It's almost three. Kennedy called. We've got a plane to do coming in from Singapore. Got to get it right away, since it's going to be a fast turnaround."

I groaned a little, then hopped out of bed and pulled on my jeans. You always had to wear jeans, Dad said, even in summer. I found my blue and orange Mets cap on the floor to cover my greasy brown hair and scrounged around my laundry piles to find a less smelly t-shirt. An orange OP one with a blue and pink wave was close, so I started to put it on.

"Hey, wear your shirt with your name on it. Got it? We want to look the part out there. None of this hobo crap. All right?"

"Right. I forgot."

I continued the search for a golf shirt. It was Dad's thing: wear the company shirts, always wear pants, need to have a belt on. A workingman's list to follow. Down in my laundry basket, there was a light blue shirt with my name on one side and a lighthouse emblazoned across the right chest. Image from Coney Island Light and it had South Brooklyn Exterminating, Co. below it. I had a couple of these in different colors. After a quick sniff of the armpit, I fitted it over my head. Never got what a lighthouse had to do with what we did, but it was on all the shirts so we looked "the part" and "put together" in Dad's words. Dad said Mom came up with the name when they bought the company, since she collected miniature lighthouses and was into dollhouses. Still never clicked what this had to with exterminating rats and roaches in New York City, but it was our company. My mom, Casey, was in the next room asleep. Merry, my sister, was curled up next to her.

A Northwest Orient plane came in with roaches from Asia a short time ago, Dad said. That's where we were headed. Dad walked down the steps and laced up his blackened work boots at the front door. He picked up his sprayer and box and stuffed his route book into his jeans and his flashlight into its holster. I followed him sleepily to the car. He shifted away the receipts and map books on the front seat and I sat atop a pile of McDonald's, Taco Bell and Arby wrappers, scattered with some glue traps with driving directions and customer phone numbers penned across them.

An Egyptian pharaoh statue, maybe Osiris, was taped to the dashboard of the truck, alongside a great pyramid and Anubis. Dad collected pieces since his first date with Mom, a date at the Brooklyn Museum, where he impressed her with his Egyptian facts and folklore. He built a few Egyptian models in his spare time with me, when we weren't doing planes, tanks, or ships.

Dad started the car and lit up a Pall Mall. He took a long pull from the butt and stretched back into his seat. Never used his seatbelt. Not once. He looked at me for a moment, as I was busy buckling my belt into a sea of papers where it was buried. Toll receipts were stuffed into the seats. Cigarette ashes dusted the consoles, and the car smelled like a full ashtray needing a quick dump into the trash and a run through a few car washes, followed by some long ventilation. Paper was piled in the passenger's feet well for safekeeping. Gas receipts hung from the sun visor above my head. Three dog-eared paperback horror novels—two of them Stephen King—were stuffed between the seats. The shiny silver cover of *The Shining* still gave me the creeps, but I'd still pick it up when Dad wasn't looking. Behind me in the backseat was a combination of liquid poisons, bait bricks and spraying and fogging equipment. Hazmat flags, foggers, squirrel cages, a pellet and shotgun were scattered in the back of the cab.

We pulled out of the spot and drove slowly down toward Gerritsen Avenue. The car rolled on toward Knapp Street before banking down past the water sewage treatment plant to the Belt Parkway. The smell choked you on warm summer nights—the smell of processed sewage drifting north, pushed by the sea winds of Rockaway.

The Golden Gate Motel sat at the crossroads of the highway, right before the end of the road and the turn west to Sheepshead Bay. We went there for the weekend baseball card shows, but Dad said it was a place for druggies, hookers and one-night stands.

"That place, geez, the whores couldn't be worse and they don't change the sheets for a month. No wonder you see such skells coming out of there. Drugs and hookers. Can't believe they keep that shithole open. Golden Gate, my ass. More like the Golden Clap."

He laughed and I nodded and shifted in my seat. I hated these discussions but didn't ask questions. I stared straight ahead, nodded, and kept my eyes to the side of the road. I imagined other things to talk about. These kinds of Dad statements were often followed by a retelling of his early years, traveling across the country in a 1957 Chevy called *Color me Dead*, and hanging out in LA with lots of drugs, alcohol, and women. I'd heard all of them. Mom seemed to have been the saint who saved him from himself. Whatever that meant.

"Forgot to tell you," I said. "I organized all the '54 cards into number order. That way we can see which ones we're missing."

"Nice work. Keep them safe, kiddo. That's going to be worth something to you or *your* kids, someday. I'm telling you."

"I know it. Ted Williams, twice. Ernie Banks. Al Kaline. Hank Aaron. Duke Snider…"

"Some of the greats. You picked up which one for us last week?"

"Cal Hogue. Pitcher on the Pirates."

"Right. Keeping an eye out for those commons. We're getting closer and every card counts. Imagine your nanny tossed all of those out when I left for California?"

"Crazy. What was she thinking?"

"Nobody knew back then. Where you keeping it safe?"

"Keeping it in the chest at the foot of my bed."

"Good. We're going to finish. Going to get it done. Mark my words."

We were collecting the first baseball card set Dad remembered. 1954 Topps. 250 cards. He was right around my age when it came out. We chipped away at it every few weeks. He splurged on the Aaron rookie a few weeks back. According to my counts, we were 44 cards from finishing it.

"Maybe we'll catch a game at Shea this homestand? I

was thinking that some time we head out and see a few other stadiums. You know, around the country. Drive out and see what's it like out there."

"Sounds different. But, how far would we go? Just me and you?"

"Of course. Merry and Mom wouldn't be up for that. And we take our time. Maybe a few stadiums one year. Few the next. Plan it out right. Hell, we can start easily by heading up to Fenway one weekend. Easy drive. Plus, it's a good way to see what the country is like. Catch games. See how beautiful things can be as you get away from the city."

"Lot of driving, I guess. But that might be cool to see. Our city is nice, though."

"It's not everything. Lot of opportunities out there. Lot of things to see. Keep looking to the horizon. See as much of things as you can. I never regretted that trip cross country."

We merged on to the Belt Parkway with a dark sky shimmering with stars out over the bay. It was quiet and the water was still as glass. Our headlights pierced the common shore reeds and we headed east toward Kennedy. Two cars streamed ahead of us on the highway heading out towards Long Island, like they were weaving through Endor in *Return of the Jedi*. Dad pointed up to the night sky. Before us I saw the channel leading out to the sea and the lights of the Marine Park Bridge spanning the water out to Rockaway. Years ago, Dad rescued a man by jumping off that bridge. A drunk fisherman's boat had capsized and Dad ditched his fishing pole to jump in and save his life. He glanced at the bridge now and kept his eyes on the road. It was now named for his hero, the immortal Gil Hodges. Hodges once lived a few streets from us in Brooklyn. Dad bitched about Hodges not being in the Hall of Fame and how he brought the Mets a championship in 1969. We never mentioned Walter O'Malley in any conversation.

The road was peaceful and empty. Dad smoked a cigarette and let the blue smoke curl out the window and into the warm air outside. My eyes stared at the green interior lights in the console of the truck, and then I looked out the side window, watching the sand dunes of Plum Beach and then the inlets off the Belt Parkway pass in the dark. The shrubbery blocked the water from my eyes, until we drove across bridges. Then I saw the moonlight shining down into the water before me, casting flickers of light across the currents of shimmering water out there in the channels. Dad and I said little more on the drive. The wind blew through the windows and we drove in the slow lane all the way out to the airport. Occasionally a car zipped by us going 85 miles an hour, but it was no matter to us. We were making our way out there on our time.

"What're we handling?"

"Plane came from the Orient. Singapore, some shit place before that. Apparently they got roaches somewhere along the way. Crew was bitching about it, pilots bitching about it, everyone bitching about it, so that's where we get into the picture."

"How do bugs get on the plane?"

"Not uncommon. Figure planes have food and people, right?"

"Yeah, of course."

"Well, then they are going to have bugs. Bugs stowaway on the packages of food trays, people's bags and things. Sometimes they come in on people's coat pockets, for Christ's sake."

"That's pretty gross. Carrying bugs in your clothes and bags?"

"Never know who's getting on a plane and from where, you know? Hell, a year or two ago, a plane had a stowaway rat running around. Damn things always find a way in. That's what keeps me in business and you in toys and baseball cards."

I imagined bugs and rats hopping flights across the world. Jet-setting insects and vermin were flying friendly skies, maybe even setting up new families in South America, Asia, or Africa.

Along the Belt, we made our way to the airport, a vehicle stuffed to the brim with writing, receipts, and death traps, with a steady trail of blue smoke drifting out the driver side window. I closed my eyes for a few minutes before arrival.

We parked close to the Northwest terminal and gathered our materials from the back. I carried a light black box with a gas mask and some replacement cartridges in it. There was a box of aerosol cans in there. The bombs clanged in the box. Our job was to smoke the pests out of the plane and clear it out for tomorrow's travels. We walked toward the terminal, clattering our gear. The building had a faint, ghostly glimmer with the darkened skies behind it, a sea of black with only the roaring sounds of jet engines. A couple of yellow cabs waited for passengers with their lights on in front of the glowing building. A young man waited with a green military duffel bag out front, waiting for some family member to come take him home. I watched him as I passed, and he gave me as short nod and wave. I nodded at him as we walked by.

Dad's work belt was loaded with flashlight, screwdriver and hammer, and a Leatherman knife. In the back of his jeans, he stuffed disposable glue traps into the waist of his pants. His service book was folded into the front pocket of his jeans. In one arm he carried the bombs; in the other he held the silver canister of poison tightly in his fist. Security guards waved to us as we made our way to a deserted corner of the terminal. Sweepers scoured the floors with mops and buffing machines. One worker had his feet up near a counter, his eyes opening and shutting at whim, with his arms folded across his blue blazer with the company insignia.

I was behind Dad, struggling with the discomfort of the box in my hands. The handle dug into my palm, and I adjusted it and set it down several times. Put the box down, shake out the hand and pick it back up.

"Need a hand, Jonah?"

"I got this. I can carry my stuff."

Dad punched in a code on a keypad and we entered an off-limits area. In a room down a long corridor, we spoke briefly with a man holding a logbook. Dad flashed a security badge. The guy wrote down our names and the time into his book, and he told us where the plane was on the field. We walked the corridor toward the airstrip. I stifled my yawns and my limbs pushed on beyond the burn. Dad seemed to have the strength of four men. He just kept going forward.

Out there on the tarmac I paused. Baggage handlers drove carts to the terminal. In the distance, a man with two yellow batons guided a jet plane out of the terminal and toward the runway. He was wearing protective ear guards and eye goggles, and he looked as if he should be roving around Tattooeen or flying out of Mos Eisley with the Millenium Falcon. I half-expected a land cruiser to whiz past me on the darkened field. Lights on the airstrip streamed and blinked in the distance. I was far behind my father, scanning the scene before me, soaking in the images spinning around me.

Dad walked towards the plane, parked a hundred yards from the terminal building. I jogged along to catch up. We climbed the metal platform steps to an adjoining causeway. Dad placed the boxes down in the walkway, entered the plane and called out to see if there was anyone else aboard. I stared out a small window just in time to see a jumbo 747 streak down a roadway in the night and lift off the ground. The jet climbed and dipped out over the channels. Soon, it was far beyond the marshlands and out of sight. Dad never paid much attention to these things. His hazel eyes were on business ahead. He looked at our boxes and counted the bombs in his head. My eyes peered over the plane, inside and out. I took note of each bolt and the color of the Northwest Orient insignia in red on the outside. I stared at this long tube of metal and screws and paint and its idle engines and wondered where it had been. The faint rumblings of jets surrounded us. An American Airlines plane was idling, not too far away from us. The motor hummed like it just needed time to unwind before the next takeoff.

The plane was empty and the coast was clear. I was free to roam and Dad gave me the captain's go-ahead. He looked me in the eye and motioned me into the plane with a tilt of his head. I ran in and made a quick right turn to the aisle. Straight through first class, I went, running and pumping my arms up and down like an Olympic sprinter. My hands tapped the seats of every aisle, one after another, all the way to the tail of the plane. In the tail, I looked back and saw Dad watching me. I went through the small kitchen in the tail, and then right back up the other side. Dad laughed as I stopped at the front of the plane.

"Was that the two-hundred meters?"

"Possibly."

He laughed and walked toward the cockpit. "Can you believe someone knows how to handle this thing and what all these blinking lights actually mean?"

"So cool. How do they figure all this stuff out? Must take a while to get all of this down."

"Over here is where the navigator sits with the charts and radar. The co-pilot sits right over there." He motioned to the seats before us and I sat down in the pilot's seat.

"Where are we off to, kiddo?"

"Let's go to Europe first. Then, we can dip down into Africa, and continue on to Asia."

"You got it. Prepare for takeoff."

"Cleared for takeoff."

"Roger that. Who knows where we'll end up, right?"

I stared at the blinking, off-limit space. The numbers and the meters created a dizzying kaleidoscope pattern. I scanned the intricate panel of gauges and odometers and fuel level meters and blinking lights, looking for speed and height and placed my hands gingerly on the wheel before me. Dad stayed with me for a moment or two. He was behind me playing navigator for a second, giving me coordinate numbers to adjust the path of my flight. After a minute of pretend, he was up and out of the cabin. My fingers were on the steering wheel, holding it firmly and daring not to turn the wheel off course. The course was set, dead ahead. I stared out the cockpit windows at the New York terminal to the right and the endless sequence of planes coming and going out in the night to my left. I was a captain of a huge jet liner, glancing over an endless pattern of muted green and red lights, signs of altitude and velocity, direction and wing-flap adjustments. I closed my eyes and allowed for take-off to occur down that runway, soaring far out into the night sky, leaving New York behind me in the distance.

For a few minutes, I replayed Luke Skywalker staring over Han Solo's shoulder in *Star Wars*, asking him about the flashing lights and claiming he wasn't a bad pilot himself. I wanted to be both of them, but there was no way to give up Jedi powers just to fly the Millenium Falcon. Dad could be Han Solo on this mission.

Dad walked down the aisle of the plane to work. He pumped his silver sprayer with the gold handle with swift, short strokes. It was like a good blaster. His work boots pressed and dragged against the carpeted floors.

Then, there were the familiar sounds of the spray being sprung out of the pinhole nozzle and into the crevices of the plane. I looked down the aisle and saw Dad adjusting the nozzle head. He was turning the tip of the sprayer to fan-spray. The carpets were getting a light coat of chemical.

I drifted back into my imaginary captain's seat. The clouds filtered past my window. Below, I saw vast cities of the world in miniature. Great walls, mighty bridges, huge canyons, deep seas, and long stretching plains to eternities. Mountain ranges kissed the sky and high above the stars twinkled and the moon beamed a round orb of white.

Dad reentered with a couple of bags of peanuts. He tossed both to me and told me to save him one. He handed me two sets of plastic captain's wings he found in the stewardess's station. There, I clipped my wings on to my shirt. The smell of dispensed jet fuel filled my nostrils, and I loved it. I thought about where life would take me. I imagined soaring planes jetting to exotic destinations. I too could soar anywhere, be anything. Dad was somewhere in the plane, opening latches and kneeling and looking under cabinets. I was far away from him up in the front, flying the jet across the oceans, encountering turbulence and preparing for a smooth emergency landing and using the force to negotiate any imperial entanglements in my way.

After a few minutes, I walked to the back of the plane.

"Need me to do anything now? Happy to help, if I can."

"You've done all you can do for me. Coming along and keeping me company and lugging the crap is the job. Hang back for a few more and then you can help me set up the canisters."

Dad walked with a smile on his face, and I ran back to the cockpit again. Motionless flight was magic. My jet soared off again, out over the marshlands of my home. We banked sharply, seeing tiny cars streaming along the Belt Parkway to Brooklyn and Long Island. Then we caught a glimpse of the Manhattan skyline in the moonlight. The blinking red lights of the Twin Towers tapped a secret code into the dark and the Empire State building was bathed in white floodlights. In my pilot's seat, I landed in a jungle airport of South America to play Indiana Jones and then was off to the deserts of Cairo to find the lost Ark of the Covenant. I already knew what my Halloween costume would be that year, and I needed a real whip to make it complete. Mom would never approve, but Dad probably could be convinced.

In a few minutes, Dad finished spraying. The bombs had to be placed up and down the aisles and across the small kitchens in the belly and rear of the plane.

"Let's put the bombs out, Jonah. Then, you can sit with the gear outside when I start to set them off."

"I can help you set them off. No problem."

"No way. One mask, and you don't need to be breathing in this shit."

I strode back to the cockpit for one more moment to take a final glance out the windows. I grew a little sad, wondering if we were ever coming back for night service like this again. It was possible it would end. Someday it would. We'd lose the account, no longer have to come out for these things. It was the nature of the beast, part of the job; someone was always out there waiting to grab what was yours. Dad told me this all the time on the road.

I held on to each gadget as it was and copied every color of the blinking light to memory. A jet was taxiing into the terminal a few hundred feet away. It landed out there in the darkness with the blinking lights not more than ten minutes ago. I wondered who was flying in over my house at 4 a.m. What were they carrying with them? What dreams did they have, unbuckling their lap belts and reaching for their carry-on bags above their heads? A few hours ago, there were people on this plane I was playing in. Their suitcases were tossed down conveyor belts and their luggage spun around a winding carousel. In the terminal, next to me, they grabbed their gear and darted off in the waiting yellow cabs. Some were greeted with hugs and kisses by waiting relatives; some carried darker things, like a family death, as they got their bags. Now it was all just empty seats.

Out on the runway, in the dark, another set of travelers were readying for liftoff over the Atlantic. Some were heading out of town on business, or vacation, or family visitations. I imagined people like me, hurling into the sky with fresh wings for adventure, to see new sights and sounds and smells. Off into the clouds, they went hoping to see stars on their ascent and a last glimpse of their home down below. They'd see the calm ripples of the bay waters below them and the postcard image of the sleeping city off in the distance. They'd return to this place with memories, things they had to do. The coming and going, the lifting-off and the touching downs buzzed through my mind like bees entering and leaving a hive. I heard engines and wheels spinning and the bells of the cabin going on and off, telling passengers to buckle up for bumpy rides or touching down with the harsh push of the flaps forcing the air to slow everything down to a stop.

The plane was now saturated with chemicals. I smelled the pyrethroid, and it was time to depart. I felt myself coming back down to the ground from far away. I took a final glimpse at the control panel and captain's seat, and then I went to the docking area, opening up cardboard cartons of aerosol bombs. We worked quickly, a box of bombs in our hands, on either side of the passenger aisles, placing the canisters down every ten feet. When we met in the tail of the plane, Dad motioned for me to get out. He tilted his head forward and took the box from my hands. I walked up to the front and looked back when I got to the hatchway door.

Dad fitted his gas mask across his face in the plane's tail, pulling it through his dark black hair. He refitted the South Brooklyn Exterminating baseball cap on his head. I saw him, breathing air through the charcoal cartridge circles. His glasses shined in the cabin light with the plastic protective gear over his face. He looked like a Storm Trooper there, checking the Falcon for Han Solo and Luke Skywalker. Then, the subtle hissing began. The vapor drifted up towards the top of the cabin and my dad was covered in it. He held an open canister; he pointed the nozzle towards the open cabinets in the air kitchen. Steam and haze followed my father forward; a chorus of hisses echoed through the plane. He motioned me away from the door with his hand, willing me back down to the stairs. I watched from the crevice of the door. My body was pushed up against the connecting walkway with my eyes peering through the slat near the door hinge. My hand was on the fuselage of the jet. Dad was in a fog of insecticide as the aerosol cans filled the tight compartment, soon to be sealed.

In that doorway, I watched Dad work up and down both aisles, like a conductor setting off a chorus symphony of poisonous hissing snakes. He screamed me away with a violent expletive through the mask and a backward thrust of his arm, like a punch. I backed off and started down the stairs. He followed close behind, slammed the hatchway and sealed it. He looked into the black box, fished out a **Poison: Keep Out** sign with a skull and crossbones emblazoned on it, and taped it with some electrical tape to the door. We gathered the gear and Dad unstrapped the mask from his face. I smelled the traces of the fumigant on him, and it made me sneeze twice before we walked back to the underground in the terminal and headed back the way we came in. The mask was on top of the boxes. I stared at it for a bit.

"Let's hope that does it. Don't want to be back doing that tomorrow."

"It's cool thinking about all the places it will be."

"Certainly true. Think about all the places you'll be. All open for the taking. Keep working hard for it. And don't forget what you've had to work for."

"I won't."

"Someday you might miss even these night trips. Never know where things may take us, right?"

"You always say that."

"Hell, I always think what might be next down the road. Maybe not doing this forever. Lot out there to explore. Different opportunities. Back to school, even."

"Yuck."

"You say that now. But imagine killing these things forever. Sometimes school looks a lot better from where I'm standing."

We stowed the boxes and sprayers in the trunk. I climbed back into my navigator seat and before we turned out of the lot, I was drifting off to sleep. My head rested on the window ledge, opened up a crack for fresh summer air. Dad's truck wove through the looping roads of the airport, until we merged onto the Belt Parkway. By the time we reached the highway, I was almost asleep. Dad had his eyes on the road ahead. He hummed 1950s tunes along with CBS FM and tapped his fingers on the steering wheel. A lit cigarette hung from his mouth, and he spit thick saliva out his driver's side window into the wind whipping off the shore.

I awoke and cracked my window a little more and closed my eyes again. I thought of planes and airports around the globe. Dad's smoke drifted out the window, and he coughed and spit more phlegm out on the road. The faint glimmer of morning light was still a distant dream over the bay and shoreline along the Belt Parkway, as we drove home skirting the curved land along the highway over sea and marsh. In the driver's seat my father pushed his head, muscles, and bones home to bed, past exhaustion, and I piloted a jet plane somewhere over the Pacific Ocean, imagining I was a rebel Jedi in search of some lost treasure I had to find, somewhere out in the universe ahead of me in the darkness.

Office on a Dead-End Street

The office was on a dead-end street in south Brooklyn, right off Coney Island. The building had light brown shingles, and it was next to an oil truck depot yard. Two cars were out front. And the oil trucks were waiting for fill-ups. The Wonder Wheel spun in circles. The Cyclone rolled up its rickety wooden tracks. The ocean pounded against the shore. People were headed to the aquarium, where I wanted to be, all to watch the Beluga whales dive and surface in their tanks.

We were there when it happened. Merry was rolling her chair over the hard plastic that was over the shag brown carpet. She spun the chair in circles and held Strawberry Shortcake and Orange Blossom in her hands. I had my baseball glove and tennis ball, under my arm, waiting to bang the ball against the side of the office. We were hoping for a trip to the aquarium, followed by Nathan's hotdogs with mustard and sauerkraut.

The smell of cigarettes and must hung in the air. I peered into the next room, and my aunt Theresa and uncle Owen were with my mom. They were pulling out white receipts—they had green figures on them, like men and horses dancing to finishing lines.

Piles of tickets came from the drawers. Owen was shaking his head and patting my father's back. He walked in circles and spoke in whispers. Theresa's eyes were fixed on the calculator before her. She was an accountant in Manhattan. Papers were handed from uncle to aunt, and then I heard the calculator numbers, the same machine I played with to fill time in that office. She kept hitting the return button, again and again. I saw the white ribbon rolled in a bunch next to her. Mom was chain-smoking Kools and staring out the office window. Dad paced the room like a caged animal.

Merry was still rolling and spinning her chair on the hard plastic, singing a song from *Annie*. A loud fan blew hot air in our faces in the front room where the secretary was supposed to sit.

And then came the muffled sound of my father. The words like a chant, a private hymn. "Fuck me, fuck me, fuck me." He repeated the phrase like a madman praying for the end to come. He banged his fists, elbows, and feet into the desk and walls.

"We'll shutter it. Declare bankruptcy. You had no idea that he was doing this to you! We'll get out of this." Mom said.

"Motherfucker charged hookers, helicopters, and how many fucking horses that never crossed the damn finished line for Christ's sake, and who's the fucking asshole now holding the bag? Me, biggest dumb fuck on the entire planet! That's who!! That cocksucker gets to drive into the back of a garbage truck and it's all left for me to clean up his shit."

Dad punched the brown metal filing cabinets. He rocked them back and forth until they almost toppled. Uncle Owen stopped him and Dad was crying on my mom's shoulder. His veins burst from his neck like the Hulk's.

Nothing was being done. That's what I could hear. Taxes left. Supplies bills unopened. Dad passed them nightly going to his desk, but he focused on the route board, hung neatly on the brown plywood wall with Catholic school handwriting in red marker. Even I knew that was the case. He hated that paperwork crap, hated anything to with being in an office. Always did. Focused on what he had to do and trusted others to do the same. That didn't seem to be happening.

"No way I'm walking away from this shit now. Not on account of that motherfucker. It's the only fucking thing we have. This is it. Either this or the fucking house goes. All goes. I'm working this fucking thing back if it's the last goddamn thing I do! They'll have to pry my dead fucking fingers from this, if that's what needs doing."

The adults in the other room looked at each other and stayed quiet. I looked at Merry and knew she was listening.

Dad wanted to walk away. He said it on routes to me. Sell the business. Cut back and consult. Go to school. Maybe teach history. Read lots of books. Seemed like that's what he wanted and that wasn't going to happen now.

Merry stopped swiveling her chair. Her song was over. She gathered her drawing pad and pens and put them in her Strawberry Shortcake backpack.

"I think we should go out front and play something, Jonah. Think we're going to the aquarium and Nathan's anymore?"

"I think we should get the hell out of here."

"You cursed! I'm going to tell Mom."

"I think that's the least of our problems, Mer, least of our problems."

MODELS

In the basement of our green house in Marine Park, an industrial green carpet was laid with beige and black patterned lines. A fisherman's net was cast from the drop ceiling and a harpoon was anchored on the wall, next to an oar slung atop two industrial hooks. Bookshelves and cubby holes were built into the wall, constructed out of pine and cedar. It looked like a honeycomb. A couch was placed before a television entertainment center. The flower printed cover of red roses and green vines was worn away. Its pillows were depressed and its springs sagged in the middle. The threadbare fabric had black grease stains on it and cigarette burn holes. Ashes accumulated in the crevices of the couch. The nautical coffee table was strewn with glasses, bowls, cups, and magazines.

All of this was right next to the new makeshift office for dad's company, South Brooklyn Exterminating, and the brown cabinets separated the sleeping space from the office. In the back of his basement, a tool room grew with drills, hammers, saws, and screwdrivers. He stacked some of his traps and gear here as well. Then, model airplanes and ships started to follow. Row after row of model packages grew down there like weeds. Every week a few more ships and planes came into the house in plain brown paper bags.

Our weekly routine was this: Dad came home and handed dollhouse furniture to my mom and sister. Mom carried it to her space in the dining room, and then Dad and I went to work on building models in the basement. Every Friday we did this after dad's hospital work. I imagined what it was like to be a soldier, a sailor, a pilot in every object Dad handed me. My favorite one was a battleship, Yamato, which had Japanese directions, and we'd probably never open to build.

We worked past my bedtime. Dad had a fluorescent bulb overhead, which never needed changing. It burned day and night in the toolroom for years. He then had a bright lamp on his workbench to peer into the small crevices of plastic models. He had a set of paints lined up before him. There was a scalpel and tweezers arranged on the countertop. A coffee can collected his paintbrushes.

Underneath the workbench was a small collection of dusty bottles in various colors. Magazines were stacked next to the bottles. On the cold grey floor, bolts and screws were strewn about. Kitchen cabinets lined the wall of the tool room. They came down after our house remodeling. Inside the detached cabinets were plenty of spaces for children to squeeze into and play. When Dad was working, I came down here and dreamed about a place of my own inside the white cabinets, next to the workbench and circular saw. I thought about Fridays, Dad entering with models to build and stack and the time after work we'd spend together downstairs. Women stayed upstairs in the dollhouse dining room; men descended into the cellar to build models.

Dad's hands were always calloused and leathery when he walked in. They were black with grime and nicked with blood and needed to be washed with scalding hot water, Lava soap, and a bristly scrub brush. He didn't use gloves in the field, said he couldn't feel what he was doing with them. The wire mesh he fitted into roof holes to prevent squirrels from nesting was done bare-handed.

When he came in tonight, I ran to the medicine cabinet in our bathroom and pulled out Batman super-hero Band-Aids to place over his open cuts. He patted my head, and he never opened the bandage packages. He handed the packages to my mom and handed us two brownies from the hospital kitchen. They were gooey, topped with walnuts.

We ate the desserts, wrapped tightly in hot cellophane before the television. Mom and Dad were talking in the kitchen in low whispers. Faint, strange sounds, almost like whimpering, came from the kitchen. A few minutes later, Mom came with her dollhouse package and said that I should join her and Merry in the dining room.

"Why can't I go with Dad? I don't want to do dollhouse stuff. I wanna be with Dad!!"

"Give your father a little time, Jonah. Ok? For me? At least give him a half hour or so, got it? He's had a rough day at Sloan Kettering. Ok?"

"This isn't fair. I don't want to watch dollhouse stuff. It's ridiculous and stupid!"

"You're stupid!" Merry said.

"Stop, stop, both of you. Dad needs to handle a couple of things before you join him, all right? No big deal."

"Fine, but I'm staying here with my guys."

"Well, we wouldn't want those dumb Yodas, or Skwalkers, or Chewbaccas here anyway!"

"Whatever Merry, whatever."

I sat on the floor with my Star Wars action figures, refusing to join them. Every few minutes I asked to run down into dad's basement. I buzzed the house with Luke's X-Wing fighter, taking aim at Mom and Merry's houses. Lando, Han, and Chewie were in the Falcon. Han had Hoth gear on this time. Yoda trained Luke on the coffee table in the Dagoba system.

Merry and Mom opened the new packages and moved the figures from room to room. Tonight, they were hanging tiny curtains in the Victorian mansion. Merry moved the fake cat and dog around, from room to room. Mom strung up the new curtains and put the other ones away for safekeeping. I continued to attack the houses like they were Death Stars. Mom relented after forty-five minutes.

I went downstairs quietly. A Rangers game was on TV. Intermittent hisses came from the radiators and creaks from the old pipes. The faint smell of mildew mixed with the lingering odor of cigarette smoke. Dust clung to the glass of his entertainment center and his endless shelves of books, papers, and devices. Dad slept on a couch down there, said he needed the TV to sleep.

Dad wore blue jeans and construction boots every day of his life. They were in a ball on his couch, and his monogrammed work shirts hung from the pipes above—button-up shirts in different solid colors, *South Brooklyn Exterminating* emblazoned across their left pockets. His right pocket was always filled with a pack of cigarettes, a few toll receipts, and a Parker pen. His chemical-stained, hardened and muddied work boots were cast off under the coffee table. A faint chemical odor, perhaps a pyrethroid, permeated the air. The carpet was wet under the table from the periodic floods that crept through the seams of the house. A forest of mold and mushrooms grew in the recesses behind the oversized furniture. Wires hung from the ceiling; there were circles in the ceiling tiles, from where the radiator upstairs had leaked, and seeped its way below. In the office area, the light of the answering machine was blinking 3. Dad had yellow handwritten route cards in a wooden cubbyhole. A dry erase board, hung with fishing wire, swayed in space from the ceiling. Using blue and red markers, and neat Catholic-school handwriting, Dad wrote out his work days. His four-week schedule was printed there, from the Rockaway nursing homes to the racetracks, the Hunts Point market in the Bronx, out to insurance offices in Long Island. There was a steady, punctual rhythm to it. And yet, it missed the emergencies, return trips, special services, one-time stops, and countless favors.

When I entered the toolroom, Dad was bent down, working like a friar copying a sacred manuscript. His eyes were close to the table and he was dabbing glue on a plane's wing. He then swabbed the excess glue from the tail rudder and turned the decals into position on the plastic wings. My approach startled him.

"Hey, so how you doing, Jonah? Didn't hear you come down here. Pretty stealthy."

"I just didn't want to break your concentration, that's all."

"Thanks for that. Take a seat, buddy. Just needed a little time tonight, to get my head on straight. Tough day at the office, as they say." Dad pulled my stool closer to his. Before the workbench, there were two identical stools. In red and blue permanent marker, Dad wrote our full names on them. James J. Fennell. Jonah O. Fennell. The seat rocked back and forth and steadied as I climbed into it. He resumed his work.

"They're always tough, though, right? What you always say."

"That's true, boy, but sometimes certain things are a bit rougher than others, you know what I'm saying? Like different and difficult to get your head around."

"What happened today?"

"Well, I told your mom I wouldn't say it, but you can handle it. You're a man. Just don't open your mouth to Merry, all right? She doesn't need this shit so young. And no repeating it back to your mom, hear? Promise?"

"Sure, I won't say a word."

"Well, I've been seeing this little girl every week at Memorial for awhile. Not sure how long it goes back now. Probably a few months. She's been fighting cancer."

"That's terrible."

"Yeah, well, she's about your sister's age. Anyway, I've been popping in to see her every week. Bring her a Strawberry Shortcake figure, a brownie, usual stuff to brighten up things a bit, since she's going through all this shit."

"Which ones did you bring her?"

"What?"

"Which figures?"

"You're missing the…, I don't know, whatever ones I came across at Toys R Us really. I don't remember. That's not the point of the story."

"Oh, right. Makes sense, I guess. What's her name anyway? She getting better?"

Dad stopped talking and took a drink from the soda in front of him.

"Name was Carrie. And, no, not getting better. She didn't make it, Jonah, if you can believe that. What a fucking world, right? Around your sister's fucking age."

"Jesus. Sorry, Dad. It's awful. You ok?"

Dad drank a little more from the cup and tried to arrange some of his tools for the model tonight.

"That's why I needed a little time. Just difficult to swallow. The whole thing."

"Really sorry to hear that."

"Makes you think, that's all. Nothing is fucking guaranteed. Just seems fucked up that God would take a kid so young, so innocent."

"Not fair."

"Definitely not, but that's life, right? Shit sandwich sometimes. That's what you're served."

"I guess so."

"Ain't nothing you can do about it, either. Like my dad. I told you about him, right?"

I nodded and knew he would retell the story.

Dad reached for his lighter in a metal ashtray, caked with black soot, next to the workbench. Ashes and butts and wrappers were down in the reservoir, waiting for disposal. Dad filled his lighter with a blue and yellow can of Zippo every few days. It was silver and smooth to the touch, square in shape. The top flicked back and his finger clicked the igniter. The familiar click of the top, the flash of the butane, the glowing of his cigarette as the tip turned orange. He sucked the smoke into his lungs and spewed it all over me. A haze bathed me in a blue cloud, until I gasped for breath and brushed away the smoke.

"So, I used to work odd jobs here and there. We were living in Flatbush. Your nanny, Grandma, she used to work sewing baseballs in a factory. Then a chocolate factory. Cleaning houses. Anything she could to make ends meet. And then there was my father. Fennell, that's all she called him. Sonofabitch was a welder. Wicked motherfucker. He'd get his check and blow it all on booze, whores, ponies. You name it. Uncle Donny got out of there as soon as he could. And I tried to pitch in. Keep things working for the rest of us. Nanny was caring for seven of us before Aunt Rene and Donny left. A lot of shit to shoulder, especially with a thug like my father, coming home blasted, pushing her around, not coming back at all and disappearing for a few weeks."

I stared into my father's hazel eyes. He was back in the Flatbush house, and I knew the story he was about to relate.

"And you know what that prick did to me? His own son?"

I nodded and he continued.

"So, I'm working two jobs, saving up a couple of bucks to buy models and records. Be able to get some things on my own. You know, we didn't have shit. Nothing like the stuff you guys expect."

"I know, we're lucky."

"Damn right. Well, the old man comes home one day after an early toot at the bar. Starts digging around in my room, I guess, looking for smokes or cash, whatever. Sits

41

down in the chair and lights a cigar. Boom. Asshole falls asleep and burns down the fucking house. Whole, damn thing. Moron fell down the steps on the way out, too. Broke his leg, and then, then comes the best part! He tells the firemen that his long-haired loser son burned the place down. Imagine the balls? I punched him right in the face when I got home and would have dragged him down the street, if the firefighters didn't separate us. Lost my records, models, everything. Basically all the measly bits of crap I had, and he blamed me for the whole thing. I got the fuck out of there as soon as I could."

"That just stinks, Dad. I'm sorry you had to deal with that. That's when you went west to California?"

"It's all right boy. That was when I went out across the country. Shit makes us stronger, is the way I look at it. My dad wasn't worth shit, but I wasn't going to let him get away with crap like that by sitting around for more. Off to the coast. Only came back when the bum was long gone. Ghost of himself drinking ripple in the Bowery in the end. Disgrace."

"Yeah, he doesn't sound like a good person."

"He wasn't, but he taught me a lot of valuable lessons. And one of those is that life doesn't guarantee you anything. Really do have to work hard, prepare for the worst. What life always taught me."

He grew silent and drank a large gulp from the soda.

"Can I help you with anything tonight?"

"Of course. Why don't you go get some hot water from upstairs in a cup. Could use that in a bit for more decals."

I got the hot water in a few paper cups. Dad built the jet quietly. This one was almost done.

Once a model was completed and the air had dried the pieces together, we placed it carefully in an old glass display case. The case was stripped down with varnish and its bottom was lined with old wallpaper from my parents' first apartment. Tonight, Dad asked me to place the last decal into place. I peppered him with questions of what was next on the list.

"So, I say we try to do one of the submarines next."

"We'll see. I was thinking we tackle one of those tanks. God knows we're not ready for the Yamato."

"No, that's going to be epic. We won't get to that one for years."

"Probably right."

Models waiting to be built surrounded us, stacked everywhere. We had squadrons of jets and boats, tanks and trucks, ready for an impending imaginary battle. Sometimes, I imagined coming down there when Dad was away and flying the models around. They swerved through the space down below and were rearranged in the glass cases by my hand alone. Utmost care was taken not to damage a single wing, propeller, or wheel in my play. The models went back in the cases exactly as they were built and placed.

Dad had me handling the decals in the water. He set two small lids with water before me. Gingerly, I used the tweezers to dampen the stickers before placing them on the wing. My father watched patiently. The bullseye of the British warplane settled in its spot. My eyes were getting tired. To combat my drooping eyes, I reached for Dad's soda glass.

The liquid touched my lips and tasted strange. Dad's hand grabbed my arm and the glass spilled out of my hand on to the floor. His fingers pulled the glass from my palm and he yelled: "Jonah, you never ever grab a drink when you don't know what's in it! It could have been poison for all you know! Tears sprang to my eyes, as he released my arm. "But, I saw you drink it and I was thirsty."

His face was red and he just stared at me. I ran up the two flights to my room in tears, wondering what I had done wrong by sharing my father's strange-tasting soda. My mom and sister were asleep, and I never discussed it with them. A couple of weeks went by and we didn't build models anymore. I stayed away and watched the collection grow dust in stacks and on the shelves. I stared at them sometimes from inside the white cabinets where I hid.

WINDUPS

We left around 5:45 am that day. Marine Park was dark and asleep. Even the stray cats, raccoons and possums were out of sight. We packed our gear and drove toward Ocean Parkway. The truck passed row after row of single-family houses without a single light on. No one seemed up but us.

"No days off for us, huh, kiddo?"

"Guess not."

"At least we get the chance to see how the other half lives today."

"You mean the zombies?"

"City never shuts down and neither do we."

Our truck lumbered down Ocean Parkway, past Church to the Prospect Park Expressway. We weren't saying much. Billy Joel's Greatest Hits was playing on tape cassette and it was quiet outside. A couple of graffiti artists were spraying tags on the highway walls as we coasted by.

"Where are the fucking cops? Jesus. Should be nabbing those little bastards. Don't ever get caught up in that crap. Hear me?"

I shrugged my shoulders and nodded and checked out the large bubble letters taking shape on beige walls. They looked cool to me, even as the artists gave us obscene gestures as we passed.

"That shit may seem like nothing, but it's against the law, and then those fucks do that on store grates and private property. No end to it. Good way to wind up with an evening in jail, if you ask me. If I was a cop, I'd haul those little bastards in and stick the cans up their ass."

"Why do they do it? How come the cops let them get away with it?"

"Because the cops are strapped, running around after this guy and that. Everyone trying to get away with something for free, and no one works in this country anymore. Everyone's got a handout and looking for the easy way out. No one knows hard work anymore. That's the problem."

"But what does it really do? Mark turf? Respect? I don't get taking the risk."

"Maybe, more like every little shit like those punks giving the middle finger to doing what's right, you know? Everyone's got to see their name up in lights and paint. Like they're owed something, and they're all so goddamn special."

"Some of it looks kinda cool. I mean, not the same words everywhere, but the pictures and bubble letters."

"Yeah, real cool breaking the law and winding up with a record for spraying walls that are only going to get covered up anyway in the next week. And more money to keep painting the walls. More taxes for me."

We drove along, and I wondered why it mattered, either way. Must be a reason for it, must have been something to it. I had a book on cave paintings. It was really cool, learning about people happening upon these caves in France and Spain—didn't think Dad would see anything there, but he had given it to me so I took a shot.

"Dad, maybe drawing places is just what we do. I mean those awesome cave paintings you showed me with the buffalos, bears, horses, and cattle. No one knows what those things are there for. Maybe this is just the need to get something out there for people to take notice? Like when that artist in the cave left a hand print?"

"Are you fucking serious? Those cave paintings, I'm sure, were because those people were probably awed or scared shitless that they'd kill or be killed by those things. Maybe they killed them and the paintings captured their spirits. You think that crap has anything to do with those beautiful drawings?"

"Maybe it's just in the eye of the beholder. Maybe there's a reason, something we need. Maybe to be recognized some way?"

"Well, my smartass friend, this beholder says it's punk garbage and should be treated as such, and my opinion is the one that counts in this truck, right?"

"Right. Ok. Just trying to make a point and see the other side, that's all."

"Right, a wise-ass point. You'll make some lawyer someday."

"Maybe. Maybe a writer on walls."

"Watch it. A writer, fine. That's different. But you ain't writing on walls, ever. Sure you'll have plenty to say as a real writer."

He fiddled with the radio. The truck made its way through the tollbooths of the Battery Tunnel. Dad had a stack of tokens on the console and bought them in bulk. He wound up and pitched a strike into the basket and the coin popped right out onto the road.

"Goddamn it!"

"I think you went a little high and hard on that one."

"Ha. Yeah, well, I'm no Tom Terrific, that's for sure. Damn arm always gave me trouble."

Dad's arm had a zigzag across it. He broke his arm as a kid. Bone went right through the skin, and a metal pin held it in place. It looked like something out of Frankenstein, and it still bothered him. But, Dad often said it kept him out of Vietnam and filling a body bag in Asia. He said that every now and then, as if it was some miracle he was still here, as if he was always acting on borrowed time.

Dad opened the door and bent down to retrieve the coin. Some jackass behind us started to beep. This wasn't wise. A profanity tirade ensued. Dad motioned to his crotch. He flipped the guy the middle finger and then tossed the coin gingerly in the basket. This was common enough for us on the road. Dad was always ready to go to war with some fellow road-rage motorist. Usually you didn't see them this early, but this guy wanted no part of my father's incivility. He politely motioned back an "I'm sorry," and we were on our way into the Battery to Manhattan.

We drove under the Twin Towers, and I pressed my head to look up at them on the West Side Highway. Dad always had comments for people out along the highway at this hour once we were by the Towers. Degenerates. Trannies. Junkies. Winos. Prostitutes. Seemed to be a lot of them along the West Side at this hour of the morning.

"Nobody's working. Everyone's living it up. How it goes here in the Village. Wonder how the hell this place still exists."

"Yeah, a lot people out for so late, that's true."

"Imagine what kind of holes they're crawling into."

We made our way to midtown and parked the truck in the same garage on 43rd Street. Dad went to the back and gathered our requirements: sprayer, glue boards, rat poison pail, and windup trap. He handed me the trap and a box of glue board. Windups always were greasy. Often, I'd clean them off with a hose in the yard. Most of the time they lay scattered in the back of the truck with remnants of peanut butter in the bottom as a lure.

We walked to the New York Yacht Club. Some Queens' bars were on our other Saturday route. Richard greeted us from his station next to the massive doorway. He walked the halls singing opera arias and show tunes. He clicked his heels as he walked. Richard had curly salt and pepper hair in a perm; he wore gold-rimmed glasses on a neck chain, a red blazer, grey trousers and spit-polished black slip-on shoes with white tube socks.

Richard chatted with Dad at the front entrance about adult stuff related to the club, so I tuned it out, walked away. I practiced my baseball windup in the other room, imagining I was taking the mound at Shea for a save. I did this a lot. Walking out of the bullpen, I strode across the Shea outfield to take the ball and strike out some Braves. *Jonah Fennell takes the mound with two men on in the ninth and the Mets holding on to a one-run lead. Put up or shut up for the Mets closer.* I strode around the mound, looking up to the sky for inspiration from one of LaGuardia's jets passing over the stadium. I practiced my windup all the time. Sometimes I stared in and shook off a sign; other times I'd imagine some high chin heat and escalating tensions. I'd grab the toss back from the catcher and glare into the opposing hitter, knowing a curveball was about to come his way. The roar of the crowd hummed in my ears.

Dad caught me in windup mode and laughed. "Get him? Was that a slider, a curveball? I know it wasn't the heat with the break of the wrist."

"All right, all right. You got me…it was a curveball."

"I thought so. Next time, get em with a knuckler. That'll make him think twice."

I smirked and grabbed my gear. Richard walked in and sent us to the kitchen for freshly brewed coffee, cold glasses of milk and plates of cookies. The cookies were always macaroons and they were delicious. We ate our cookies, chewing off the soft tops of the macs and then eating the crusting bottoms. Richard joined us in the kitchen for a goblet of black Russian tea. He smoked a black skinny cigarette and stirred his tea with the end of a kitchen fork.

The model room next to the kitchen had cases of miniature model yachts and sailing trophies. The maroon carpets were thick with rich floral prints. Lights were always dimmed or out altogether. The centerpiece of the room was a vaulted fireplace, with an oil painting of two ships sailing over calm, rippling seas.

Dad and I ate and drank and strolled around the hall. The only light came from the brightly lit kitchen. Banners were hung from the mahogany walls. Sailing regatta photographs hung on the walls from years ago. Black and white pictures displayed in rich silver frames. Miniature replicas of Yacht club vessels sat in glass cases around the room. The oaken walls blended with the maroon carpeting. The room was always prepared for a cocktail party, for a regal celebration of victory, where a new trophy would be toasted and placed in among the cups and awards of the past. Large leather chairs were scattered around the room.

In a place of glory, alone in the corner of the dining hall was the Club's prized possession—an America's Cup in a case of its own. Dad walked toward it and then bent down underneath it to check a glue trap. I looked at the etching in the silver. It glistened, as if polished by staff on a daily basis.

"Can't beat this room, huh? The details of these models sure beat the ones we slave over. Look at those things. Like professionals build them or something. That would be some job. Model replica builder."

"These things could probably sail across a pond if need be."

"Funny you say that. You know there's a park in Paris where they do just that. Kids push the boats across the fountain to each other with sticks. Sturdy ones, I'm told. I've only seen pictures of it. Luxembourg, I think. You'll get there some day."

"That sounds like something to see. These things would probably hold up fine. Maybe we'll get there."

"Also read that Place de La Concorde over there has an Egyptian obelisk. Always wanted to see that too. Some ugly history in that spot, though. Executions."

"Guillotines???"

"You got it, my friend."

"Pretty awful."

"That it is, but that's how it goes. You should put those on your list of places to see, kiddo. Good, Bad, and the Ugly of Paris."

"I will. All of it. What were you talking about with Richard?"

"Mostly the usual crap. A few rumblings here and there, though. Lost the cup to the damn Aussies last time around. They'll get it back. Heard the keel was winged or something, whatever that means. 130 YEARS they had that thing…something like 25 challenges and still they held it. Some kind of crazy kangaroo intrigue to take it away."

"Doesn't sound right. I mean, but you got to lose sometimes, I guess."

"Not around here, according to some of the regulars. Not how it works."

"I guess there isn't much losing. Place is super cool, though. Wonder what it would be like to be a member here."

"Little over our paygrades, son, but not a bad dream. Think you might have to have a boat to sail in first, and we barely have a pot to piss in."

"Lights would be a start so we could see everything."

"Yeah, engineer's control panel is locked. Only us, right? Even the Yacht Club saves money when they have to. We've got flashlights to get us around."

I stared at the big shiny cup and wondered what it was like to race sailing ships on open seas. Pictures on the walls showed men in white shorts and some had billed captain caps. A bearded man wore his captain cap proudly. He had a blue blazer and white pants and he looked far removed from seaman duties. Lots of men with bronzed skin and white tennis shoes. It didn't fit with my distant comic books of the seas. I thought about *Treasure Island* and *Swiss Family Robinson,* about marooned families in intricate treehouse nooks and then stowaways climbing up the crow's nest, scaling up the rigging and working high atop the masts. The whaling ships at sea were searching for mighty white whales in *Moby-Dick* where the entire crew seemed a ragtag bunch of races from all around the world. My *Moby-Dick* comic was one of my favs. Dad said I'd eventually graduate to the novel, but that thing was massive and gathering dust in my room.

Sailors here were in ascots and white shorts. They weren't the dirty pirates I imagined, where cabin boys jumped into pickle and apple barrels to overhear plots to overthrow the crew. My favorite was still Iris Vinton's *Look Out for Pirates!* Captain Jim outsmarted an entire ship of pirates with just two in his crew. They even used beehives to get the pirates and steal their ship. Dad and I thought that was awesome. I'd probably read that a thousand times with him alone.

Dad and I did the place together. We wandered the labyrinthine basements in search of waterbugs and mice. Richard tipped us off to problem areas. He listened for the news from workers in the lockers and kitchens.

Dad always gave Richard some glue boards and roach stations for his apartment. We walked along the corridors down below the same way as always. I sprayed the walls. Put droplets of poison in the corners. I spritzed around the workers' lockers, making sure not to spray anyone's shoes stored beneath the compartments.

All was dull and predictable. Occasionally you'd find a water bug in the basement, scurrying to the corners for safe harbor. Today was no different, until we returned back to the ground floor. Richard was in the kitchen again. He was singing a song from *South Pacific*, badly off-key. *Gonna wash that man right out of my hair, and send him on his way…* He entered with a lit black cigarette and a half-empty tea goblet.

"I completely forgot to ask about mice in the banquet room. I did see our little friends the other night. Mickey and Minnie came to visit me as I walked around, so I clicked my heels like Cinderella and off they went back behind the paneling."

"Thanks for reminding me. We're going to get the flashlight and give a check in there in a few. I left a Ketchall in the fireplace last week. See if we got anything."

Richard shook when my father said this. The heebie-jeebies took hold of him and worked up his spine. He closed his eyes and started to walk away. "I'd rather not be there for that. Thank you very much. I will let you boys attend to that business on your own. Good luck, young man. Toodles."

"Yep, leave that to the working men, Rich. Catch up when we're finished."

He was off towards the front entrance with a glass cup of fresh, steaming Russian tea. He was again singing *South Pacific* off-tune, and I was stuck in the kitchen. I wasn't as fortunate. I left the remnants of my cold milk glass and walked behind Dad back into the darkened hall. Dad pulled out his black chargeable flashlight from the looped notch on his belt and shined the light toward the fireplace. His beams looked like dancing ghosts on the walls. The fireplace hadn't been used. I stared at the large painting above the fireplace—two ships at sea on calm waters, a serene mix of blues and greens. The ornate, carved-stone fireplace rose to the ceiling in curves and patterns. It was difficult seeing the figures in the dark. The room was warm and the windows were cloaked in heavy, dark curtains. Dad turned around and handed me the flashlight. My eyes darted around the room for a light switch, even though there wasn't one to be found.

Dad moved the metal grate and pointed to the trap in the far end of the fireplace well. "Shine the light on that for me, ok?"

I nodded, but then reared up and walked away. "Got to be a freaking light in here somewhere. I mean, why doesn't this room have any light?" I asked.

"I told you before and you know this. Light's

controlled at some engineer's panel we don't have access to. Come on. Come over here and shine the light for me for a second."

I walked over slowly and deliberately. I muttered about the light and flickered the flashlight on and off with my thumb. Dad bent down towards the trap, and a sound reverberated in his hands. I stopped dead, frozen like a statue.

"Look at that…" he said.

I didn't want to look, now or ever. A powerful jolt of revulsion surged through my body. It was involuntary. I wanted to run back into the lights of the kitchen and drink the small drops of milk in my glass and find more cookies. My face flushed like the crimson carpet. Cold sweat developed on my neck. Something was about to occur. I felt it deep within. Something awful was stirring inside. Something was alive in that trap in the fireplace.

Dad picked up the cage with his bare hands and it bounced around. The cage was greasy and dirty, as they all were—it had not been properly washed. The winding gears had a layer of black grease or dirt on it. The cage rattled back and forth in my father's calloused hands.

"Easy, fellas. Whoa."

"Fellas? More than one?"

"Two, it seems."

"What are you going to do?"

Mice were in there, real ones. Alive. Dad took the

flashlight from my hands and pointed the light through the holes of the metal cage. Two sets of black eyes glared back at me from inside the trap. Dad peered in at them. The bellies of the two mice were expanding and extinguishing air rapidly, panting and moving about frantically, realizing the end was near.

My mind was paralyzed with fear. *Why don't we just put it down, go back to the kitchen, and forget all about them here.*

The words ran through my brain like a skipping record. *Put it down, go back, forget them.* Again and again the phrase rolled through my mind. I didn't want them to die. They were Mickey and Minnie. They were scared. Finally, I blurted out, "Let's just put the cage down, go back to the kitchen and forget about them. I mean, what can we do. What can we do with them anyway?"

"What're you talking about, Jonah? We can't just leave them here for two weeks. They'll stink up the place something awful. That's all we need. And I'm not making a special midtown trip in three days to remove two rotting mouse corpses. You know how bad they are going to smell after a few days? You know the stench."

I did know it, all too well. And anything was better than that. But I also knew I didn't want to see it.

"Well, what are you going to do?"

"What do you think I'm going to do? I'm going to kill them. That's what. What we're here to do in the first place, remember?" Dad said, his own question answered, unfortunately.

Somehow death was abstract up until now. It was what we did, I knew. But it wasn't real. I sprayed and left poison, never saw it with my own eyes. Just spread the stuff here and there and took off. Death and dying occurred somewhere else, behind a wall, in a pipe or down in the underground caverns below. Wasn't part of my reality. It wasn't usually in my father's hands, inches away from me. But it was now.

"Dad, can't we just let them be? I mean, how are you getting rid of them, I mean, killing them anyway?"

"I'm going to open the top of the trap a smidge, then shut the lid on their heads and put them out of their misery."

I watched Dad fill a bucket to drown a rabid squirrel. He dropped the cage in a pail of water after we trapped it. That was pretty awful, and I walked back to the truck to avoid seeing it, really. No such luck here. Nowhere to go. My mind battered the ideas of drowning and smashing skulls around. Neither seemed to work. I paced the rug, searching the walls for something to focus on. Terror seized me. Panting stomachs of the mice were my only consideration, and I knew why we were there, finally. The milk and the coffee and the cookies weren't real. They didn't matter. These trophies and models weren't here for us to look at. We were there for things to die.

I stopped walking around and returned to my father's side.

It was time to be strong. I pushed the squeamish feelings down into my tummy and felt my body tense up. My body tightened as I clasped my hands into fighting fists. I was a team member. I was an exterminator, or the son of one, there to kill things, period. Being disgusted was unmanly. I pushed it all the way down, as I watched him slowly pull the top of the cage back a smidge. The fatal lid was about to break the necks of two mice. Every part of my brain and body prepared for death and I prayed to God for the mice to die quickly.

In a flash, two mice were out of the trap. They hopped on to the red carpet and scurried between my legs. I jumped and yelled out. "Whoa, Jesus Christ!"

Two mice scuttled toward the kitchen and down the stairs to the basement below and were gone from sight. My father laughed and I was panting with revulsion. My first words were a mixture of veiled machismo and relief: "Oh my god. So, what do we do? Go down after them and see where they went? Whew. Can't believe they got through that little slit in the opening. Yikes, they took off fast, huh? Right through my legs. Almost was able to stomp them with my sneakers."

My words were rapid fire. My stomach was in knots. My eyes were glistening in shock and relief.

Dad smiled, and he knew full well that my feet were

floating inches off the ground when those mice flew out of the cage. He sensed it and said nothing. He raised his index finger to his lips and shushed me. "I think you ought to consider the high jump, my friend. That was quite a leap. Not sure baseball is your sport, boy. Maybe the hurdles."

"I wasn't expecting that. That's for sure."

I giggled nervously and Dad smiled. I was still stuck on their escape—they got away! Out of the trap and down into the basement below. The scurrying mice frenzied my brain, and the image of them fleeing was set in my mind. Thank God, they were gone. It was over. Or so I thought.

Dad shrugged. He was secretly happy they were gone, too. I could tell. His movements suggested some get away and some don't, and that was all right. A sigh of relief came from my lungs. Tension drifted out of my limbs. I sensed he had let them escape for my sake. I was pretty sure he did. He was about to rewind the trap and replace it in the fireplace when he paused and looked down into the metal cage.

"Ah, check that out. There were three of them in there."

That phrase froze my soul. I walked toward Dad in a zombie trance and looked right into the basin of the metal wind-up trap. Dad was quite right. Three mice were in that trap. Two had escaped through my legs not more than thirty seconds ago. The third one was in the trap. He had become breakfast, lunch, or dinner for the other two. Carcass was there. I stared at it and couldn't look away. A bit of the tail lay curled in sight. Blood in the cage bottom was mixed in with the paws and some scraps of the head. The insides of the creature were eaten away, gnawed at with tiny razor teeth. That third mouse was considerably smaller than the other two. Death occurred right there in that fireplace, maybe the night before, maybe a few days before. I smelled faint whiffs of death, rotting flesh, coming from the bottom of the metal trap.

"That's how it works, I guess."

Dad walked the trap to the garbage pail in the kitchen, opened the lid and tapped the mouse remnants into the can. I followed him silently, as he went to the slop sink to clean and wipe down the trap.

"Bigger ones ganged up on and ate the smaller one. Cannibalized him in order not to starve to death in there. After a day or so more, two left would eat each other. Survival of the fittest, nature red in tooth and claw…"

As he strode back to replace the trap in the fireplace, he saw my face. The struggle inside that trap was on replay. I was the little mouse, about to be eaten by two other mice with beady black eyes, glaring at me from across the cage. The ending couldn't be changed. Yachting paraphernalia was visible through the slats in the metal. Glorious photos and cups kept getting further and further away. Smiles and sails and trophies gave way to squeals and squeaks of the little mouse. I tried to push the picture from my mind, but it was stuck on a loop. All hope lost. Two predators moving closer in close quarters. Fight was all that was left. Flight was lost. Trapped in a windup.

Dad sipped the last drops of his cold coffee, and I peered down into the garbage can for one last look at the carcass. Remains sat atop the glue traps we tossed in earlier on top of a slew of cans and cups and paper napkins and two used tea bags. No way for me to shake the image. The last bits of the tail, the missing midsection, where once the stomach hung close to the ground, and the eyes, open in death.

Dad didn't speak about it. He picked up the gear and walked toward the entrance, where Richard was on duty. He stayed silent about the mouse getaway. Richard wished us well and signed the service ticket with a large sweep of the pen. His signature looped all over the bottom of the page, a dramatic last dot atop the "i" in his first name. He was humming his song now and blurting out *And send him on his way* every now and then. I stayed quiet, stuck in a reverie all my own. We hit the street and Dad lit a Marlboro with his silver lighter. He sensed something stirring inside me.

"So what bothered you back there?"

"The mouse in the trap."

"What got to you?"

"I dunno. It's horrible. I mean, what a terrible way for anything to go…"

"Yeah, but that's how it works, Jonah. We're here to get rid of them. What we do, son. No one wants those things where they live or eat, right?"

"Guess I never really thought about it actually that much."

"Well, maybe you should. That's one of the reasons why I want you to come out with me. Want you to stay in school so you don't have to see and do this shit for a living. Maybe it's important to see this stuff sooner than later. Toughen you up."

"I'm tough. It's just that third one was….brutal, when you think about it."

"Life can be pretty brutal, kiddo. You know that. Not all games, toys, make believe and dreams. It's fucking cruel and nasty sometimes. Sooner you learn that, the better. Will wisen you up to a lot of things in life."

"Yeah, but even you have to admit that was really nasty. I mean…think about it. Imagine being trapped like that…no escape. Horrible."

"It's tough, you're right. No, it's *not* pleasant. But you see it all the time. That's life, pal. Sometimes that happens to people. You get stuck in tight circumstances, tough times, you never know what's possible. Sometimes those survival instincts kick in and people do some pretty horrific things as well."

"I can't imagine doing something like that. No way. There's got to be something that separates us from that…"

"Imagine you were starving, or if someone was trying to hurt you or someone you love—you can't always tell what you might do. Brains, book-learning, imagination… all great, don't get me wrong, but sometimes people just operate on animal instinct."

"Fight or flight, right?" *But with no flight chance in sight.*

"Exactly. Got to keep toughening you up, Brooklyn boy, if you're getting antsy about a dead mouse in a cage."

But it wasn't only the mouse in the cage.

"I guess so." I paused weighing the moment for a question. "Dad?"

"Yeah, son?"

"Ever feel pity for them? Regret killing things for a living? Does it ever get to you, what you have to do?"

"Rarely. Sometimes you think about it. But, I always come back to something. You don't want these things running around your house, where you eat and sleep. I mean these things are commensurable pests. They need to live and sleep alongside us. That's what mice and rats do. They survive off us and do it well. Hell, they're the second and third most successful damn mammals on the planet. Behind us, of course. But they carry disease, filth and excrement everywhere they go. You don't want to share space with these things, right?"

I didn't want to know what commensurable was. The mice lived with us, off us. That much was understood.

"No. I want to keep them out, get rid of them. I just don't want to think about killing them like that though, not like that."

"You just don't want to see it and think about it, that's all. It is not the most pleasant thing to do in life, but it serves a purpose, a real one. It may not be glorious, but the world needs what we do."

"Yeah, I know. I didn't want those mice to die in there."

"I know, Jonah. They didn't. They got away."

But the little one didn't.

I kept to myself as we drove out of the garage on to empty Manhattan streets. I closed my eyes, trying to shake away images of rotting mouse flesh in dirty silver cages. Dad smoked, letting the blue haze drench my clothes before billowing out of the rolled-down window. In the darkness of my eyelids, sailing cups disappeared into blackness. Sailing ships slalomed through buoys out in tranquil bays and then vanished. Then there came the deafening shrieking of the mouse. My heart began to race with the sight of the beady eyes. Sharp teeth were on flesh, teeth gnawing at veins pulsating in the neck, and excruciating pain. Predator eyes ablaze and engulfed in consuming flesh. No escape.

I sat up in the car seat and looked out the window. Must have fallen asleep. We were on Ocean Parkway, the mall of trees stretching down to the sea. In a few minutes, we turned left and headed back home. I squirmed in my seat, moving the route books and dirty maps from beneath me. Fast food wrappers and cigarette ashes dug into the carpets underneath my shoes. Staring ahead through the front windshield, I watched the windshield wipers push streaks across the glass as a gentle rain tapped on the car. Wipers pushed the water beads to the side and its rubbing sound on the glass soothed me. The blades moved faster across the windshield and the rain dripped in through the open side window.

I thought about baseball and pirates, sailors and ships. My windup, the books and movies about pirates I loved. But for the moment, only traps came to mind. Real ones. I wondered if Dad felt trapped by the endless day-in/day-out routine of place to place, stop to stop. Every day, without end. Winding the trap up, coming to check on it, dumping the bodies, doing it again and again. An endless cycle of killing, just to make a living for me, Mom, and Merry. I wondered if he regretted it. Surely he must have.

"Going to be quite a storm. It's good we got our stops done already. Not sure we'll get in your game later."

I nodded and blocked out the image of a dead mouse. Time for cold rain to fall on my forearms. I opened the window to feel the raindrops in my hands and wiped the water down my arms and on my cheeks and into my hair. I didn't want to look inside metal wind-up traps ever again.

BLISS

We drove on the BQE and passed over the Kosciusko Bridge. Dad mouthed the name every time we went over the bridge. He spoke it with gusto, as if he were a Polish immigrant. He repeatedly told me how people butcher immigrant names and how important it was to pronounce places correctly.

"*Kosh chush ko*. That's how you say it. Once knew someone who said: Koch e as CO. That used to make me nuts."

I repeated the name to show I had it right.

"He was a famous Revolutionary hero, an engineer and freedom fighter, but you don't get the real interesting history in school. You only get the big shits like Washington, Lincoln, and Franklin. Good stuff is the local history, seeing how people influenced communities, left their mark on neighborhoods. And this guy was an immigrant like us. Gives a better sense of how little people can leave big marks if you look for it. You know?"

"Like how Gil Hodges lived by us on Bedford? And the Lott House, right?"

"Exactly. You'll remember that and pass it along to your kids. Tell them about the Lott House and how George Washington stopped to use the mill by Gerritsen creek during the Revolution. That's the cool thing about real history. Local stuff that makes you get where you're from and what happened around there. Like when the Lenapes had all of it. Then those Dutch settlers. They had all of that farmland by us and now look at it."

"A lot of history by us. Like the marsh and crazy stuff we found at Bottle Beach."

"Don't say that too loudly. Stuff we collected down there technically belongs to the feds and you can't remove it, but no one needs to know that."

"But it's garbage on the shore. No one wanted it."

"Right. But the feds say it has to remain where it is. Floating in the waters off where we live. Like that makes any sense, at all. That's why Dead Horse Bay is so freaking strange, and it's right in our backyard. No one knows a thing about it."

Dad brought Merry and me to Dead Horse Bay months before. He said nobody went down there. That's why we went. We went down with a bucket and collected bottles. Perfume bottles from the 40s. Beer, soda, you name it. All washing up there for years. Some spots could even find newspapers stuck in the dirt and piled upon for generations. Dead Horse had been a glue factory long ago when horses pulled carts before cars and you could still find horseshoes washing up there. Back then it was a city dumping ground, now federal parkland. It was right at the base of Gil Hodges Bridge. You could see the city skyline and planes from the beach, heading out over the marshland.

"Still tough to believe they used to turn horses into glue there. Smell must have been horrific. People lived down there, too, right?"

"That's right. I'm telling you. Forgotten, working class New York. That stuff is worth saving. How many know about things like that? Tip of the iceberg, if you ask me."

Below the highway, lights of the city were blinking. Smoke rose from the stacks of industrial Queens. White smoke was drifting up into dark space and bright lights were shining out from a city asleep. Trucks sped by us on early city delivery routes. An ambulance passed with its lights spinning and sirens off. We made steady progress out to Woodside, where the elevated train carried immigrants in and out of their apartments and back and forth to the city.

We parked on the road, maybe an avenue with a number attached to the street signs. Never really fully understood the streets in Queens. We were headed to exterminate the Bliss Tavern. A group of teenagers milled outside the bar. One of them was leaning forward with his back to a wall. Orange vomit at his feet and splatter marks on his sneakers. His friends laughed at him and a girl twirled her arm in the air, with a boy spinning her back and forth in a drunken waltz. Street was quiet except for these stragglers from the underage bar. We collected our gear from the truck and carried two tin tanks filled with heavy smelling chemicals and the black box with glue traps and snap traps. The canister dug into my palm. The young drinkers watched us, and I felt embarrassed to be here. Here I was hauling gear and working with my old man. They were only a few years older than I was, out and about at 5:30 am on their own.

Dad laughed when he saw them out in front of the bar.

"Reminds me of nights out at Marty's in Flatbush when no one wanted to go home. Had to be dragged out as the bartender closed up shop. Everyone poured out to the diner, or went home with somebody. Whatever was on tap for the next day."

"Whatever."

I looked away as I passed, and they yelled out to us as the only others on the street.

"Different times back then."

"Hey, exterminators, you tell that bartender to let us back in for another."

"Yeah, we promise to behave. So what if he puked. Got all the shit out. We are all set. There won't be another mess."

"Check out these guys with all this shit, yo. Bug Killers."

"Maybe you promise to behave…I ain't promising shit."

Laughs resonated, and I prayed Dad wouldn't respond to them.

Dad smiled to the group and knocked on the door

with his flashlight. Charlie asked who was out there.

"It's me, Charlie. Jimmy Bugs."

"All right, Jimmy."

"Jimmy Bugs! Hahahaha." The group laughed at my dad and called out his nickname. I concentrated on the door lock and getting inside.

Charlie opened the door with a turn of a deadbolt and we were inside a dimly lit bar. Voices from outside changed, and angry curse words got closer. A bottle smashed on the street, and Charlie closed the door behind us and locked it tight.

"Little fuckers won't go home. Been giving me trouble for the last few weeks. Kid of one of the partners, but the prick is pushing it. He gave them such shit in here last night. Privileged, obnoxious little prick. Cops called twice."

"Yeah, that's not good. Maybe the kid needs a little ass-whipping."

"Son of a bitch is going to get his skull cracked. Started two fights, they told me. Running up a massive tab and shooting his punk-ass mouth off. He's got to watch out. His father doesn't want the state to come in here and see them serving all these minors every Friday. Bad news if you ask me."

A fist pounded on the door behind us.

Charlie yelled obscenities towards the door, telling them to go home, call it quits for the night, and to go to bed. A half-filled Bud bottle slammed on the locked door, and Charlie went for the bat hidden beneath the bar. He opened the latch, with my dad right behind him with his flashlight in hand, and the group was gone, running down the avenue to some other corner underneath the electric train tracks above.

Inside, the lights were on in the dining area. Spilled beer stuck to my sneakers. I sloshed through the bar area, where young faces had been three deep, seeking refills from taps and bottles. Before me, a Spanish man with a *New York Post* spread out on the bar. He had a sweating glass of rye on the rocks with a half-filled bottle next to it. He was wearing a security guard uniform. Three seats down there was an Irish construction worker. He was watching soccer scores on the television above the bar. He had a Heineken bottle before him, an empty shot glass and a steaming cup of coffee. Charlie rechecked the door. He had a bucket of wet soapy suds ready to wash down the sticky beers spills. Cigarette butts were all over the floor. A patch of vomit was underneath one of the tables in the hotly lit dining area. Peeled beer bottle labels stuck to the tables in heart, cross, and plus patterns of Bud, Heineken and Coors Light. Someone spat a wad of blood next to the labels.

Charlie ran behind the bar and poured my father a mug of hot black coffee. He grabbed a glass off the shelf and poured me a fountain Coke from the hose, holstered at the edge of the dark mahogany bar with cigarette burns charred on its top. Charlie tossed coasters down to us like Frisbees, and my father and I put our drinks on top of them and took stools at the bar. Charlie offered me a hamburger from the grill, but I refused. Burgers at 5:30 am seemed like a bad idea for any stomach.

Dad talked with Charlie and the regulars down at the other end of the bar. Seamus was the Irish construction worker from County Kerry. He was friends with Charlie, did side weekend jobs with him, and carried his gym bag filled with tools everywhere he went. He spoke in a brogue and drank beer all the time. Ricky was the older Puerto Rican man reading the paper. He wore a white shirt and blue tie and had a grey uniform blazer with a security company patch on the chest pocket. It was draped behind his barstool as he drank his glass of rye. A glass of water sat next to it. Charlie filled the glass of rye for Ricky and he popped open another Heineken for Seamus. The regulars chided my father to have a drink with them. He lifted the coffee and tipped it back.

"Working fellas. Trying to take it easy."

Seamus and Ricky waved their hands at him and went back to their drinks. It was time for me to work. I walked around the bar and filled my glass with ice. The little button was pushed for Coke, allowing the pressure to pump the liquid out in spurts and stops. I sipped and smelled the bubbles from the top of my glass, and Dad motioned me to start spraying chemical and placing glue traps. I walked the dining area with my sprayer, a stack of glue boards in my hands. In the corners the glue boards were tented and placed. Old ones were removed, the ones covered in beer from two weeks ago. They smelled stale; some were drenched or crushed. I held them in the tips of my fingers, trying not to let the disgusting liquid corrupt my fingertips. Drops of beer fell to the floor from the soaked glue boards. Mice were never on them, only a rare water bug stuck on the glue, caught between kitchen and dining room in the darkened corners. Charlie hadn't mopped yet. My drips and drabs of spray were useless once the mop went through, but it was necessary for window-dressing, Dad said. Many places wanted you to stink up the place, make it smell like a toxic cloud had been unleashed, so they knew you were doing something every week.

Dad did the kitchen alone. He ducked underneath the bar and flashed his light in all the crevices. He did the kitchen and behind the bar. I did the dining area and basement. That was the deal. After the dining area, it was downstairs for me. Behind the half-naked picture of a blond, shamrock-clad woman, holding a beer bottle, was the basement stairs, where kegs were kept and boxes of empty and full cases of beer were stacked. Cartons of liquor lined up on the walls and puddles formed from drips filtered down into the cellar. The door was open a crack and I felt around for a light switch. A center bulb cast faint light into the darkness. A scurrying sound of feet was heard as the mice made their ways to the corners. Rickety steps buckled under my weight. The door was always closed and locked behind me. Charlie closed it so patrons didn't get any ideas to head down there for booze, even though that was unlikely right now.

On either side of the stairs were piles of bottles and pint glasses from the night before. Used condoms were left on the steps and cigarette ashes were flicked on top of black bubble gum patches. Patrons used the stairs when the bathrooms were full. Pretty gross but it wasn't my business. Bottle caps were tossed at the bottom of the stairs and broken glass from brown and green bottles speckled the dirty grey basement floor. My feet stuck on each step. The basement was twenty degrees cooler than the bar. The dinghy basement rooms had waterbugs and mice. Lately a rat or two made its way in from all the construction going on. Pools of muddy water gathered in the center of the room. A steady trickle of water ran down the walls. Cardboard boxes buckled from the leaks, and bottles lay strewn across the ground, spilling out of filled return boxes.

I walked the perimeters of the cellar and checked my glue boards. Old, moldy ones were replaced with fresh ones. I tried to write dates on the top as I placed them gently on the wall, in runways. My shiny tin canister of poison dug a red trench into my hand. I inspected my fingers and palms and a faint whiff of poison mixed with a metallic odor. I shook my hands to relieve the weight.

It wasn't the only thing I was shaking off. Eyes peered from the holes in the basement and then came the groaning sounds of the cellar sagging and moaning above me. Cracked concrete hung like stalactites from above. Upstairs dripped down through the floorboards. The trap door at the front leaked water. Rat trap boxes were placed in each corner.

Black rat bait traps, I hated them most. I approached a black box with caution, making as much noise as possible. I kicked the top and jumped away, hoping that a rodent wasn't inside having a meal. Something was this time. A dark streak exited and darted behind the boxes. In terror, I jumped and yelled, "Holy Shit."

Dad opened the door upstairs. "You all right? What was that?"

"I'm ok. Just something ran out the box before I opened it."

"Told you there's construction going on all around here. Make sure you bait those boxes well. Been rat infestations around here lately. Want to make sure we stay on top of it. And none of that shit of sticking bait blocks in the openings. I don't want that shit pushed out into the open. Got it?"

"You got it. I'll open 'em up."

I did toss bait bricks in the opening to avoid opening traps. Most of the time I lied to Dad about baiting boxes. I didn't want to be afraid, but I'd been getting jumpy with these damn things. It was wrong for an exterminator's son to be like this. Mom told me that it might be musophobia. Thought that was bullshit, but I didn't tell her that. Mom sometimes prayed to Gertrude of Nivelles for me. Dad would have laughed his ass off if I told him that. He thought Mom's holy water from Lourdes didn't magically reappear when she used it or that the head of the cracked infant of Prague didn't show up when it was lost. He secretly thought she refilled it with tap water when no one was looking and hid the head when she felt like it. Maybe she did.

I bent down and pulled out the box key from my pocket. I hated opening these things, the same way I hated dark rat burrow holes in general. I placed the key in the slot and pried both sides open. Inside was a dead baby rat. His black eyes were open. I cursed under my breath and jumped away. Knew I had to get rid of it. Gingerly, I approached again and stared down at it.

Truth was I was terrified of these things even dead. Dad told me plenty of stories. They caused the Plague and could bite. I even heard they'd go for your neck if trapped. I dreamed about being a Pied Piper of Hamelin and merrily leading rats out of town and into a river.

Play your little flute, do a little jig and lead all these damn things out of your houses to their watery deaths. This wasn't the case. They moved behind the boxes, crept up and down the walls, and tightrope-walked the pipes overhead. I hated this creature, its goddamn single-mindedness. It was the only thing I really hated, except the great white shark, but even I knew that was dumb. *Jaws* wasn't a part of my life. These things were.

The rat was different. I winced at the image of filed down teeth grinding through the walls, nipping and gnawing food scraps and each other. And then, there was the relentless pursuit of our castoffs. Rats lived with us, fed and thrived off our garbage. I gently picked up the trap in my fingers and turned it over. The carcass fell softly on the ground near my feet. I let it sit there for a moment, staring at the disgusting flesh-colored tail on the grey concrete.

"Dad, check this out!"

My father came to the door and down the steps.

"Little one, huh? Where'd you find that?"

"In the box. Must have eaten the poison I left. There was another in there too. Also pretty small."

"Yeah, well, let's get that in a bag and out of here. Good work. Fully re-bait that box and put it back in their runways. Wonder what we have ahead of us later at the new bar. Probably going to be running."

I swept the rat up with a broom and shovel, tossed

the body in the trash and thought about what was ahead. The bar owners had a new place in the works a few streets away. If Dad said it might be running, I filed that for safekeeping. This morning, I walked the perimeter like a robot. Pump, pump. Spray, spray. Chemical pooled in corners and cracks and crevices. I wanted to be elsewhere, away from smelling mildew and stale beer and listening to the shifting sounds of a basement, the echoes of the footsteps up above.

The door at the top of the stairs was closed behind me, so I walked around in circles and listened. Something happened upstairs every time when I was down here. This basement could be done in five or ten minutes. Each morning I wandered around, baiting the same boxes, spraying the same corners. I listened and heard dad's voice having a stiff drink with the regulars. He needed it to get through his day, I guess, like they did. He just didn't want me to see it. I figured this after the first few times doing the basement. So, I did my work and let him have it in peace.

I sat on the rickety steps, covered in sticky, grimy beer and black circles of spit gum, and waited. I dreamed about writing. About being a musophobic forced to exterminate. Then, I heard rustling behind the beer cartons. I took the flashlight from my pocket and shined the light in the direction of the sound. Probably the damn rat from the box before. It had to be somewhere.

Dad would have hunted that thing down. I knew it, but I sat on the rickety steps and waited to be paroled from the basement.

I felt my breaths grow faster and dared not go to pound my fists on the door above. The rat peered out from behind a Budweiser box, and I grabbed and threw a beer cap in its direction. Damn thing barely moved. I stomped my feet hard and made noise, cursing the thing furiously. Slowly, I stepped toward the direction of the rat. In a flash, it darted to a large crack in the building's crevice and was gone.

I sat back down, waited and stared at the space. Dad always said working hard was the way out of this. This, sitting on basement bar steps and throwing beer caps at the rats in the corners. I wondered how long to wait. When would it be enough. Dad's laugh came through the door. Then, squeaks came from near refrigeration units. I jumped up and hyperventilated a bit. First thought was ignoring it. It was loud. A creature in pain, and it was from a gluetrap location I had just placed on my circuit.

I got off the steps and walked to the spot. Dad would hear the squeaks when the door upstairs was reopened. Fridge motors turned on and sounds of a passerby banged on the sidewalk grate overhead. Customers upstairs chuckled again. Cold sweat formed on my neck. It was time for me to kill. Really kill. Not just toss and run. I could do this. I didn't want to look weak and scared. Put something out of its misery. Avoid being a coward.

It was a glue board, a fresh one, one that sat been placed no more than ten minutes ago. My flashlight shined down on the tented white cardboard. The tent read "Catchmaster: Sticklers for Quality" with a painted red and white mouse emblem painted on it. Its words below read: "Keep out of Reach of Children and Non-Target Animals." Small directional words instructed where to fold. It was non-toxic. On top, there was a record keeper to chart the days you checked the trap. My handwriting was atop the tent.

Sticking out from the glue board trap was the body of a tiny rat. It wriggled back and forth and was moving the trap. Its front legs caught in the adhesive, body struggling to escape. Long tail, small body.

Not many options. Leaving it stuck to starve was wrong and cruel. My responsibility. I did this, this time. My mess to clean up. I glanced at my shoes. They seemed ready. My red and black Air Jordans were sturdy and laced tightly. Squeaks came and went for a few more seconds. Rat was moving back and forth on the ground, furiously. My flashlight beam steadied on the glue board tent. And I looked upward and waited to pounce without looking again. The light was averted from the white tent, and the squeaks grew silent. I said a prayer for something I was about to kill, and then every ounce of force in my Air Jordans descended.

The process was repeated, several times. I stomped the trap until my legs hurt from the pounding. I heard nothing, felt nothing beneath. The flashlight turned again to the folded tent. I tried to anticipate the sight under my foot. A mutilated body wasn't sticking out from the tented glue board. I reached down and touched the squashed trap gingerly. I picked it up in my fingertips. An unsteady beam of light shone into the tiny harborage trap. Nothing inside.

I gasped and tried to steady my breaths. I took a closer look inside the crushed glue board. Debris in the trap. Rat left some whiskers, gnawed off one of its paws to get away. The arm and paw were there in the tent. A small amount of residual blood was there as well. The glue board was coming upstairs with me and I had had enough.

Enough waiting. I walked toward the rickety steps and collected my gear. I pounded my fist on the door blocking my exit. Dad opened the door and he looked down into the darkness behind me.

"You all done?"

"Yep, you won't believe this. Check this out."

He took off his glasses and looked inside the compacted tent.

"Damn. He found a way to get away, huh? Chewed off his paw. Damn. Don't see that every day."

"Yeah, I walked over to squash him and put him out

of his misery. He must have just got through doing it. Crazy right?"

"Nuts. Damn things survive. Guess we have to step it up down there. Must be a good number of them still. This one probably doesn't have much left in him with a paw missing."

The glue board was folded up and tossed in the trash behind the bar.

I saw Charlie remove an empty glass. Probably a whiskey. Dad's gear was right behind the stool. He said his goodbyes to the men on the stools, and then he asked Charlie for the set of keys.

We were going to the new bar. Demolition was taking place, getting the place ready for opening. Dad was doing demolition baiting. Rats were running wild and the contractors were complaining. I stared ahead in silence. The working day wasn't over and we were heading to another basement in a few minutes.

The basement of the new bar had rats. Lots of them. Not like the few stragglers I had just seen or little ones. Charlie grabbed the keys from behind the bar and looked sternly at us. "Good luck over there, boys. Guys there said that place was running last week. Had free reign over there for years. Little demolition and BOOM, they're everywhere. Some nasty crap you boys have ahead of you."

Rats were smart. They avoided new things. Fed at

night. That is, unless the population was so big, and then the big rats pushed out the weaker ones into the daylight. They took the same paths each night to get to food. If something got in the way, they gnawed through it. They bit off their arms to get away. Paths imprinted on their brains, in the bones. Follow the muscles back to where you feed. Do what you have to do to get what you need and want.

I hated them more than anything else. Feared them too. Something in the eyes did it. I shook thinking about them in burrows. Sleeping and waiting, knowing exactly where to go for food. Nothing else besides that. Eat, reproduce, and survive.

Dad collected the signature from Charlie and we walked back to the truck to stow away our gear. I kept to myself. Dad tossed in our gear and opened the doors. The sun was beginning to rise over the elevated trains. Ricky was one of those walking to get the early morning train. He waved as he walked past. Dad placed the key in the ignition and turned to me. "Good work, Jonah. Could have gotten me to take care of that trap."

"I can do it. I'm not afraid of getting my hands dirty."

"I know that, but you don't have to prove anything to me. I know you can handle yourself. You've seen some shit these last few weeks."

"It's all right. I can take it. That's how it is, right? Get used to it."

"That's how it is. But, you don't see chewing off your paw to get away every day, huh?"

"Never seen that. But, got to do what you've got to do."

"Maybe it's about time we kept a list of these things. You know, write em down for our craziest hits or something. No one would believe this crap we come across."

"You're right, there. They keep you on your toes. Might gross people out though."

"True. But important to show they're not as dumb as people make them out to be. Sometimes, we're the dumb ones. We hunt them, but it's a losing battle with some of our *brilliant* fellow humans. No one cleans up after themselves. Worth a story if you ask me."

"Pied Piper. Black death. Rats of NIMH. Yeah there are some stories there. For sure."

"Melville had a whale, right?"

"Don't know if Norway Rats can measure up to that, Dad. Come on."

"Don't underestimate small things with tenacious agendas, my friend. Shit, people here in New York called our people rats coming off the boats when they landed and went to the Five Points. All how you look at it. All I'm saying. Sometimes you have to look small, at your feet, under your nose. Maybe more interesting and more telling."

"Maybe. They are smart and interesting, even though I do freaking hate them sometimes."

"Me too, kid. Me too. Relentless buggers, give them that." He lit his cigarette. And started to look around the pile of receipts for a phone number. We had to call the owner before going over. Confirm this and that.

"You hanging in there with school?"

"Yeah, I'm reading some good stuff. All kidding aside, maybe I do write about this someday. Being a writer would be pretty cool."

"Back up plan for the majors, I assume."

"Yeah, something like that. Plan B or C."

"No exterminating?"

"Maybe that's Plan D or something. This stuff is hard work. See some crazy stuff."

Dad laughed. "See, that's why I want you to tag along. You see and do this shit and there's no way you don't stick in school for something better. Even though these working days will stay with you. Build you up. Toughen you to some things. All counts for something along the way."

Dad adjusted the radio as Don McLean's "American Pie" came on. He sang along a bit. "Now that was a loss. Buddy Holly. What a talent."

I'd heard this all before, so many times. Dad loved rebels who died young in the saddle.

"*Drove my Chevy to the levee but the levee was dry. And*

good ole boys were drinking whisky and rye, saying this'll be the day that I die, this'll be the day that I die…"

He sang and I stared at the sky. I liked this song a lot, too…

Now, for ten years we've been on our own.
And moss grows fat on a rolling stone.
But, that's not how it used to be

When the jester sang for the king and queen
In a coat he borrowed from James Dean
And a voice that came from you and me

Oh and while the king was looking down
The jester stole his thorny crown
The courtroom was adjourned
No verdict was returned

And while Lennon read a book on Marx
The quartet practiced in the park
And we sang dirges in the dark
The day the music died
We were singin'

We drove the car a few streets. I didn't object to the singing. Dad loved this song. It might have been his time on the road. Maybe it was wanting more in America.

Maybe he didn't want to come back from California, and I wasn't sure about any of it.

Dad finished singing, dropped the lit butt out the window and looked at me.

"Listen, it's going to be running here from what we both heard. You can stay in the car, Jonah. Stay put, listen to the radio, keep the air on. I can take care of this. I'm just going to set a bunch of snaps to start. That's all. Come back tomorrow to clean em off and start again."

"I'm going in to help you. Not staying in the car. Are you kidding? I'm not afraid of some freaking rats. I'm your son. I'm here to help you, anyway, for *Christ's sake.*"

Dad nodded, half-heartedly. He looked down at my shoes. My Air Jordans were red and black and sturdy.

The words of *American Pie* trailed off. Dad jingled the keys in his hand and shut off the engine.

"So these keys only open the shutter grate in the sidewalk. No idea about lighting."

"Got it."

"Stay right behind me, all right? If there isn't a light down there, we'll have to use flashlights. No splitting up. I don't want you wandering around down there. We could be walking into a real mess, so stay behind me."

"All right."

This was not a good sign. He was never concerned about jobs. Ever. I nodded and swallowed. The metal grate in the sidewalk was padlocked and covered in strange graffiti. Besides the ordinary tags, a laughing demonic face was on top. It smoked something, winked, and laughed. Down below were rats. Dad paused as he walked around to the trunk.

"You sure you don't want to just stay put, keep the car running? No biggie if you just stay put and relax."

"Dad, it's not like I'm not used to this stuff already. I've seen and killed mice and rats."

"I'm just saying. You've got nothing to prove, kiddo."

"I know, and I'm going anyway. Here to help. Not sit in the car and listen to the radio."

"Ok. We'll give it a look and then come back and bait the snaps. Grab something at the grocery store around the corner. Get something cheap to throw on there when we set em."

In the pit of my stomach, a battle was raging. Juices were flowing and nausea crept up and into my throat. I swallowed whatever was making its way up into my mouth.

Dad smiled anxiously. He pulled a pellet rifle from a black plastic holster in the back. The end of his flashlight and his keys were poised in the other hand. We walked to the hatch and put the key in the padlock. He turned and pulled the latch and noises came from every direction. Faint squeaks and movement under the hatch.

An uncontrollable shiver struck me. My sweaty hands

fidgeted. As Dad slid the lock from the latch and pried the gate open, I heard the sound. Movement inches away from us. Dad lifted the hatchway and light poured down below the ground, two skinny tails darted down the stairs and faded away.

Dad moved down the steps and rat chatter came from below. Scampering of feet followed, movement in every direction. Creatures were scurrying away from the light. Dad shined his flashlight beam. The beam caught peering eyes. Rats up on tables feeding on leftover sandwiches and discarded pieces of fruit. Dad stepped heavily down the concrete stairs. My feet were floating like feathers. My foot arched and toes gently tapped the steps before me, barely letting my heel touch the ground. There were well over a hundred rats, on ceiling beams, on tables, and in the corners. Everywhere I looked. I tried to step harder on each step, driving away fear.

As Dad reached the last step, a screech rang out. Squeals careened and caromed. I adjusted to the darkness and looked down in horror, as Dad stepped back and reached with the muzzle of his gun to flip over the plywood. Rats darted out from under the board, scurried in all directions. Dad swung the butt of the gun down on a rat's head while one attached itself to the end of his pants. I screamed as the creature dug its teeth into Dad's blue jeans, seeking to bite him. Dad grabbed it by the tail and swung it in the air and down to the steps, smashing it a foot in front of me. I shrieked in terror and Dad didn't utter a sound. He tossed the lifeless body on the ground and I froze for a moment. A spasm went from my core to my extremities. The squeals gave way, and Dad aimed his gun at a rat on a table. He let off one pellet shot and the rat spun in midair and darted away.

Blood was on the end of Dad's gun. On the floor before him was a smashed rat body. Its head was bleeding from its mouth and ears but its belly was moving. A gasping sound escaped from me. Dad crushed his boot heel down upon the rat, and the creature stopped breathing.

My frozen spell wore off. A few defiant rats were still eating, picking away at something about twenty feet away. Dad shined light over to it. It had feathers, must have once been a pigeon. I galloped up the stairs to the sidewalk above. It was over in seconds but didn't feel that way.

I walked in circles up on the sidewalk. Hands on my hips. Deep breaths heaved out of my lungs. Hyperventilation set in. Dad walked out of the hole. He looked like he was smirking, right until he saw my ghost-white face.

"How ya doin', pal? You ok? That was a little intense."

"That fucking thing was trying to bite you. Did it get your leg? Did it hurt you? I can't believe that shit."

"I'm fine, Jonah. Fine. He didn't get through my jeans. Not a scratch. That was a bit nuts, if I do say so myself. You all right?"

"I thought he got you. Is it true that they go for the neck if they can?"

"Yeah, it's not a good idea to mess with large numbers of rats. Nasty things. That's why you got to respect them. They fight for every inch, every scrap. We walked into something else down there."

"I don't want to deal with them, not ever. I don't want them to bite you, get us…"

"They didn't get us, son. They won't. They're just living off of instincts. They are much more afraid of us, than we are of them. They come at us out of fear or desperation. There's just a lot of them competing down there for morsels. That's all. That rat only bit because I stepped on it…"

"Well, don't step on them, goddamn it!" My body convulsed. And my frame shook as if casting a demon off from the base of my spine.

Dad reared back, as if on unfamiliar ground.

"Let's go grab a couple of sodas from the deli. I could use a Coke or a root beer or something. Rats can wait for us a few more minutes, right?"

I nodded and walked behind him to the bodega.

We walked into the store and stared at the endless possibilities. Cherry Coke. Sprite. Pepsi. Gatorade. Schweppes Ginger Ale. He grabbed an AW Root beer and two Gatorades and I opened up the fridge and let the cool air pour out on to me. I grabbed a Mountain Dew, after having my hands on a Dr. Pepper.

"Get two, kiddo. Save one for the ride home later. I got Gatorades for both of us later as well."

I grabbed both drinks and we walked to the counter. Dad got two packs of cigs, a Pall Mall and a Marlboro. We walked back to the truck and sat on the bumper, opening our drinks.

"So, that shit we just saw reminds me of a supermarket I did years ago. Morons lost the lease, or something like that. Maybe illegal dealings. And they basically just shuttered the place. We walked in there and those damn things had the run of the place. Like wild kingdom. They were everywhere. Kind of like what we just saw, except unlimited food. I mean, it was like nirvana for rats. Like the dinner bell went up for miles around to come running, and believe me, they did."

"Sounds dystopian."

"Damn, nice college word there. Dystopian? What do you know about that?"

"Read *1984, Lord of the Flies. Star Wars* can kind of be something like that with the Empire, if you think about it."

"Damn right. Sometime, maybe when you get a little older, you've got to read *Hero with a Thousand Faces*. Basically, George Lucas's inspiration for *Star Wars* when he was laid up after a motorcycle accident. And I might add, the first movie we ever watched together."

"A classic. Although *Return of the Jedi* is the best of the bunch."

"I'd hazard to disagree. I'd always go with the original. Some would even say *Empire Strikes Back* is the best. Kind of like *Godfather II*. Might surpass the first. Rare."

"*Empire* is cool with Hoth, Lando, and Cloud City and all, but Luke loses his hand at the end and finds out Darth is his dad."

"I think that's what makes it unique. Defies expectations, you know? Well, to be continued."

We drank our sodas and I began to calm down.

"Up for a return?"

"Yeah. I'm ready. Thanks for the timeout."

"My pleasure. So, unfortunately, we have to clean up after these bozos. Grab a trash bag from the back. You follow me and we'll grab whatever crap they left behind."

"Dad?"

"What is it?"

"Mind if I take a shot or two with the pellet gun?"

"What is this *wat* season, like Elmer Fudd?"

"I get it. Wabbit. Funny, Just would like to take a shot at one or two."

"Be my guest."

He pumped the pellet gun and handed it to me, and I walked over to the open grate. Dad walked behind. His flashlight stream darted and danced around the basement. In the corner, I got sight of a hole. A rat darted out and along the wall. I asked Dad to dim the light. My eyes adjusted to the dark. We sat on the steps leading downstairs. All was quiet. Only a few sounds of movement here and there. I waited and Dad sat with his arms folded, silently watching. A rat came back towards the food. I saw it stop and pause, trying to figure out if the coast was clear. I waited again for another second, more sounds heard in the far corners. They were coming back.

Rat looked out from a crevice. It was headed back to the feathers, so I aimed my attention directly at it. As it made its way from the wall to the pigeon's corpse, I fired and hit. It spun in the air and went right back into the dark crevice.

"Nice shot, boy. Little game hunter right there. Maybe not Hemingway shooting water buffaloes and rhinos, but hey, you got that one squarely."

"Felt good, actually."

"Well, take a shot at one more, and then let's go get those snaps baited. Not going to sit down here shooting at shadows all day."

I looked around. Scurrying rats were moving behind the walls and behind some of the construction materials. They didn't leave. I followed one as it darted behind some concrete bags. I went towards the direction; my rifle pumped and ready to fire. As I got closer, a rat went for the hole in the corner like a dart of lighting. I fired and the pellet ricocheted off the wall. The rat was back into hiding.

Dad opened the contractor bag and started to dump trash into it. He cleared off the remnants from the table. With his gloved hand, he walked over and picked up the remains of the pigeon corpse. I set the rifle down by the stairs and helped him. We worked quietly, clearing out the garbage. I carried the bag upstairs and Dad was close behind me.

"All right. Let's quick run to the supermarket, and then we're ready to get baiting these things."

"What do we get there?"

"Let's try a bag of shrimp. Something tempting and smelly. We barely need anything with what's happening down there. Set em, put em out, and watch em snap."

Dad and I went to the corner FoodTown. We grabbed a small bag of shrimp from the fish counter.

"What do you call a guy who sells fish, Mr. Dystopian?"

"Fish Seller? I don't know."

"A fishmonger, genius. That's your word for the day. Want to know where I've seen the most rats lurking around?"

"Where?"

"Fulton Fish Market."

"Guess they like fish."

"Like the rats are built for that part of Manhattan. Like they ain't going anywhere. Ever. No way to get on top of that, especially with the city handling it. Hell, I was asked to bid years ago on the subway. Those morons basically wanted you to use anything that isn't toxic. Like they're more worried about some homeless moron eating the shit than they are about getting rid of the damn things. Hopeless if you ask me. I wouldn't even bid on it. No way you would even make a dent with the crap you were allowed to use."

We went back down the grate into the basement. Dad and I grabbed the snap traps and began baiting.

"Now, you take a shrimp, leave it here like this, and then set the spring back. Don't let it the snap off on your finger, all right?"

"Got it. One shrimp per trap."

"I'll put them in the key runways. You set em up, I'll put em out. Deal?"

I set the snaps gingerly, making sure not to snap the metal spring on my fingers. Dad grabbed three or four at a time and started placing them all over the basement. Intermittent squeaks resonated. Once again, I heard dad stomping. His flashlight light illuminated the blackness, as he placed the snaps. Soon, most of the rustling in the shadows dissipated into the voids of the walls.

Then, a snap sounded in the far corner.

"Wow, that's fast. Barely put the damn thing down."

I walked toward the sound of the snap like a radar ping. It was the direction Dad was going as well. A juvenile was dead on the trap. Dad reached down and undid the latch. The corpse dropped to the ground.

"Most humane way to get rid of em, ask me. *Bang.* Done."

"Reset it?"

"Let's put out a clean one right there. My guess down here is that we set fifty and we're clearing off fifty in a day or two. It's bad."

Snap. Behind me, a snap trap went off in the darkness. Dad walked away and I moved toward the noise. He was shining his beam far away in the distance. He seemed far away. I walked toward the snap. Along the side of the basement wall, there was a dead rat smashed on a trap. My flashlight centered on the corpse. Another juvenile rat. My work gloves were in my bait pail, and it was time to put them on. They were durable—they had blue and red lines on them and were grey in coloring. My hand grasped the beast by the tail. I pulled it from the wall and walked back to the steps. Body was removed, its head was split by the metal spring. It took seconds for it to be over, not like the agony of a poison, which made them bleed out. This death was just a trip of a lever, and light was snuffed. Darkness set in.

Dad walked over.

"That's a young one, huh? Poor bastard didn't know what hit him. It's the older ones—the king rats, dominant males you have to be smart to get. They avoid new things at first. These guys we're getting now are the teenagers. Just young and dumb. Big hungry colony though."

"Wash the blood off to reset it?"

"Good idea. Rinse it off and reset and replace it for me. Thanks, Jonah."

Dead rats began to pile at the bottom of the stairs. Dad was right—they were mostly juveniles, rats who hadn't reached maturity and never would. In the slop sink, the snap with its blood and fish was washed off

Dad kept baiting and setting the traps. Soon, we were out of materials and it was time to leave the dark cellar and ascend to the sidewalk.

"Hopefully, we will get a few of the ringleaders of that colony down there and get on top of the problem."

"Yeah, we'll get on top of it."

"Jackasses need to stop leaving the goddamn garbage down there. We might need to come back, clear em off, and reset in a day or so." We started stowing away our gear in back of the truck.

"No problem. I'll give you a hand."

"Gracias, amigo."

"Why would they do something so dumb? Leave trash and crap down there. So dumb and lazy."

"It's really why we're in business. We don't clean up after ourselves. You're right, we are lazy, us humans. Leave it for someone else to pick up. Not my problem. Toss my garbage for someone else to handle. And guess what, pal? Me and you are the clean-up crew when it gets out of hand, unfortunately."

"Sucks. Those things are nasty."

"True. And smart. And they reproduce at quite a clip. Sure could have dystopian attached to their story, if we don't pay attention."

"Maybe we have it coming with leaving crap behind for others to take care of?"

"Quite possibly. All I know is its epidemic. Leave it for someone else. All around us. Certainly no perfect world. No Bliss here, eh?

He laughed and I smiled as we got back in the crowded red truck. Driving home, it occurred to me Dad's breath smelled like booze and soda and smoke. We had a few small stops to do on the way. I looked up to the elevated train and listened to the train, rolling into the station up above. The wheels of the train screeched and skidded to a stop. People exited the closing doors and went about their day. And I was glad to be back in the truck and away from the Bliss.

CLEFT

We did the Century Club twice a month. Two weeks prior, Dad told me it was started by William Cullen Bryant, a poet to look up sometime. Last week, I thought I'd give him a shock. In his old books downstairs, I found a collection of American verse and read "To a Waterfowl" and "Thanatopsis" to impress the old man with a few lines.

"Century first today, right?"

"*Jawohl*. Off to hang with the writers, bright and early."

"Got something for you."

"Really? Shoot."

"Here's a little bit of Bryant:

So live that when thy summons comes to join

The innumerable caravan, which moves

To that mysterious realm, where each shall take

His Chamber in the silent halls of death,

Thou go not, like the quarry-slave at night,

Scourged to his dungeon, but, sustained and soothed

By an unfaltering trust, approach thy grave,

Like one who wraps the drapery of his couch

About him, and lies down to pleasant dreams.

It's the finale from 'Thanatopsis.'"

"Bravo, my friend. Even well delivered. Maybe a bit

bleak for an early Saturday morning… but I'm impressed to hell."

"Thanks. Thought you'd like it."

"You were paying attention a couple of weeks ago."

"That I was."

We parked and approached with our gear. The door of the club was heavy and imposing. Inside was a cold marble hallway where security guards waited for visitors. Probably the service entry where workers came and went. It was sparsely lit with a buzzer off to the right. Every morning, two guards took turns at desk duty. While one sat at the entrance desk, the other roamed the halls. Jean and Hector were the two guards on weekend duty.

Hector Alvarez lived near Marble Hill in the Bronx. He worked two jobs and had three kids and a wife. Hector and Dad argued sports every week. Hector loved the Yankees; we loved the Mets. Hector offered us coffee from the kitchen and exchanged Century Club news with my father. He told us about any problems or complaints from the kitchen or from guests, and he greeted us with a smile and a handshake.

Jean Toussaint was from Trinidad in the Caribbean. I had no clue where he lived now because he never got into it. He once mentioned Eastern Parkway. Jean looked straight down his nose at us. Today, he was seated at the desk and we watched him reading the newspaper by the green lamplight. Some days we saw him sleeping in his chair. Our boxes were heavy and our canisters were filled with weighty poison. Dad had a fifty-pound black box with his gear and supplies tucked into it. Hector always sensed us on the street and jumped to greet us at the door. Jean didn't give a shit and liked to have us sit outside and wait. This morning wasn't any different.

Jean was lounging at the desk when we rang the bell. He shifted in his chair slightly. I saw his eyes through the steel-rimmed glasses that were attached to a chain that hung around his neck. His eyes closed again and his head bobbed. We rang the bell again. He awoke and looked towards the door, peered down at the paper on the desk before him, and he started to walk the other way. Dad fumed as he watched Jean disappear from sight.

"That fucking son of a bitch." Dad rocked and rolled in his boots and put the gear down. "Going to pull this shit again, huh? That routine again?"

In two minutes, Jean was sauntering back to the desk with a handful of letters. He placed them on the desk and started to thumb through them. Dad took the end of his flashlight and pounded on the door. He rang the bell for the third time. Jean motioned us with his hand and began to make his way towards us. Dad was ready to explode.

"This fucking guy. I swear to Christ, I'd love to beat the living shit out of this lazy fuck. Always screwing with us."

"Don't let him get to you. Like a game with him, every time. Gets old."

Jean strolled to the door and then turned around to go back to the desk. The keys sat squarely in the middle of the table next to the letters. Jean walked back to the door deliberately, shaking his head. Dad gripped his canisters. Under his breath, the profanity welled up to the surface.

"That fucking bastard…I'm going to fucking kill this guy…rip his head clean off his shoulders. Piece of crap."

"Easy. He's not worth the aggravation."

It was time to drift away from here. An inner squirm was coming on. Explosion was imminent. It was building across the austere hallway with the marble floors. Dad's fists tightened on the poison canister. He tapped the glass door with his flashlight for good measure as Jean walked his way across the marble.

Jean fiddled with the keys and spun them around his index finger as he walked. He looked at the walls and was sure to check the clock hanging next to his station. He leered at us from over the rims of his glasses as he placed the key in the lock. A calculated smile curled upon his lips as he turned the key. Then, he opened the door and said, "Don't you be hitting that door with your flashlight, man! What's wrong with you? You leave a mark on that door and it's your ass. And my ass too. You wait 'til I get that door, man. I hear you."

He didn't look at us when he spoke. His head swayed back and forth; his eyes looking toward the ground.

Dad stared straight at him and growled, "Well, get off your fucking ass and get the door then. We're hauling fifty pounds worth a gear in our hands and you're sleeping at the desk and sauntering around like it's a goddamn rest home, playing with yourself in there. Get your ass up outta that seat and let us in. We've got fucking work to do and stops to make."

"I do my job the way I like. I ain't running to the door for you. I don't care how hard you slam on that door. You know I will get there…you can wait."

"Seems like taking your sweet ass time is how you do things in here. Guess answering the door is too much when your job is sitting at the doorway waiting to let people fucking in. Doorman, right? I don't want to tax you too much. You might have to check with the union if opening a door is part of your job description as DOORMAN. Moving your ass from the desk may qualify for fucking overtime or worker's comp."

"You just bitter cause you dragging your ass around the city in da middle of the night. I can't be responsible for your choices, man. Shame on you, have to drag your son's ass outta bed to do this shit."

I was far away now. The black box was down on the marble. I shook the wrinkles from my hand and studied the grooves on my palm. The words fired back and forth, but I wasn't listening anymore. Attention only focused on hands, shaking them out as if the sting of the spray canister was still bothering me. My single callous was inspected like a rare specimen under a microscope and a faint smell of chemical lingered. My hands were soft, not like Dad's hands, which were rough and darkened. His hands smelled permanently. His knuckles and palms had gashes where blood had pooled and dried. Heated words were said, hard words of hatred. A black man from the Caribbean was shaking his head and smiling. Dad pointed his cracked fingers at him and the muscles in his neck were pulsating. The blood was rising in Dad's face and there was a steady stream of hate flaming in his eyes.

I looked away with an uneasy grin on my face. I was sitting on one of our black plastic canisters, waiting for divine intervention. I kept waiting for the bell to ring, where everyone went to their corners and toweled off. Jean was averting his eyes and making his way back to his chair. A wry smile came across his lips. Soon, he motioned to me.

"Why you bring your boy along? Want him to learn the bug-squashing ropes? Why not let him sleep? It will do him better. He still has a chance to do better."

"You're doing plenty of sleeping for all of us, pal. Some people have to work at jobs rather than clock hours on their ass. It's the way it works. I'd rather be lugging this shit and calling my own shots than be sitting at a desk with a log book in a monkey suit for eight hours."

More jabs continued. Hector walked down the main stairs, and Jean stopped the jabs and turned to business, started to give orders to my father.

"So, you need to do the kitchen thoroughly. The cook says he sees roaches and that is not acceptable. Guests are on the top floors, so stay away from that. We don't want them to see *you* about." Jean spoke to us like we were iterant workers, the hired field hands to be kept far out of sight.

Deep inside, I despised Jean. I wanted nothing more than to scream for how he made me feel. We were hired working slobs, carrying gear on our back. We were dirty, entering the service door to do the job no one wanted to touch. Our soiled hands had to be kept to ourselves and we had to move through invisible corridors to avoid respectable eyes from seeing our dirty business.

I really didn't like Jean. And I had been taught to give everyone a chance, no matter what. Jean stared at us like we were not fit to peel gum from his fake patent leather slip-ons with white tube socks inside. I despised his white shirt and red striped tie and blue blazer and grey trousers. I hated how he made me ashamed to be there, mortified at my father's work. Up those stairs was the escape.

Hector came from down the hall, and I thanked God he was there. "Jimmy, Jimmy. Glad to see you, my friend. Come with me a second. I just need to go over something with you in the lockers before you start the place."

It was a Hector intervention. He put his arm around Dad. The locker room visit was just to calm him down and get away from Jean. Hector spoke rapid fire. "So, those Mutties of yours are looking good. Still a long way away from pinstripe power my friend. One of these years, you will see the light." Hector shook my hand quickly before they made their way down the hall.

I heard the baseball chatter drift away with them and soon I was alone with Jean in the hallway.

"So, you gonna be a bug squasher like you daddy?"

"We don't squash bugs. We control pests."

He laughed a bit and stared back at the paper on his desk. "Well, your father claims you smart. Let's hope he's right and you stay in school to avoid tis kind of thing."

Every nerve in my body arched in defiance. I wanted to whack him with his slip-on shoes. I ground my jaw a little and looked away.

"Let's see if that Catholic school pays off. I'm from Trinidad. You know where dat is?" Jean asked.

"It's near Tobago. It's a beautiful country in the Caribbean."

"That's right. Now, in Trinidad…"

I cut him off mid-sentence. "I have one for you. My father's family is from Bonavista Bay. You know where that is?" I asked.

"That is the town in Ireland where you black Irish escaped from," Jean said, condescendingly.

"Incorrect. It's a town in Newfoundland. You even know where that is? Or what country?"

Jean adjusted his seat and remained silent for a moment.

I continued. "That's a province in Canada, by the way. It's a land of fishermen. It's a tough place. Real men are raised there, like the iron workers who built this city of ours, like my uncles with their bare hands. You may have even seen my uncle in *Lunchtime Atop a Skyscraper*. Pretty famous photo, if you ask me. Shows work and courage. No fear. No settling. We work hard for a living to get ahead and aren't afraid of real work, getting our hands dirty. I guess you wouldn't know much about that, huh?"

Jean didn't speak. He looked out from above his glasses with a stern face. He didn't expect this from the quiet, baby-faced worker. My blue eyes were dead set on his, peering at me from behind glass and steel and chain.

"Hmmm… defending your daddy. Priceless. Won't be too long till you are following Daddy around all the time, then. Squashing bugs, chasing mice, living

111

underground. Or maybe better. Working fifty stories up, drinking bottles of rubbing alcohol for lunch. Now, that's just what I like my son to do."

I was about to scream my uncle was the guy without the shirt, eating the sandwich, but I stopped. It wasn't worth it.

Jean laughed as he picked up a magazine from the desk and walked toward the bathroom. In Jean's world, it was simple. Sure, I wear a jacket, sit at a desk, and let people into a club to do work. But my hands are clean, and my muscles don't ache. I don't have to risk much here. You? Your hands are caked with filth and death. You roam from place to place in the middle of the night. I am better than you. *My job may be bad, but it isn't as bad as yours. I've got ease, you have toil. And I'm here to remind you of that.*

"It still must be tough walking the same halls on a graveyard shift. Punching clocks and wasting hours and picking fights with a kid must get to you. Plus, you got to wear that silly uniform every day."

Jean glared back, but the talk was over. Inside, the wrestling and churning in my stomach intensified. The push of fight surged. Then, something else came in. Respect elders. Mom would have hit me with a Sermon on the Mount or some shit like that. Jean shuffled off with a set of keys to take a dump. As Hector and Dad returned from the lockers, Jean dragged his slip-on shoes across the cold marble, making his way to the old service elevator down the hallway. He pulled back the cage door, pressed the buttons for the basement and was gone.

The pain in my stomach intensified. I heard Mom reminding me to turn the other cheek. Treat people as you want to be treated. All that shit. But it was hard sometimes—hard with some of the people we met…

I looked at the red carpeted stairs before me. Dad gave the nod, and we were headed upstairs with the gear. Upstairs was a different world from down here.

"What was happening with you and him back there?" Dad asked.

"I just didn't want to keep my mouth shut as he shit on us. He's an asshole."

"I know it and you know it. We both got a little pissed off. But you let me take care of that. No need for you to get riled up over a guy like that. He doesn't know shit."

"I know, but it's like he looks down on us. All the time! And you have your own company! I don't freaking get his problem."

"Well, there's more there than we can figure, but that guy is always looking to put someone in his place, no matter who it is. Better those talks come from me as the boss, rather than from my assistant son, right?"

"Yeah, I'm sorry, Dad. It just made me mad, and I hate when he pulls that crap with us."

"He thinks he's got something over on us by sitting there and getting paid. Like it's some kind of racket. In most cases, people see we're in the same boat. Not that clown. Meanwhile, let's face it. We're all here working for crumbs compared to what's happening up here during actual club hours. This is the REAL racket, if you ask me."

He spread out his arms to the club's library before us.

From the cold door with the buzzer to the staircase was a short distance, but it was a different world. Once you reached the top of the stairs, the desk and the logs and the clocks disappeared. Upstairs was all mahogany walls, oak panels, and richly embroidered, regal red carpets with swirls of elegant leaf patterns woven into its fabric.

Floor-to-ceiling bookshelves with wooden stepladders on tracks lined the rooms. Sculpted heads and paintings in gilded frames, each with a private light at the bottom to illuminate its detail. Large armchairs were arranged in corners. The fireplace was darkened with ashes in the grates. Imaginary parties ranged through the rooms, the kinds where people drank cognac in large glasses and bartenders sat behind mahogany counters in white jackets, ready to pour drinks over the cold jingling rocks. Oriental rugs covered wooden floors. Floor lamps were lit in corners. There was a new nook and cranny in every room. Bookshelves reached the tops of the ceiling. I scanned the room freshly each time. Beautiful, priceless paintings hung on every wall and in each alcove.

Dad followed behind me and got to work.

"So, you know the deal. Roam around and soak it in. Just keep the flashlight out and pretend you're looking for infestations. I'll be in the kitchen."

"Sure you don't me to help?"

"What I need you to do is take a good look. How many kids get to walk around and look in a place like this? Not many, I'd say. I'll let you know if I need anything."

I roamed through the rooms, looking at books and gazing over paintings, never touching a thing. Not a single book. I got close, but my fingers never touched an object, fearing that I'd get caught and tossed out. Touching anything was sacrilegious. Volumes on the shelves were old, fragile-looking, but they were safe here. They had been idols in someone's imagination—years of labored composition. Now, they'd stay in this cathedral space on a sparsely lit library shelf, surrounded by portraits and landscapes.

These books were sacred treasures. Each room was a cove of wonder. I made my way back and forth, hoping never to find people reading or taking volumes off the wall. My feet creaked and cracked the floor beneath me and I was far away from my dad spraying into the crevices and eons away from the poison gel he was injecting into the wallboards. My mind was soaring through high culture, conjuring a day of membership in this place. At leisure I walked through the rooms, looking up at the holy stacks with sacred scrolls on display.

Someday I'd pick a volume at random to read in a secluded corner chair. The words were on crisp, heavy stock paper. I'd sip from a cocktail in a crystal goblet, allowing the sweat of the container to run onto my fingers and down on to the knee-level table next to the chair.

The paintings vied with the books. As I strolled about, I caught my dad taking a closer look at a painting before he went to the kitchen. I stood back, watching him from the other room. He examined portraits of members and studied landscapes. He turned and saw me watching him and motioned for me to walk over to him. He pointed to a Winslow Homer landscape, placed there without pomp or circumstance, and motioned me to follow him to another wall. He pointed to a lush forest scene, drawn as if the painter was sitting on a mountaintop looking down into a valley of lush green trees, some snapped branches in the foreground and slight storm skies in the distance.

"This is an Asher Durand. Hudson River School. He was a member here. I'll have to take you to see more of these sometime. This one is my favorite."

"This is really beautiful. Definitely my favorite. Portraits are cool, but there's something about this one."

"Priceless. And you'd never know it. Just here, no major fanfare. This is the first American school of art. What makes this country unique and different: these incredible landscapes. Nature's nation, you know. We should go up and visit Church's Olana and Thomas Cole's place sometime. Cole was friends with Cullen Bryant, who started here. You'd probably like it. And it's right there in Hudson Valley."

"I'd like to see those. Fit with Bryant's poems. This one right here is magical."

"That's the Hudson Valley for you, and not too, too far from where we're standing in this concrete jungle." Dad bent closer to the frame and looked at the title. "*Kaaterskill Clove.* Now that's a spot to visit some day when you get a chance. He did another one like it called *Kindred Spirits* that reminds me of it. Put two figures on the cliff looking out, Cole and William Cullen Bryant. Poets and painters. You and Merry. Another to put on the list of checkouts."

"Most definitely. Both of em, agreed. Going to remember it."

He nodded and went back to work, and I stood staring at it, long and hard. The cut felled logs looked like fingers pointing to the center. The pine branches on the left seemed to reach to the heavens, despite the cut branches down below on the trunk. A haze seemed to cover the valley and there was a light in the center, a feeling of whiteness in the center, despite the slight clouds above the cleft. No humans were in sight and there didn't need to be. Dark and light greens. Heavy browns. And wisps of pure blue.

It was instantly my favorite painting. It was almost hidden in a hallway, next to a short strip of a bookcase. I walked away and made a cursory circuit of the rooms and came right back. I wanted to remain in this same exact spot for eternity. I remained fixed in silent reverie for minutes until I heard the rustling of Jean's slip-on shoes in another room. I noted the location of the Durand for future reference and scurried away.

Jean came and went quickly, jingling keys through the halls. I wondered if he ever stopped and looked.

The atmosphere floated like wildfire in my imagination. I scoured the rooms looking for treasures and admiring the setting. Nothing in those rooms should change. Right down to the ashes in the fireplace grates. Dad let me roam freely. He waited and delayed finishing up for my account. I caught him looking at volumes as I mapped the rooms. I drank in the cloistered space like a saint at a holy shrine. I sat in secluded chairs and prayed to be allowed back one day. Someday a reentry had to occur, and my fingers ran over the shelves at liberty. I'd take books off the shelves and the spell would be broken. I'd read the words of a book I had never heard of, staring at the large windows on to the silent street below.

Dad started to pack up the gear, so I had to take the last gaze. Time to walk gingerly down the stairs to get a signature, go to the next step and then home. As we walked down the stairs, I thought about being an outsider. We were outsiders in that world. Our world was one of deference, of listening to high-class complaints, and knowing one's place. Jean was down there with a logbook. He tossed it on the brown desk and filled in our times, in and out of the building. He didn't look at us, nor say a word. Dad signed the book and flagged down Hector to sign his route book. On the paper, he listed all the chemicals we used, and he shared some thoughts with Hector.

I'd return, someday. I was sure of it. They'd ask me to come in for a late afternoon cocktail party, to watch the sunset through the open windows, with the curtains pulled back. Dad walked by my side in this reverie. He was old then and he led me back to the Durand. His old wrinkled eyes stared deep into the forest with the impending storm and he was happy. We toasted each other and walked the rooms together, and we weren't working.

We walked toward a greasy spoon around the corner for breakfast.

"Some place, huh? Quite a spot, and interesting to see how the other half lives."

"I'll get back there some day. Be a member."

"Not a bad goal to have. A writer, my son. Like when you wanted to be a sailor at the Yacht Club. Far away from being an exterminator's son."

"Anything's possible, right? Way you always put it."

"It is. Work hard. Stay focused. That's the beauty of it all. And focus on doing things you love, so you don't have to be doing things just to put food on the table and keep the roof over your head. That's why you're out here with me. Remember that as you keep working through school. That's the point. Why I encourage Mer to paint, you to write."

"I know. I'll do it. Set my mind to the task and just do it."

"That's it, my boy. And have that Plan B in the back pocket just in case it doesn't work out as planned. Gonna be the first in our family to graduate high school, let alone college. Going to happen."

"I know. It is pretty cool having some of these stories to tell. Who gets to see stuff like that?"

"It is quite a range of stuff we see, is it not?"

"Yeah, one end to the next. That Asher Durand was so cool. I'm going to see a lot more of the Hudson River School. Maybe even hike up there sometime."

"Sublime. It's a beautiful neck of the woods and not too far. New York State of Mind. Worth a trip."

We entered the diner and Dad talked pidgin Spanish with Papi, the waiter.

"Papi! Coffee, amigo. Gracias."

"You got it, Jimmy Bugs. What can I get you hombres?"

"Bacon, egg and cheese on a roll, Papi. Thanks."

"Wow, going against the grain? No bagel this time around?"

"Switching it up on you today. Going to try something new as you keep telling me. Keep you on your toes. Like reading Bryant and checking out Hudson River painters."

"I am impressed. Striking out for new territory and giving something new a try. Maybe we all need to do that from time to time. Beats the same old, same old, every day. Wears on you, wears you out."

"Sometimes got to think about bigger things. New things. I get it. Even if it seems like something small."

"True. The rat race and the constant grind will wear you out pretty quick, if you let it. Keep trying new things."

I'd shock him again when I made it back to the Century, not to work. I knew it was there for the taking. I would never make people feel bad for the work they had to do to get where they needed to go. I waited for my sandwich with a cup of hot black coffee, thinking about Hudson River landscapes and leather-bound books. Dad looked at his route cards and counted the money in his pocket. We had a long way to go.

Room of Anchors, Whales, and Ships in a House of Cards

My mom came upstairs and woke me from a toss-and-turn sleep. I knew something was up. Merry was staying at a friend's in Rockaway and this was never a good thing. Dad stayed out when Merry was away. One night I came downstairs to find Mom on the couch and Dad asleep on the sun porch, covered with a white sheet like a sleeping ghost. Some nights he didn't come back.

"Something's wrong tonight. He has a real strange look in his eye. I told him to go downstairs and sleep it off. He must have taken something."

"What the hell is going on? What's happening down there?"

"He's on something, or lots of somethings. I don't know what. Doesn't even seem like him. I've never seen anything like this, ever. We need to stay out of his way. Hopefully, he'll just go downstairs and pass out soon."

My drowsy eyes adjusted to the light coming down from the circular, frosted fixture in the center of my rugged, plastered ceiling. One spot in the spackle cracked and peeled and hung like a patch of dead skin. Other spots looked like cake frosting dripping from melted heat. Mom looked out the window and she sat down on my treasure chest where my baseball cards and comic books were kept. The 1954 set that we had collected was in there. I guarded it with my life.

Mom lit a Kool cigarette and walked to my door. She closed the door, jammed it shut, even though it didn't fully close. She pulled my bookshelf in front of the door to block the entrance. I'd never seen anything like this before and started to become afraid.

Two floors below, dad was drunk and high, walking around the basement. You could hear his rantings echoing up the stairs. He picked up a golf club and smashed his own glass entertainment cabinet with one swing. In short succession came sounds of smashing glass and doors being torn from the hinges.

"Oh my God, he is breaking up the house. What are we going to do?"

I had no clue and pulled my hands through my hair, like it was in knots, ready for untangling. Nothing came out of my mouth, so I got out of bed and looked out the window. Mom's eyes didn't have an answer, and she was praying. Rosary beads were in her hands and she was moving her fingers across the blue pebbles, noiselessly mouthing her words. I didn't know what an Our Father, Hail Mary or Glory Be was going to do at this moment. I tried to say an Our Father with her, but the words didn't help. Not then. *Hallowed be thy name. Thy will be done. On earth as it is in heaven.* God's will had nothing to do with what was happening. I was certain of this and this was no time for God or heaven right now.

Something was ending. This was different, and I knew it. It was coming closer and closer by the second and Mom was praying for help. I sat on a cold radiator and felt the grooves underneath me where steam used to rise and keep me warm. Gifts surrounded me. I looked at my drawer filled with toys and noticed the bull-horned handles of my dresser, which kept all my clothes. I touched a few things scattered on the floor before my bed to make sure they were still real. I started to pick up my clothes and toys and looked around for my bat.

Noises downstairs got closer. Dad was in the kitchen now, breaking glasses and plates and toppling our kitchen table over and over again like he was a troll trying to push an immovable boulder to clear a mountain pass.

"We have to do something. Call the police or something. Get someone in here. The phone's in your room. Just call!" I screamed, wanting action of some kind.

"No, no, he will calm down. He'll go back downstairs. God help us and protect us. God help us and protect us. He won't do anything to us, ever."

My house was being broken below. Mom's tears flowed. She wasn't going anywhere or doing anything but praying and pleading.

"If you don't do something I will. He is destroying everything!! And he's out of his fucking mind! You don't think he'll make his way up here soon?" I insisted.

"Just wait. He's going to stop. Has to. He won't want to wake all the neighbors and get the cops here. Not the neighbors. He doesn't want to be arrested!"

"You think he gives a crap about neighbors at this point? Are you kidding?"

The Norman Rockwell plates, hung on our dining room wall, were dropped, one by one. Many broke clean in two. Some didn't break at all. A couple he flung like flying saucers out into the street. The words came in like waves. They came rising up the stairs: "Fuck me. Fuck me. Fuck me…." He repeated the phrase again and again with every broken piece of glass and mangled piece of furniture. He broke one of Mom's dollhouses with a swing of his club, a place where Merry and Mom spent hours putting all the little pieces together.

I wanted to not exist, to disappear. Mom wept uncontrollably. Dad wanted to exterminate everything in that house. Get rid of it and us. And I knew it, as I paced my bedroom in circles, thinking of a way out.

We were trapped. Dad's work boots were kicking over our coffee table, where hours before I played solitaire and watched TV. I thought about the TV he was going to break. Hours before, I was watching *Nightline* with Ted Koppel with Mom. It was the last thing on before bed. He signed off with his signature "*From ABC News, Goodnight.*"

I couldn't believe that might be the last thing I'd ever see on it. And I wasn't sure why that came to mind.

Mom went to the door and cracked it an inch. She listened for a few seconds and the sounds came and went. For a few minutes all was quiet and Dad was probably refueling with whisky from the not-so-secret stash down below.

"That will be it. It will be ok. You can go to bed, Jonah. I'll wait a few minutes and then go down and keep an eye on him. You know Hannah's brother choked in his sleep ten years ago. God rest his soul. Gotta make sure he is sleeping on his side."

"He's not done, and you know it. And Hannah's brother, are you kidding? We need to get out of here, now, while we can. Go to Auntie's or something, anything, anywhere."

"No, no. He's done. We have to take care of him. Just so hard on him with the business. He's running himself into the ground after Teddy's death. I can't believe Teddy did this to all of us."

"Teddy's an asshole, but he's been freaking dead for months! This is happening now, right in front of us and Dad could kill us. Not Teddy. You know the gun's down in all of this mess."

Mom crossed her arms and lit another Kool. She went towards the door to listen.

I stared outside at the streetlamp. A jet plane high

126

above the lamplight carried my eyes with it until it curved past the branches of the trees and was gone. I wished I was on it, knowing anywhere was better than here. Anywhere away from here.

Jim Fennell was back in our living room. He tossed a dining room chair out into the front yard. A glass goblet from the china cabinet went sailing toward the tree at our curb and shattered. Pictures went out the door next and then the chairs out in front of the house went careening into the street. I watched our memories crashing out in the street, tossed from the doorway below, and I was frozen at my window. Then, I saw his face for a second. He stumbled out from the front door alcove, pointing at the other houses. His eyes were glassed over with drugs and whisky and the darkened shadows of the trees kept him covered and shrouded.

"Fucking keep looking. My house. That's fucking right. And I'll do whatever I do with it, fucking busybodies, getting rid of fucking all of it. Done."

He sure was. He staggered to the truck and continued yelling at neighbors. Only a few lights seemed to pop on. The rest were content to ignore him.

"I will go down there and stop this. This has to stop. He is destroying our lives and it's got to end," I said, making a movement towards the door.

"No, Jonah! Stay here. We have to stay put, right here. No choice tonight. We can't go down into this. He'll…."

"He'll what, ma? Kill me, right? Kill us? And you won't call the fucking police?"

Mom feared for our lives, but no way she was calling the cops. I didn't go for the phone, either. I became pretty certain it would be all be over, all of it, and I knew Mom and me wouldn't do a thing about it but sit and wait for it.

I went under my bed for weapons. Underneath my bed, next to my dirty socks, muddy sneakers, and Victoria's Secret catalogues, there was a baseball bat. It was a Reggie Jackson special, a black bat with a white trademark. It was the best thing I had. Bat had red masking tape on it because my team was the Reds last season. I pulled it out and gripped the handle tightly in my fists and took a couple of level swings.

"What is that for?"

"It's for if he comes in after us. I'm not sitting on my hands. No fucking way."

"You'd hit your father?"

"If he tries to kill us."

If Mom wasn't here, I'd probably hide behind my bunk-bed dresser drawer and pretend I didn't exist. But that wasn't happening. There weren't many choices left.

I tried not to think of construction boots coming down on me. My bat swings wouldn't work. He was too strong for them. I thought about climbing out on the roof and escaping down the porch roof below, but he might meet me jumping into the front garden and there was no way I was leaving Mom in my room to die.

The voice downstairs came in waves. It thundered out into the night, addressing street lamps and dark homes, and it cursed women and children, especially me and Mom as blood-sucking, life-sucking leeches. Sounds slurred and words cleared. He was on the front doorstep and called out to the night to listen. He spoke to cars and neighbors peering out their upstairs windows to the scene of blind rage and fury below.

"That's all there fucking is. Work till you die trying to keep ungrateful bastards from eating you whole, taking every last thing you've got to give! Every fucking piece of you. And who gives a shit if it kills you?? Nobody!"

He pointed his finger to the neighbors, and they didn't even call the police.

"Oh my God, he is going to wake the entire neighborhood and get arrested. Please God, please let him go to bed. Please, mother of mercy. Just for tonight, let him stop and go inside, go to bed."

Mom pleaded with an indifferent night.

Soon, the noises ceased at the front door and our things lay broken out there on the lawn, sidewalk, and street. Our picture frames looked like seaglass out on a deserted beach in the moonlight and the furniture pieces looked like driftwood spars washed up on rocky shores. I leaned my bat on the radiator as I listened to silence.

Police sirens didn't sound, and no one congregated in the street. All of them ignored us, as he cast our belongings out. I asked God for the gun to disappear from his mind. It was my only request for divine intervention. I looked around my room to take stock of what I had.

The wallpaper had blue and green anchors, whales, and ships. My favorite colors and some of my favorite sea images. And I had never once been on a boat. I had a Jonah and the Whale bank on my workbench. You shot pennies into the whale's mouth. Dad got it for me when I was born. On the workbench was my Star Wars collection. Everything from the Millenium Falcon to X Wings to Jabba the Hut to Boba Fett to Lando. Creatures from Hoth, Tattooeen, and Endor. Jawas and Storm Troopers. Ewoks and Sand People. They were all there. I had figures from Indiana Jones, Eagle Force, GI Joe, Batman, Spider-man, and large rubber WWF wrestling figures from Hulk Hogan, Junkyard Dog, Ricky Steamboat to the Iron Sheik, Nikolai Volkoff, Captain Lou Albano, Randy "Machoman" Savage, Tito Santana, and Andre the Giant. I loved these things and took them all in during the quiet. Hours spent moving them around, whether across the universe to battle, through the deserts looking for holy treasure, or bouncing off the ropes for a clothesline…it all was so distant, ages away now. Another galaxy from where I was now.

Silence unsettled me. I watched the door and tried

not to sleep and started to lose a sense of what time it was. My bookshelf was jammed hard against the door. On the shelves were my Harvard Classics and my Hardy Boy novels. There were illustrated classics on the second shelf, and I read a bunch of them. *Treasure Island. A Tale of Two Cities. The Prince and the Pauper. The Man in the Iron Mask. Moby-Dick. Dr. Jekyll and Mr Hyde. War of the Worlds. Twenty Thousand Leagues Under the Sea. Huck Finn. Tom Sawyer. Oliver Twist. Adventures of Sherlock Holmes. Great Expectations. Call of the Wild. Mutiny on Board the HMS Bounty. Robinson Crusoe. Count of Monte Cristo. Wizard of Oz. David Copperfield. The Oregon Trail. Adventures of Robin Hood. Black Beauty. The Three Musketeers. Captains Courageous. A Connecticut Yankee in King Arthur's Court. Little Women. The Last of the Mohicans. Around the World in 80 Days. Tales of Mystery and Terror.* All came from my father, and they were in the hallway, barricading my door. Stupid as it was, I thought about all the ones I promised to read some day. I thought about the stories I had read. Ones I liked, others I didn't. I promised I'd read 'em all if I survived tonight. I imagined faraway places I wanted to visit and wanted nothing but one of those classics and a quiet nook in some safe place, like a private club in Manhattan. An island alone, blazing a trail somewhere, robbing the rich to feed the poor, making it on your own, fighting for what's right. All those stories, and they all seemed too late for me now.

The upstairs parquet floor creaked when we walked across it. Always did. It was an old patchwork floor, sagged in the hallway and splintered in spots, and you could hear every footfall.

I watched the door and grew tired. My eyes drooped. My heart was still pounding. The danger subsided and we listened for more noise from below. Mom was slumped near the radiator on the floor. I sat down on the edge of my bed. The silence scared us both. Somehow, we imagined him asleep below. Mom would cover him in a white sheet wherever he fell and slumbered. And that would be it, for now.

It was a silent eternity, and then without warning, his boots smashed the inner panel of my door. We never heard a sound and he must have climbed over the railing and avoided the floor, like a sailor scaling the rigging. His fists followed, and the door was splintered in seconds. He pulled the door off the jamb and began to kick the bookcase blocking his path. Mom screamed and the bookcase broke into pieces like the doorframe. He kept repeating one phrase, *fuck me, fuck me, fuck me.* That was all he said. No warning. He moved like a machine. The chants stopped and the ravings were replaced by calm swift kicks and punches to the only impediments left. He tossed my Illustrated Classics and Hardy Boys books behind him, calmly, like Michael Myers in *Halloween.* He threw a few volumes down the hall towards the bathroom.

I stepped forth, clutched the bat and cocked it behind my head. I was a lefty hitter in position for one swing. I don't know what came from my mouth. I just knew I was about to die. Death would come with my weapon in hand. I stepped in front of Mom to fight. Mom yelled Dad's name as she retreated back towards the windows in my room and crumpled in a ball on the floor. I was twelve.

I assumed a gunshot was to be fired. The gun was tucked in his workbelt, right behind the worn notches. Next thought was a pummeling to death with his fists with my skull bone caving in on my brain. No place to go, no time to exit. Flight impossible. I screamed bloody murder back at him: *What the fuck are you doing? What are you fucking doing? What the hell is wrong with you?*

Then, he stopped with a splintered shard of wood in hand. There came the most terrifying words I've ever heard uttered. First, his eyes rolled back in his head and they scoured the ceiling. He craned his neck in a lilt and opened up his mouth to reveal his teeth in a twisted smile. He looked like a bird of prey, ready to drink the blood of his victims and pick the flesh from their bones. He said in a Southern drawl: *"There ain't nothing wrong with me. Nothing at all. Ain't nothing wrong with me, boy."*

He looked like a deranged Edgar Allan Poe and it was not the voice heard previously. I didn't know where it came from or who it was, but the words sent chills down my spine. His eyes didn't stay focused on either of us. A dark, twisted leer burned over his face. His hazel eyes were distant and demonic behind his glasses, and his arms were down by his side, with a spike of wood in his fist, ready to strike. There was a stain on his shirt, probably from spilled bourbon or whisky. A smell of hard liquor filled the room and there was no escape. He was about to kill us. All he had to do was act. He entered the room a step beyond the doorway. I gripped my measly wooden bat for dear life and summoned every ounce of courage left inside my body.

Mom yelled out in agony. "Jim! Jim! It's your son! It's Jonah. You wouldn't hurt Jonah. He's your son, Jim! You can't hurt your son. Please, Please! Please stop. I beg you! Go back downstairs. Don't hurt Jonah, Jim. Jim! You can't hurt Jonah!" Her pleas were spoken from her knees, her body crumpled by the radiator, near the window.

My name was repeated like a prayer. It broke his drifting eyes and somewhere inside my father looked out on the scene before him through the haze of alcohol and drugs. He repeated the phrase again. "*There ain't nothing wrong with me.*"

I moved forward, screaming, threatening. The bat was in position for repeated strikes. My breaths were hard and fast. My heart raced and began to hurt from pounding. My eyes fixed on him, forcing every nerve in my body forward. My brain seized with anger and fixation.

He laughed and looked straight through me without a shred of recognition. His eyes continued to roll and he repeated the phrase again through the Southern drawl, and terror seized me. *There ain't nothing wrong with me.* Angry incoherent words were my last resort against it. His glassy orbs held the devil in them. There was no stopping it if it came forward. Mom cried and screamed and her words disappeared into silent shrieks. I couldn't hear her anymore and her words were incoherent.

The bat was cocked back over my shoulder and fear turned to rage. My jaw tightened and locked. My teeth ground together and my face clenched in resolute hatred. Every bit of me said fight and die if you must.

"What the fuck are you doing? What the fuck is wrong with you? You sick, twisted fuck. Get the fuck out of here! Get out before I fucking kill you, you fucking devil!"

I screamed with all my might across the void between us. My door lay in shards and my books were cast in piles at the exit. Dad's eyes roved the room and then he turned to my wall. He ripped the Keith Hernandez poster off my wall with a flick of his fingers. He did the same to the Michael Jordan one next to it. He left the new print of *Kindred Spirits* in the far corner. He moved towards my workbench and grabbed an X-Wing Fighter and threw it like a paper airplane out the broken door and chuckled.

"Twelve fucking years old and playing with toys. Time to grow up, boy. Be a man. You going to be a man, right? Going to be a man tonight? Take matters in your own hands. Like you know how to use that thing except for playing with balls and sticking it up your ass."

"Fuck you, you fucking asshole!! Demented fuck. You're a sick motherfucker!!"

"I told you, *There ain't nothing wrong with me. Boy.*"

He laughed, opened my trunk and flipped the contents out on the floor. For a moment, he glared at me, then he saw the cards scattered at his feet. The 1954 set was right in front of him, in a green binder with our names and 1954 in his own Catholic-school handwriting. He stared for a second, kicked the binder with his foot and then turned around.

He staggered toward where he had entered seconds before, and I moved behind to kill him. Mom reared up from the floor and threw her arms around me.

"No, Jonah, no. Let him go…it's over. It's all over. He's going. It's all done, son. Over, it's over."

"Get the fuck off my arms, Ma!! Get the fuck off me!! I'm going to kill that sonofabitch and be done with it!"

Dad walked through the door, then turned to me, "You ain't gonna touch me, boy. Better pray that I don't rip your sorry smartass head clean off your body and throw it out front, you puny little bastard. You ain't shit. Never will be." He chuckled, as he was leaving. I froze in place. My words were my only defense.

"Go back to fucking hell!! Get the fuck out of here, asshole!!"

Mom released me and stood next to me as I went to the broken doorway, screaming as he exited the parquet hallway to the stairs. He turned only once as he strolled across the creaking parquet floor. Noise echoed after every footfall. He smiled back at me and raised his finger to his lips. He shooshed me from the top of the stairs and made his way back down the steps. His feet plodded ahead robotically. He walked deliberately, stepping up and down. He was like a madman serial killer, proceeding down the stairs without a rush, as if he knew the victims never got away, no matter what, even if they hid, ran, or fought. He never looked back up the stairs; his eyes were focused downward, and the grin across his face tortured me with fear and hatred.

Mom held my arm and dropped to her knees in tears to pray. She was still clutching a broken string of rosary beads. I was still holding a bat, sobbing in deep heaves, and looking at my broken things.

We waited together for fifteen minutes, crying and praying and looking outside. The noises downstairs ceased in the green house and Mom started out the door and down the stairs. I followed close behind with my bat.

Downstairs, our house was in shambles. It was like a tornado had blown through the dining room and all our crystal goblets had been tossed against the walls. Fine china was shattered on the floor and the cabinets were cracked. The shelf where the Rockwells rested was pulled from the wall and hanging by a single screw. I surveyed the damage silently, shaking my head and cursing under my breath. Mom sobbed for her home in smithereens. The world she had assembled lay in broken shards of glass, and crumpled pictures and torn pieces of wood.

"Holy shit."

"We need to get things inside quickly."

Mom ran out into the street to collect the pieces of our lives, and I followed blindly and silently. She found wedding pictures, baby albums, and household decorations. Pieces of furniture and broken videotapes were out in the street and at the curb. A harpoon stuck like a flagpole in the lawn, and I picked this up and held it with my bat. The houses around us remained dark, with few exceptions. A few people peered out through the curtains, as Mom worked like an elf, carrying her things quickly back inside, clutching photos close to her heart.

I was drowning. Tears covered my face, and I didn't want to see any of it, anymore. I picked up some of their nautical antiques and went to a mossy cave from a magazine in my mind, where gentle octopi roamed, fish darted through seaweeds and eels ducked their head out of rock crevices. The sunlight shimmered through the darkened waters and my eyes were behind a scuba mask, and I was far away from Marine Park, for good. On a boat with an anchor, I was somewhere, diving with a harpoon, looking for something better in underwater wreckages with sea creatures and looking for gentle whales breathing water out into the air.

I dropped my harpoon and bat amid the rubble. I pitched in with bringing things inside. Glass jutted from the carpet fibers and the house was a shipwreck. Mom was collecting debris and bagging it. There was driftwood and detritus to scan through, searching for some hidden gems left in the wake of the wrath.

My weapons were down when I heard rustling in the kitchen. He looked in at us amid the broken spars and masts of our lives and drank one more gulp of whisky. He vomited on the tile floor, as if he had swallowed seawater and expunged it from his system. He didn't say anything anymore and went downstairs. I was numb and finished.

Mom found her plastic statue of the Infant of Prague. The Infant was headless, and she started to look for the glue for the plastic statue. I took the statue from her hands and tossed the saint on the floor without speaking.

"We have to clean this up, so Merry doesn't see it. She is too young to understand what happened. Fuck, no one can understand it. I'm sorry, Jonah. You have to help me for a bit, ok? Please?"

"She's not going to notice everything's broken?"

"Of course she will, but she doesn't have to know about this. We'll figure something else out. Like an intruder or something."

"She'll know. She's not stupid. We can't hide this. Not anymore."

"All right, we'll tell her. But let's just salvage what we can, ok? No one needs to see this as bad as it is."

It wasn't okay but it was done. In silence, we collected it all. Mom had glue and she set broken pieces together with large dabs of adhesive. She held the salvageable pieces in place, even though the scars of the breaks were visible and obvious. Mom and I cast the broken furniture out in the backyard with the ivy and wisteria.

At daybreak, I dragged my weary body to bed and Mom tucked me in beneath my *Star Wars* sheets. When she left, I went under the bed to sleep.

There was a nightlight on, which I hadn't used in years. I stared at my blue and green sea wallpaper. Anchors, whales, and ships surrounded me, and I wanted them to take me away, far away from here. It was time to pull up anchor, get aboard a ship, and go seek whales. It was time to get away.

In the morning, Dad was in the basement, drugged and unconscious. Mom was on the basement steps smoking Kools, watching him sleep and breathe.

Gun, Pills, Booze on the Kitchen Table

It was that damn six-shot pistol. He carried it around in his belt. And we never got rid of it. Sometimes it flashed before my eyes when he left the house. Sometimes he stuffed it under his driver's seat with the paper receipts and fast food containers.

Mom forced me back out to work with him. We didn't say much about the drugs and alcohol and his destruction of the house. He came and went like a shadow, day and night, working fifteen hours a day. I minded my business and kept to myself. The family ignored it, and he just kept working. And we went on, ignoring everything that happened.

Merry painted and kept to herself. She knew something happened, but we didn't give the details. Mom fixed her dollhouses and took a part-time job. I read, wrote, and practiced graffiti.

It was summer, and I stopped working for a few days. I started to look for some off-the-book work elsewhere, away from him. My buddy Paul Costello and I were practicing tags on the garages of the black alley down the street and behind garages around the neighborhood. Paul lived down the block. Some kids tried to rag on him for having a big schnoz, but he owned it and started writing BEAK. I was working on TALE and VERE. In a week or so, we'd hit the junior high near the park. Our tags looked fresh, big-bubbled letters in black outline and white centers. Or a cool mix with red, white, and blue.

For a while, we worked on designs in spiral-bound notebooks. My sister gave me help with some colors, even though she didn't get what we were aiming for. We sprayed up the garage behind Paulie's house. We wanted to get it mint, before we tried something out where people could see it.

One day, we saw my father's truck pull up. I thought little of it. Mom was doing part-time work as an optician at a local eyeglass place for extra income now, near the mall about a mile away. No one was home.

"What's your pops doing home, man?"

"No idea. Fucker's probably downing a quart of something and going to pass out. How it is when he's got a free minute to collapse."

"Should we give a look? Not like him. He's usually out till ten pm, right?"

"True. Not like I give a shit anymore. Let him do what he wants. I don't care what he does."

"You don't want a repeat of that shit, man. And that's not true. He's your pops. I'd take a look and see what he's up to."

"Fine, let's take a walk down there and see what's up. Can grab my glove, while we're at it."

We walked down to get my baseball mitt. Paul was outside, waiting in the yard, throwing a tennis ball into the air above his head. I walked into the kitchen and there he was. Before him on the kitchen table was the pistol. The metal was worn; the handle was brown. Four bottles of pills were scattered haphazardly. The white tops were off, and the brown bottles were empty. Two bottles of liquor were there on the table and three packs of Marlboro cigarettes. The Jack Daniels bottle was half-full. The Smirnoff Vodka bottle was drained. A cigarette butt burned and smoldered in the ashtray beside the red and white packs.

"What's happening?"

"Come, sit down. I'd like you to see this."

My feet stopped in the archway of our kitchen. Flight was my first thought, but my eyes froze on all the objects on the table.

"Paulie's outside. I need to…"

"Send Paulie away. You got to do something important with the old man."

"Ok, hold on. I'll tell him."

I ran to the front door and told Paul to get help, lots of it. He saw my eyes and knew the deal. Paulie had asthma but he jetted down the street. I returned to the kitchen, walking deliberately through our living room, through the dining room to the kitchen. Most of the stuff was back in some order. A lot had been replaced. Broken stuff was tossed out or taking on rain and vines in the backyard. I sat down at the table. He had the gun in his hand now.

"Have a drink?"

"I guess so."

"What do you mean? Not want to drink with your old man one time?" he asked, slurring his words.

"I just haven't ever, that's all."

"Get a glass. This won't take long."

He picked up the gun and held it awkwardly in his hands, as if he didn't know how to grip it. He moved it near his temple, then towards me. His right hand placed it back on the table.

The glass in my hands was a McDonald's collectible from 1977, a set of four. I chose Grimace on a pogo stick. Mayor McCheese held his glasses; Hamburglar was riding a train, and Big Mac was sliding along on roller skates with a whistle in his mouth. The whole set was in the kitchen cabinet.

My father poured a glass of Jack Daniel's. The bottle missed the glass, then the amber liquid settled by the drawn-on springs of the pogo stick.

"To you, boy. Drink"

I tasted the liquid and winced.

"Why are we drinking to me?" I asked.

"Because I really fucked up royally with you…I really fucked it all up, didn't I?"

"No, no you didn't. We're doing ok."

"Probably fucking scarred you for life. And you know what?"

"What?"

"There are fucking days when I wished you and I weren't born. I mean that. Both of us. I worked my fucking piece of shit ass off all my life and for all of you in this house. And for what? For what? What do I get?"

"I know you did. But it's not my fault I was born."

"True. Not your fault. Right. Right."

"And I know you're working yourself into the ground, but what the hell is this going to do? Just going to make it all worse."

"What do you mean? Worse? How? I work like a fucking dog, and I'm gonna be remembered for a night of hell I can't get back. Fuck it…all done in. Blink of an eye. Just because you can't take it anymore, break down, and let loose. All falls to shit."

"So now what? Shoot both of us? That's how it's going to work. Because I don't give a shit anymore."

"Who the *fuck* said I'm shooting you? Taking care of my mess once and for all. You're the witness."

He was slurring and drinking.

"It doesn't have to be like this. Can always get better, Dad. We can make it better."

"LIKE HELL IT CAN. I'M WORKING MYSELF TO DEATH FOR THIS HOUSE AND YOU'RE ALL EATING

ME ALIVE."

"I can eat less. Promise. I won't take seconds anymore. I'm sorry, I mean it. And I'm out trying to find a job. Ask Paulie. We scoured the whole neighborhood the last few weeks. I know I need to pitch in more."

He pulled the strands of his dark hair in his fists and started to weep. His head was swaying a bit, and his eyes turned to look out the window. His garden was a tangle of vine and leaves. He hadn't tended it because of work. The wisteria twisted itself in knots and ate everything in its path. It snaked across fences, ran up the mimosa tree, and threaded itself around anything in its path. The vine had a chokehold on St. Francis. The entanglement worked its way up the trees to the sky. Bamboo he planted in pots had migrated into the yard, and the stalks shot to the sky and shimmered in the wind. Some broken pieces of furniture sat in the yard with the wisteria, ivy, and bamboo.

As he stared into the yard, I took the gun with a quick reach. For a few seconds, he didn't turn his head to look for it. I wanted to call 911, but I feared he had a few bursts of anger left in him. He saw the gun in my right hand.

"Going to shoot me? End my misery? Not the first time you thought about killing me, I'm sure."

"Don't give me that shit. I'm just not letting you off yourself. That's all. What the hell am I supposed to do? Let you kill yourself?"

He laughed for a moment and then grew silent. His eyes

were out in the garden as if he saw someone approaching through the tangle. He rubbed his eyes, and his steel-rimmed glasses fell from his face. His eyes were bloodshot and watery. "Fuck. What a piece of shit I am. I tried, I really tried…"

The room was silent, but he acted like someone was laughing. He told them to stop laughing, to fuck off, to die. He spoke words to a closed window without anyone present.

"I am not you…" the words whispered from his lips. They didn't seem to be for me.

"I know you're not. It's going to be ok. You're not yourself right now and we're going to fix it."

He wasn't listening and asked me to shoot him once in the head. Just once, he said. Pull the trigger. He folded his arms on the table and placed his head on top of them.

"We can figure it out and there's no way I'm doing that."

"I'm sorry, boy. I let all fuck me up. I should've known better. Should have seen it coming, should have been better to you, to everybody…"

"We're going to make it better and it's not this way…"

"So much we never got a chance to do…and see. Finish…"

Sound of rushing feet came from behind me and Paul and his uncle Vito entered the room. Vito was a restaurant owner with a trucking company on the side.

His hair was thinning, slicked back atop his forehead. He had on black leather shoes, black suit pants, and a white, striped silk shirt, with the buttons opened to reveal a large gold cross in his chest hairs. He entered and worked quickly, like he'd seen this before.

"Jimmy, buddy, how's it going here? What did we take? What did we take??? We're going to get you out of here, Jimmy. Let's go, boys, let's go."

Dad didn't move, and Vito pushed the table away, grabbed my father around the arms and lifted. Paul and I grabbed his legs. Vito kept talking to my father in rapid succession. "Jimmy, what did we take, buddy? What's on the table? Paulie, grab the fucking pills and put 'em in a bag."

I grabbed Dad's legs and Paulie collected the bottles.

Dad's head swayed in position; he said something incoherently. His gibberish was inaudible, but he repeated things he hadn't finished. Paulie grabbed the other leg again and we were moving toward the front door. Vito had his car idling outside. It was a black Cadillac sedan. Dad slumped on the backseat—I sat next to him. Vito and Paul jumped into the front seat. The tires screeched as he accelerated down the street against traffic. He beeped the horn and swerved away from oncoming cars.

I don't remember approaching the hospital. We jumped the curb. Vito pulled Dad out by himself and dragged him from around the waist. Paul and I followed, and my dad's lifeless form was on a gurney, and Vito was motioning for doctors to help.

Paul pointed to my waistline. The gun was tucked there in plain sight. "Give me that fucking thing."

I handed it to him mechanically and he tossed it into the Cadillac.

"What the fuck, man! Jesus Christ." Paul was breathing heavily.

My best friend pulled his hands through his hair and then took a puff from his inhaler. He reached over and flicked my shoulder with his hand.

"Don't mention the gun. Just forget about it. We'll figure what to do with it," Paul said, pacing around the car.

"Maybe we should keep it?"

"Fuck that. You're fucking crazy."

"Maybe." I walked in a circle around the Cadillac and leaned on the bumper.

Dad's stomach was pumped. He was admitted for psychological evaluations.

Vito emptied the cylinder when he got back, letting the bullets fall to the carpeted mats of his front passenger seat. "Put this damn thing out of sight. Don't tell anyone where you put it," he said to me, handing me Dad's pistol.

I nodded and took it back from him when he dropped me off. I hid it in the basement behind the washing machine. I couldn't bring myself to smash it.

The doctors at Kings Highway Hospital saved him. They transferred Dad to a mental hospital in Manhattan. The next time he came home, he was in hospital pajamas, a comatose zombie, and went back after a short stay. It took him six months to come back home. And then he went right back to work.

Kelson

It all seemed off. Mom never relented with the back-to-work exterminating crap, to keep things together with Dad. Keep an eye on him, feed me to the wolves, or whatever. Who knows. And I wanted nothing to do with him. Didn't want him at games, or asking me questions, about anything. I told her I had other plans to figure out. Kept my mouth shut to him. Come to think of it, the last real exchange we had was over cards. Dad came in and handed me Yogi Berra and Ernie Banks for the 1954 set. Must have costs a few bucks. My exact words were: "Cool. I'll put 'em where they belong. Done."

I raided Dad's toolroom and stole a whole bunch of things. All of it went into a canvas burlap bag. I'd get better use of them and build something cool. I took Dad's pistol from behind the washing machine and put it in my bag for safekeeping. Plan was to build a boat and sail it on my own, somewhere, but probably down in Gerritsen Creek. Bag was also a good place to keep my aerosols for practice tags without being caught. This was all I was really interested in, and maybe hanging a little with Paulie. Merry said I was becoming a shadow, and I liked that. She painted pictures of me as a ghost and superhero, and I hung them in my room.

Diogenes "Dee" Santiago held Dad's business together

as he recovered. I helped Dee a little with a few jobs, but that was about it. It was all I could take. Dee wasn't bad. He split tips and picked me up for work in a tan Chevy Malibu and bought me Taco Bell. Dad found Dee living in the horse barns at Belmont like eight years ago. Dad said it was hell and Dee was smart and scared. He was living in a barn, ten feet from million-dollar thoroughbreds, infested with rats, a 17-year-old kid with nowhere to go, nothing to say. No papers. Getting food and a few dollars to send back to his family in Ecuador. Dad liked him, talked to him in pidgin Spanish, and set him up with a diner owner in Sheepshead Bay washing dishes for some extra cash. After a few years, he hired him as an apprentice exterminator and got him licensed. Dee called him "Mr. Jimmy" and only shook his head when Dad's name came up during work.

"Your father. *Mr Jimmy.* Good man. Many demons. *Loco,* even. But he always was trying to do better. Get it right. He'll get back on his feet. You'll see."

"Have my doubts with that, amigo. He's loco."

"Not that much. You'll see. He'll be back. Better. Just need to screw his head on straight. No more booze, drugs. They kill him. No way to be."

I went for a job at the lumberyard in Sheepshead as stock boy, off-the-books. I lied about my age. They didn't care. They gave me a locker and I stored my bag in it. I wanted to be a yard worker and hang with the older guys.

Occasionally Jay, who had a crewcut and black belt in judo, and Keith, a wiseass Italian kid from Bensonhurst, brought me out to the woodpiles to saw a sheet of plywood in half. They counted my fingers after the cut was done. And they laughed and made me go flirt with the girls at the beverage and recycling center across the street. I restocked shelves with nails, sealant, cleaning stuff, gloves, you name it. And, I entered numbers in a nicotine-stained computer terminal to keep things up-to-date.

One time, the foreman caught me hanging out with Keith and Jay in the yard, loading the truck for a delivery. I wasn't in the union, so he decided to exercise lumberyard justice. In a raging thunderstorm, foreman sent me out with a clipboard, twenty sheets of blank paper and a pen. My job was to count the wood, all of it, during a torrential downpour. Took me a few hours, but I did it. And he crumbled up the saturated paper and tossed it in my face when I was done. I stopped going out to hang out in the yard after that.

My tool bag had what I needed to split. I was thinking about building homes, measuring inches and writing marks with fat charcoal pencils on wood beams for precise cuts. I listened to tips from all the contractors and took down everything I could in a notebook. I always tried to keep tabs on things I need for jobs, and all my tools doubled as weapons. And the bag was just the right place to hide my spray cans and Dad's empty gun.

I walked the neighborhood to stay away from home. I spent long hours out there and tagged up deserted stretches along the Belt Parkway. Paulie joined me sometimes. He said the Irish were stubborn as shit and that's why everyone went back to business in my house and Mom wanted me back out working with Dad. I shrugged. Probably right. Seemed a long while before I could get out. Bide my time and do things I wanted to do until then. Paulie and I tweaked our tags out in the marsh, where no one would find them. BEAK, TALE, VERE. I made up cool slogans for what VERE and TALE stood for. Better Earn And Kill. Take Aim Look Everywhere. Vice Endured Respect Earned. We fought the beach rat kids of Gerritsen Beach every now and then when we found them in the marsh.

The burned-out cars provided refuge. The tidal waters ebbed and flowed. In the mud, I dug with my bare hands and found a little arrowhead and a ceramic pot from the 1940s. The common reeds and mugwort swayed in the gentle breezes and the cordgrass rippled in mighty storm winds. I wrote more and more. Poems were penciled in a slim notebook, toted in my back pocket. I read books about the American road that I found in Dad's library. Dirt and mud trails led to the sea where I took cover sometimes, watched lovers and teenagers come and go through makeshift trails in the reeds. I was alone for long spells of time, writing in my notebook and practicing my tags.

Sometimes, a fire began in the salt marsh. The flames rose hot and wild during dry summer days. The fire department came and put it out. Firefighters doused the flickering reeds and next day the burnt-out stubs of grass and reeds felt warm to the touch. I wrote down poems about everything. And wondered who set the fires. Sometimes it was careless couples tossing cigs into dry brush. Sometimes it was a party that let the firepit get away from them. Sometimes I saw an arsonist skulking through the reeds, wanting to burn it all down to ash.

Bayberries were hidden amidst the tall grass. Pleasure boats and jet skis darting through the hidden channels of the marsh. Under my feet, sightings were jotted in random order. Most of the poems and short pieces were about characters and things in the marsh. I discovered car motors, rusting along the muddy banks. Old fishing boats with holes in their hulls, sunk in the mud of the shore. The washed-up boats, cast ashore here in the middle of nowhere, made me dream. I wondered about fixing one of these small skiffs and rowing out to explore the islands beyond me. An unreachable, uninhabited island was just off the marsh shoreline called White Island or Mau Mau to some, and that's exactly where I wanted to go.

In all weather I was out there on the shore, dreaming

of sanctuary in the stream, lurking out there in the inlets and across the salt marsh. Not far away was Dead Horse Bay. Every day I sought solace in a salt marsh, and I'd make my way down to Dead Horse to collect treasures from decades ago. The tides came in, pushed things out. The shore by the Gil Hodges Bridge used to be a glue factory and garbage dump decades ago. Broken glass lined the shore like pebbles and seashells and it gleamed in the summer sun like jewels. Dad showed me this place years ago.

The birds flew in and sat atop the pylons of the old mill. I studied a black cormorant, sitting and drying its wings, then plunging down into the water for fish. The black bird spread its wings and let the sun glisten on its wing, drying its feather slowly and patiently before taking off for nether ports of call. It swooped down into the channel for small fish.

The pylons were where the mill ground flour with the help of the tides during Revolutionary days. Old Hugh Gerritsen's mill was scarcely visible at low tide. Washington stopped here during the Revolutionary War. It burned down in the 1930s. Probably arson. Another useless fact from Dad. All that was left was a few wood markers in the water, standing stationary against the tug of the salt water pulling currents far away to the sea and returning in waves as the ripples covered the mill in daily floods.

Dad's tools were in my knapsack. I had a saw, two hammers, three screwdrivers, planer, wrench, mallet, tape measure, a box of roofing nails, a journal and pen and an unloaded gun. They came with me everywhere. The jangling of the tools sounded my approach, like a leper walking with bells attached to his cloak. I needed a project and gleaned more knowledge from contractors. How they did this, what to do with that. I wrote it down during breaks. Mostly, men in the yard sent me away now and back to my floor-mopping, stock-shelving, and product-counting. Too many questions for busy guys on the clock, but I kept asking.

The garbage collected in the reeds and the muddy trails. Soda cans and fast food Styrofoam containers multiplied by the hour. Glass jars and plastic bottles and aluminum cans bobbed up and down in the surf, and oil slicks were seen glinting in the sun-streaked ripples of the water. Sometimes a stolen bike was down there hidden under the branches of a low-hanging tree.

Our marsh was a garbage dump and graveyard for burnt cars. In those cars, I sat and wrote poems. I collected thoughts about relics and trash and birds and raccoons and hermits. Occasionally, a hermit crab walked along the shore and watched my movements with an eager eye. The seabirds swooped down into the current waters out in the channel waters, seeking fish.

This was my place. Motorized dirt bikes buzzed

down murky trails towards the sea. Bikers jumped dirt hills and turned along mazes carved through common insidious reeds. Cordgrass and reeds forever swayed in sea winds and the sounds of the avenue faded away. The salt marsh kept the currents at bay, a buffer for the shore for days and nights of high tides and storm surges. Objects choked its efforts and I walked around, collecting them in piles for the rangers and can collectors. Garbage drifted down off the avenue and collected from teenagers' parties. Fires burned holes through the heart of phyragmites, and bayberries fought against the weeds to find sunlight amidst the undergrowth. Sometimes I imagined working for parks out there, the mysterious one collecting trash in piles for the parks rangers. Maybe someone would notice. Maybe they'd care.

One day, I found my project in a solitary walk, taking down tidbits of what I'd come across. Like a rowboat hidden among the reeds, far out of sight. Deep in the undergrowth of the weeds, I spotted an old hermit's camp. A homeless man set up shelter, down in Gerritsen Beach. He made a fire with a stolen barbecue, roasted mussels and clams, polluted from the expunging of the sewer treatment plant two miles away in Sheepshead Bay and a stone's throw from Dead Horse. I watched him, an old homeless Vietnam Vet who set up camp and drank himself into oblivion with Ripple for a few weeks. He recited lines of something and laughed himself to sleep. Sometimes, you'd see him staring out to the water, staring out at the bridge. I started to imagine what his story was, but I was too afraid to talk to him.

One day, paint ballers shot the camp up with splashes of color. Hermit must have moved on. Camp hadn't been used in a few days. The shells were picked through, along with the assorted discarded fast food containers. His boat had a hole in it, and he didn't use it, and I imagined the old man spent his days here, holding on to a broken boat with the hope he'd use it to fish and clam in the marsh, before moving on. He was eating things he wasn't supposed to and drinking alone, at night before a makeshift campfire. In one firepit, bottles of Night Train and Cisco lay charred and broken. He probably drank during long nights to forget. I wondered what he was forgetting and wrote about where he cast off to, or if he died somewhere in the marsh and nobody knew yet. A couple of times I went looking for him, hoping to find him alive, or dead, so I could get him a proper burial.

On one return to the camp, I decided to patch his boat and use it again. Hermit wouldn't mind anymore, I was sure. My tools could be put to use, finally, for something besides protection. With some effort and luck, my tools could make the rowboat seaworthy. Dad had an old oar, hanging on his wall downstairs, which was mine for the taking. The rowboat soon became my restoration project.

I spent an early summer here, avoiding my dad. I took wood from my lumberyard for my boat patchwork along the muddy shore. My less-than-minimum wage was assuaged with the scraps of timber at my disposal.

Still, working alone was good. Dad passed me in the morning and we didn't say much. Occasionally he handed me a 1954 baseball card, as if it would start a conversation. I stayed quiet. Re-launching that rowboat and sailing it to the untouched bird sanctuary out across the canal to White Island was my focus. Geese nested out there; buffleheads and mallards paddled about the creek waters. Some seagulls lurked on the shores. Plovers, herons, and cormorants were out there too. Snowy egrets and laughing gulls were out beyond human paths. The boat patching started to take place on the sand, secluded by swaying reeds. A piece of driftwood was my bench and two barrels balanced it as table legs. My tools stayed dry in my canvas bag. I found a nice bit of stump to prop up the boat and rolled it into place. I covered it with a blue tarp I found along the edge of the water.

Weeks went by and my work neared completion. I planed and hammered away at the hull. I wanted nothing more than for the boat to float down the byway, even once, and cross from shore to shore. It was all trial and error. I caulked my patch job and used sealant on the cracks and crevices. I fitted my piece with daily saw shavings and whittling of wood into place. The date for my launch neared. Before me was White Island. The bottom hole was closed up and globs of goo dripped from the cracks. It all looked in place. The pieces dried and the boat was covered under a blue tarp near a burnt out, stolen car. After a few days drying, I dragged the boat down to the water's edge. I had a small shovel with me to row. The oar was too risky to steal. Someone at home would notice. The boat touched the dark water of the creek and I hopped in to the captain's seat. We slid on to the surface of the water. With my weight, water seeped in through the cracks. The boat and I were out on the salt marsh, headed for White Island when we began to sink. Water gushed in from the patching. I stopped and watched the bubbles rise in the water amassing in the bottom of my ship. I didn't jump. I let the water rise and felt the bottom of the boat drift slowly beneath the glimmerglass. Soon, I was swimming in the creek's murky waters. The journey ended in five minutes, an abysmal failure. My boat was slowly sinking, a ghost heading to the bottom of waters once fished by Indians.

As I stepped on to the sand, I saw them there centuries ago, swimming and using canoes and pulling fish up from the depths with nets. Their boats didn't sink, and they picked oysters and clams from the banks in knee-deep high water. The Lenapes looked back at me, here alone. I wondered if they laughed at the sight of a lonely white boy, trying to make it to White Island, sanctuary for seabirds, and sinking slowly beneath the waves. My repair work now added to the debris under the shoreline. I tossed a rock into the water and gave up. I was wet and my tool bag had a grey and pink bathroom towel in it. I dried myself off. Only a ghostly image of the boat was visible in the murky water.

A laughing gull grabbed mussels from the seabed. It squawked and fetched its prize and dropped it on a rock. Over and over again, it tossed the shell on the hard surface to get at its prize. The bird got the mussel. I was going home all wet. My dumb rowboat sunk. Tools were useless in my hands.

Footfalls approached through the reeds at a short distance from my spot. The makeshift camp was hidden. Someone must have been watching, probably a park ranger, ready to scold me or arrest me for disturbing the water. Flight was my first thought, then fight came to mind. Perhaps the homeless hermit returned to beat me for stealing his campsite and sinking his boat. The hammer was in my right hand; my left hand explored the bag for my empty gun.

In a second, Dad appeared in the clearing in the path. We hadn't spoken much in months. Our passings were silent nods. He often tried to discuss sports and school with me. I met questions with a stark silence, or a matter-of-fact, two-word response. Right now, it was uncertain why he was here, why he followed me. The tools were still clutched in my hands. He saw the gun.

"How's it going, Jonah? Didn't mean to disturb you."

"You following me?"

"I wanted to see what you'd been up to. Knew you've been spending time down here. Just curious to see why. Sorry if it was spying."

"Well, whatever. Figures you'd watch me fail with the one fucking thing I wanted to do on my own."

My eyes focused on the ground, reassembling and packing the tools for transport.

"I can help you. Give me a chance. I know you've been avoiding me like the plague these last few months. Shit, can't say I blame you in the slightest. Been some pretty dark times at home..." His words trailed off in shame.

"You can say that again."

"I'm sorry. I wish I could change what happened, but I can't. I can only work to change things right now. Maybe you can learn to look beyond the past, let me make amends?"

It was AA, I was certain. Maybe I was a step, or something, but I decided to play along. Mom said he was going to meetings during the day on his routes.

"So, what can you help me do?"

"You want to rebuild that boat, right? How 'bout it?"

"How about what? It sunk."

"Well, let's get some waders and go get it. We can

163

throw it in the truck, bring it to the yard and fix it up. We can get it to float," he said with confidence.

The idea was insane enough for me to like it.

"I'd give that a go. Beats trying to buy one. Certainly won't have the cash for that."

"Guess we're a ways off from buying something to dock down in the marina."

"Can say that. I can't even get rowboat to float."

"I don't exactly like the idea of you walking around with that gun in your bag."

"Well, it's staying with me for now, thank you very much. Doesn't need to be in anyone else's possession and it's unloaded."

"All right. Be careful with that thing. Not a toy."

"Don't I know it."

"Glad to see you're getting use of the tools. Lumberyard treating you ok?"

"It's a job. They give me castoffs and I'm picking up things here and there."

"Not sure if I approve of the spray cans."

"What is this? Think this is up to you, right now?"

"Listen, I'm still your father. And all I'm saying is be careful. You don't want a dopey thing like that to give you a record. Not worth it in the long run."

"I'll be the judge of that."

"Fair enough. Just remember your record if you get caught."

"I won't. I do this for myself. Not destroying anyone's property."

"Ok. Give you a lift back?"

"Nah, I'll hang back a bit."

"Get some stuff to work on it tomorrow?"

"Works for me."

"See you back at home, Jonah."

The next day, we purchased waders at the bait and tackle in Sheepshead Bay. Dad bought us both Roll N Roaster for lunch beforehand and we ate it in the car. Two roast beefs, two cheese fries. Iced Tea for me. Coke for him. By mid-afternoon, both of us were in the channel up to our waists, pulling out my sunken ship from the muddy bottom. We dragged the boat back through the cordgrass, mugworts, and common reeds, across the sand and through the muddy tracks near the shore. Small wonder the rangers didn't stop us. Seemed like we were wading into waters for sunken treasures.

Once the rowboat was pulled from the water and carried to the back cab of the truck, we tied it down for the journey back to the green house. Outside in the yard, we scrapped and cut and measured. We rebuilt the broken hull. Dad helped fit a rudder to the back. We sanded down the splintery plank seats. The wood was stripped, treated and repainted. The two of us worked on it in late afternoons. Dad took time from work; I left the lumberyard with daylight to burn.

"You know what the middle part that holds it together is called?"

"Not a clue."

"Kelson. Ever read Whitman's "Song of Myself"?"

"Don't think I have. Should I?"

"I think you should. I got you a copy, if you'd like it. Mom says you're writing a lot."

"It helps me keeps things together, in perspective."

"I get that. Well, Whitman mentions a kelson in that poem. Says a kelson of creation is love. I think it's the best American poem we got—our epic, so to speak. And to top that, he's a local, working-class guy. Born on Long Island, but did most of his work down in Brooklyn Heights. Teacher. Journalist. Carpenter. In fact, one of his houses is still standing."

"You and the local guys. I did read 'Crossing Brooklyn Ferry' once. Was pretty cool being about Brooklyn and all. Didn't realize he was a carpenter."

"Yeah, his dad was a builder in Brooklyn. They bought and mortgaged a bunch of places downtown. He did a lot of things. You'll dig the rest of 'Leaves of Grass.' It's worth some serious reading, especially if you're into writing poems. He was a nurse in the Civil War, too. Whitman's really a working-class Brooklyn guy."

"Got to know how to work, right?"

"Mom said that's what you've been writing. And working, of course."

"Think it's what I'd like to give a go. With some backup plans, of course."

"Naturally. But maybe not a builder?"

"Maybe not a builder. Rub it in."

"I'm just kidding. You've got patience, kid. Just have to practice the right craft, that's all. Like anything else."

We painted the boat blue and green, colors of the sea. Paulie and I put a few tags in the inside when it was done in the yard, but he said he'd never get in the damn thing. He only did the doggie paddle and he thought the whole rowboat thing was cuckoo. Merry drew a whale, harpoon, and anchor on the outside of it for me. It looked seaworthy and pretty cool. With repairs completed and paint dried, we lifted the boat over our heads and put it back in the cab. I feared another sinking, another epic letdown. The rangers were sure to be on duty, watching for the boat to be brought down to the water's edge. We parked along the quiet, deserted road past midday. We moved quickly, carrying the boat over the silver guardrails of the marshland, through the tall weeds. The matted floor crunched under the weight of our boots. We passed plastic discards and metal poles, soda bottles and beer cans, sauce jars and wine jugs.

"Place is kind of a dump, huh?"

"Yeah, but I like it."

"I see that. Still could probably use a clean-up."

"Sometimes we all need that."

"Touché."

Silently, we slipped the boat down onto the mud. Fiddler crabs darted into their holes in the mud as we approached the shore. Dad went back to the truck. I waited by the shore and he returned a few minutes later with the oar from home. He had lacquered it to make it ready for water.

"Figured we needed something real to paddle with, right? Mom and I picked this up when we collected nautical stuff for our first place in Mystic. Think it's from a whale boat."

"Always liked that thing. I was going to steal it, but I got cold feet."

"Now or never, right? Want to paddle for the old man?"

My head nodded swiftly. Park police were bound to jump from the reeds and arrest us. Sun was glowing down out across the waters. Seabirds were far away from us. A gaggle swooped up into the sky, heading out over the island. A few gulls were in the distance, their bodies cast in shadows by sunlight. The matted debris of the reeds faded. The circles of the tufted weeds looked like straw. A few of the patches close to us looked like huts, formed by the swirling winds coming in from the sea. I absorbed every detail, down to the moving form of a horseshoe crab down below the surface. He was moving along the edge of the shoreline, tacking here and there over the assorted scraps of shells, rocks, and wreckage in the marsh. Somewhere along the shoreline the horseshoes used this space to roll over and mate. The rowboat would be a good place to find the horseshoe sanctuaries in hidden coves.

We placed the rowboat at the edge of the water, boarded and pushed off. The park rangers didn't prevent the launch and our remade vessel made its way into the channel. Dad had his hand on the rudder. The oar was in my hands. I paddled with short, thrusting strokes. Port to starboard.

"*Tho she may creak she holds!*" my father said, as we made our way across to the island before us. We had that phrase posted on a sign on the steps of the basement of the green house.

"It's working! This thing floats!"

"Damn right it does."

"Holy crap, wow. This is freaking cool."

"Just think about the Indians using this place. Heading out to new territory with a little work and invention."

We had little reason to go to this place. My eyes were ahead. A jet took off from the airport and banked left before us, heading out over the Atlantic. It was quiet, except for the occasional quack of a duck, sounding its displeasure at an approaching boat. In a few minutes, we were on White Island, not far from Dead Horse Bay. The green and blue boat was on the sand in new territory. A silence lasted for minutes as we both searched the horizon before us.

"So, now what? What made you want to come out here?"

"Not sure. Walk around, check it out. Maybe walk down to that abandoned bridge. Just seemed like a secluded place to escape to, get away. Check out some birds. Be somewhere where others can't be. Nobody comes out here."

He lit a cigarette and then stamped it out instinctively on his boot. His eyes apologized for the mistake.

"You know, when I followed you down here, I figured it was a place to think. Kind of get things in order."

"I needed that. Place has been important for me. Really like coming down here and walking around. Just wanted to set up a camp out here away from it all, watch it float by me, unseen. You know, just stay here with the seabirds on the shore. Watch it pass by me, laugh at the whole mess."

"You know…I'm really sorry for all I did. I never said so, but I am. And, I'm really grateful for what you did. Took incredible courage to be there, keep it together, through all of it."

My feet tapped mud off on the rock.

"It's over and done with, right? No reason to get stuck in the past and what we can't change. Time to move on?"

"God grant me the serenity to accept the things I cannot change, Courage to change things I can, And Wisdom to know the difference. That's the way I see it. It's time to move forward. You've got a lot ahead of you, kid. A lot of good ahead. And interesting chances. And I'm not standing in the way of that."

"Not happening again, right? No retreats into that madness?"

"Not going back to that. And we do have to move on. It won't be so bad back over there, I promise. And there's a lot to be grateful for. I know it's been rough and confusing for you, and everybody back home, but we can do something about that. Piece it back together. It would be good to get my work partner back with me."

"We did this thing, right?"

"That we did. That we did. Let that be the start of something better?"

"Can't be all bad. I didn't like not helping. I just needed some time to sort some things out."

"I get it. Believe me, I do. And I can't tell you how impressed I was with you working, writing, taking things on yourself. Shows character."

"If you need an extra set of hands, I'll pitch in when I can. Beats counting lumber in a rainstorm."

"Is that what they did to you?"

"Yeah, they got a big laugh out of that."

"Nothing like telling you who's low man on the totem pole."

"Yeah, I've learned that lesson pretty well."

He stuck out his hand. It was the same, still soiled with dirt, hardened by callouses. Cuts from wire mesh fencing were still visible. I shook his hand and then hugged him. It was two awkward hand pats across shoulder blades, but it was what we mustered.

"You handling things better now? Know there's been a lot dumped on you."

"I'm owning up to things. And figuring out when I need to fix things I broke."

"Good to hear. Must be tough to do."

"Tough to admit you fucked up. But it's probably a lot worse when you don't. That regret isn't something you want to carry with you. And booze and pills don't make the load any easier. Actually cloud shit up a lot faster."

"I'm here to help when you need it. And don't stress yourself out about me and this crap I'm carrying around with me. I've got stuff under control, and I've got things I want to do."

"I know you do. Just be careful there, Mr. Tale. Or Vere, whatever."

"They do look cool, right?"

"Still knuckleheaded, but I'm not the best one to point fingers."

"Only do it for myself, really. No property. Just something that means something to me. Tough to explain."

"I guess that's up to you. Never did figure out the meaning of those cave painters, did we?"

"We didn't. And maybe it's not as cool as those awesome bears and bison and horses, but it's meaningful right now. Guess we have to keep working at it."

"Merry got the anchors, whales just right. Maybe you stick to words, Mr. Stick Figure. Maybe that's where you've got something to say."

"Try to keep my options open. Not bad being a Jack of All Trades in the long run."

"Keeps things interesting. Remember when you wanted to be a pilot all those years ago? Baseball player. Scuba diver. Boat captain. Archaeologist."

"Jedi. Well, I can now check off boat captain. It's a career start."

"Need a first mate?"

"Sure."

"Maybe we get rid of that gun sometime. Don't think we need it."

"We can get rid of it now. I carry it to look cool, and if I need to scare someone off down here."

"That might not be the wisest idea."

"Better than putting it loaded to your head."

"That may be so, but it could get you killed if someone like a cop sees it. Not worth it."

"Toss it? Want the honors?"

"You do it. You're the one with the arm, right?"

I smiled and then I wound-up and pitched the pistol far into the channel. After a quick splash, the gun was settled down in the canal to rust.

We began to row off the island. It was beautiful at sunset. A serene wind swept along through the channel, squawks of seabirds sounded in the distance. Far off, along a pylon we watched a cormorant. The big sea bird was drying there. He was still and glistening, perched atop the wooden log jutting from the salt marsh waters. He eyed us for a moment—a single bird lording over his domain. The geese flew overhead. The buffleheads and mallards paddled by. The sun began to set.

"Make a couple of burgers when we're back? How 'bout it?" he asked.

"Really wish I could stay right out here sometimes, you know?"

"You mean nowhere? Don't get me wrong, I know what you mean about trying to escape. Understandable sometimes. For any of us. But the whole world's ahead of you, boy. You have a lot to do before becoming a reclusive hermit. Got work to do, lots of it in whatever you choose to pursue."

"I know I do. Just nice being out of the fray for a bit. Nice place to escape."

"Yes, it is, but we've all got to face things sometimes. It's the way it is. Believe me. I was trying to run off for too long. And you're too young to make this your Walden."

"Another thing I should read, I assume?"

"You got that right. Except he really wasn't a local. Massachusetts, mostly. Visited, though. Visited Whitman, in fact."

"Always back to the locals. Still, like having this place to turn to."

"Amen to that."

Silently, I settled the spot. Away from the green house and the other splintered clapboard homes of Marine Park, out on an island in a littered salt marsh.

"I have been writing about the marsh a lot."

"It's good. Interesting place. Write about what you know, that's what they say. No one would believe this is Brooklyn."

"It's really got so many stories to tell, I think. Even just looking at the stuff we leave behind. The detritus."

"*DETRITUS*. These college words are too much for me, sometimes. Always been the case."

The boat made its way across water. It held together. The patches adhered. The glue and nails held the patchwork scraps of wood where they needed to be. The paint job was clean and colorful. In my mind, there was a fisherman's hut with a writing table, out there in the island, outstretched to greet the horizon at sunset. There, I could find the space away from my home between city and sea. My imaginary hut had a scattering of objects collected from the sea drift. Cordgrass was woven together in bands to keep out the rain. The burning streaks of daylight dried the cormorant fishing for food on the pylon.

We kept our shipwrecked little boat in the water for a bit and sailed for a short spell across the salt marsh. The rowboat was going home into the backyard.

"Any other places to take this thing?"

"Dead Horse Bay, of course. It's a local, undiscovered treasure for most New Yorkers, you know."

"That it is. Sounds like a cool trip. Just be careful of those crazy jet skiers out there."

"Aye-aye."

"And read that Whitman poem. He really gets to the heart of what matters."

"And a local nonetheless?"

"That's right."

Paddling back, I knew it was but a short time to be back working besides Dad. We carried the rowboat back to the truck, secured it, and stowed it behind the arbor in the backyard. It's still there, turned over to keep out the rain. Eventually wisteria will envelope it, but the journey served the tools, and I knew I'd take it back down to sail at sunset or sunrise and feel the oar cut through calm waters and rudder through the channels in the marsh. And I knew already what Whitman meant when he used *kelson* in his poem. It's funny when you just know things, even without reading them.

Burrows

New York Racing Authority stopped paying extra for barn service in late summer. Some bright exec figured they'd save some change and we weren't doing it for free. The old man told 'em to go fuck themselves. We waited for the call back.

We went to Aqueduct and Belmont for a few weeks and sprayed the grandstands and a few offices of the big shots for a month or so. The guys in the barns kept hailing down the truck when we came through the gates. We told them to take it up with management. Dad smiled and waved and threw up his hands as we passed. Then the neighborhood calls started coming in. Rats running all over Ozone Park. And the bright exec was shown the door and we were asked back to exterminate burrows.

It was over 95 degrees when they called. Dad came downstairs and I was playing Zelda on my Nintendo.

"They caved. We got to get out there today. You game?"

"You got it. Just let me save what I've got."

"Yeah, I'll show you later some of the stuff I found. Been making maps of the lair."

"Have the patience of a saint for this game. I just want to find the things I need already and do some fighting."

"Patience is a virtue, kiddo."

"Wish I had it."

"You'll get there. Listen, we're going to have to blitzkrieg this fucking place the next few days. Going to be running."

"No worries. Today? I'm meeting Molly tonight for the movies."

"Going all right there?"

"All good, except for you walking in to the living room and saying, *who the fuck are you?*"

"I was just bustin' chops. She knew that."

"I know, I'm just kidding. She handled it fine."

"Don't get too serious there, boy. College is coming. Going to be a whole new world for you. You don't want to be covering up tattoos on your arms like me when you're in over your head. Take it slow."

"Maybe I should stick around here, you know. Going to take the firemen's test soon. Not sure what I want to do, really. I just go back and forth with how to proceed."

"You're all over the place, my friend. Weren't you writing your way into the Century Club? Boating your way into the New York Yacht Club? College is the way out of this shit. All of it. Not too long ago, you were going to be a carpenter, for Christ's sake, and build boats."

"I suck at measurements, as you know."

"Well, college is where you're headed, where you belong. First Fennell to do it, as you well know. That shit isn't something to pass up."

"Maybe I just want to write my own way. Forget going away. Figure out a job that has benefits and stability. I'd be a captain. Raise a family. I don't know yet. Can always write on the side."

"Listen, this is to be continued. You busted your ass to get through high school. Now's not the time to stop and smell the fucking roses. Got to keep going. You have a lot of choices ahead of you, but I'm thinking firemen and carpenter should be lower on the list. All due respect."

"Whatever you say."

"Listen, we can dissect the bullshit later on. Get your gear on and meet me in the truck."

"I'll just throw on a shirt and boots and we're good to go."

"Get jeans on. Going to be running out there."

"It's 95 fucking degrees out. No way I'm wearing jeans. Not sweating my balls off out there. Hot as hell out there as it is."

"Genius. They haven't paid for service out in those barns for months. Going to be a shitshow. I'm telling you. Listen to me."

"I'm fine. It's too fucking hot to wear jeans. Period. I'm going like this. Will throw a shirt on."

"Whatever you say there, genius. I won't say I fucking told you so."

"Don't worry about it, old man. I'm fine. You know I

can handle myself."

"Right. You're fine. I'll keep my mouth shut."

I laced up my construction boots and found a South Brooklyn golf shirt in the clean laundry pile. We went in the backyard and unlocked the cabinets for Eaton's bait blocks. We had buckets of them on standby when the track came to their senses. Apple and Peanut Butter blocks galore. Buckets of poison bricks to make rats bleed out until death from within. Lovely business, these anti-coagulants, but that was the only thing we could use. Snaps were too dangerous with cats, dogs, and chickens roaming the barns. We'd be putting this crap everywhere, in every burrow under those barns we could find.

We loaded the truck and drove out to Aqueduct on the Belt. The windows were rolled down and Dad smoked into the hot, humid air.

"Ever going to quit that garbage? Disgusting."

"Probably not. Something's going to kill you, right? If not one thing, it's another. Sure, a helluva lot better than what I used to be doing when I was doing coke, pills, and booze."

"Shit is poison. It's going to catch up with you, just like that other crap."

"Can't live forever. Shit, without this crap, I'd want to blow my brains out."

"Dad, Jesus Fucking Christ already."

"You're right. That's too much, way too soon. Sorry, Jonah."

"You don't make it easy."

"Ain't that the truth. At least I'm a consistent pain in the ass."

We pulled into stop and go traffic. Heat shimmered off the roadway, and the boats out in the channel fished for catches under the Gil Hodges Bridge.

"Nice to be out there right now, instead of doing this."

"True. I told you about the time…"

"The time you jumped in and saved that guy when you were fishing with Uncle Donald. Of course. A dozen times."

"Well, excuse me. Threw the guy a lifeline. Like how my brother hung in there for me with my old man. Shame what happened to him. Too soon."

"Uncle Donald sounded like a good guy. Rheumatic fever, right?"

"Yeah. Had it as a kid. Great guy, he was. Poet like you. Played guitar. Fixed cars. Heart gave out on him driving home from the garage. No one realized that fever had done so much damage. Crashed right into a telephone pole. Fucking shame. Your cousin was on the way, and he never even met him."

"Sucks royally."

"That's why you don't take shit for granted and do what you can, when you can."

"Right, right."

"I'm serious. That guy had so much ahead of him. Seize it while you can."

"Carpe Diem and all that bullshit."

"You'll get it someday, just don't be a punk about it. Donald had it all going, and then boom. Reminds me of you. Jack of All Trades. Up for anything. Thinking about art, music, writing, history, working… And then, boom, all done, gone. Blink of an eye. No one saw it coming."

He smoked. His arm was on the driver side door, his scar like train tracks in the sun. He pulled the butt into his lungs and let the smoke fill the cabin. His pack was in his breast pocket—and he chain-smoked all the way out to the track.

Traffic cleared and we made our way past a three-car pileup, where a woman clutching a baby kept screaming and a police officer kept pushing his hands down to keep her calm. It wasn't fatal, probably a bumper tap, but she was freaked out. The guy in the other car leaned against the guardrails. An older woman was lying on the ground waiting for the ambulance to come. She had a neck brace on.

"Always something."

"We all make a mess of things, bang things up. How it goes. Just matters how you rebound and learn to react and keep the dents to a minimum."

"Like that crazy lady right there?"

"Got to walk in someone's shoes every now and then, Jonah. Hemingway called courage, grace under pressure. Some people just have more opportunities to test it."

"We read Papa in high school. He lived quite a life. Fishing. Hunting. Bullfighting. But Father Taylor says he might be falling out of favor. Liked the stories though, and *The Sun Also Rises*. Father says he might be read less now. Something about problems with super masculinity. I don't know..."

"I think people should read the man. Don't listen to those fools trying to censor shit about what people should and should not read. That's crap. Next thing you got is super safe, no boundaries, PC world. Everyone treated with kid gloves. I say read what gets under your skin and challenges the shit out of you. Better that way. Toughen people up."

"I see what you're saying it. Read it for yourself. Walk in someone's shoes."

"Right. Find out what works for you without someone providing a damn bumper rail. Who learns shit about anything that way? Just reading people who see things exactly as you do? That's ridiculous."

"It's like when we read Jane Austen and Ralph Ellison. I didn't think I'd like either. Turned out I got something from both of 'em."

"And that's the way it should be. Lady from another country, another century, and a black guy writing about Harlem. All goes to crap if we people can't read something because it doesn't fit some political agenda."

"Yeah, what good writing does, I guess. Let's you see things from another perspective."

We drove through the gates and waved at the guards. They started clapping when we came through. I saw rats running in the barns on our approach. I'd never seen this. Not like this. Sure, you saw rats out there. But not like this. Not during the day.

A pile of dead rats lay between the barns. Some crazy fucker took to shooting the things in his spare time. They'd burn the bodies after we got a chance to see the handiwork.

"I figure me and you shoot a bunch of them first. Then we'll start baiting."

"This is fucking nuts. Shitshow here."

"It is what it is. You stay by me and don't fucking shoot me, you hear? We'll pick off some, get them running, and then starting baiting."

"This is worse than I thought."

"I told you it would be running."

"Holy shit."

"Is this an *I told you so moment.*"

"Fuck off."

Rats were everywhere. They ran between stalls. They ran overhead between the beams. They burrowed through the hay. I'd never seen so many rats. In the emptied stalls, dark holes burrowed in each corner. The hole led under the structure, into the dirt, where they lived, where they bred. Intricate tunnels dug under each barn and there were thirteen barns to be done today.

Dad went to the back and got the pellet guns.

"We stay together. These barns are emptied, but let's not be yahoos or cowboys here. Could be a walker or two in there."

Walkers were Mexicans. They lived somewhere out there on the grounds, probably dorms, and they were usually illegal. We exited the truck and I pulled my socks up and re-laced my construction boots.

"Told you to wear jeans."

"All right, all right, you told me so."

He handed me the air rifle.

We walked into the barn and the rats didn't care. They ran around the corners, down into the holes. Dad aimed and fired. I waited. I shot one eating a pigeon. Dying pigeons lurked around holes, waited, like they knew. The rats came and got them. I shot a pigeon to end its misery. We went from stall to stall, shooting rats. Dad had lots of rounds, and we used them.

I aimed at a rat lurking in the corner. It stared right at me from the dark hole at the edge of the barn stall. It didn't move until the bullet made it shriek. When the bullet came, it flipped itself and squealed and ran down into the hole to die. The healthy ones would eat it, as it tried to go underground and die.

A rat ran from the hole and tried to run down the barn lane, where horses used to prance. Dad and I both shot it. My shot ricocheted and we both ducked.

"Fun, right?"

"It's kinda cathartic."

"No shit."

"I'd say we finish the clip and start baiting."

We shot a few more and went back to the truck. I put my work gloves on and started pulling out the pails of bait block.

"Same deal, I think. You do a stall. I'll do a stall. And we stick together."

"You got it."

"Keep those socks up. Just in case."

I pulled up my tube socks again and we started baiting. The rats peeked out of the holes and I stuck poison blocks into their holes. Every stall, I kicked the barn door and they scattered. They'd flee right before my feet, seconds before I entered and baited the holes in the corners. Sometimes they'd rush into burrows, other times they scooted under the barn doors and down the barn.

Hundreds of green bait blocks in the holes, until I came to the end of Barn 4. Dad was behind me, when I saw the rat sitting in the middle of the stall. Its eyes were straight ahead at me. It didn't go for the hole. Waiting.

I put down my pail of bait blocks. I was going to kill it. Kick it into next week and stamp it out of its misery, if need be. Dad would see the whole thing and see how far I'd come. I walked in, and just as I was about to kick, the fucker ran up my socks and latched on to my shorts.

I wheeled about in a circle and spun around trying to shake it off. Dad grabbed it by the tail. He was right behind me in seconds and slammed the rat's head into the barn door. In seconds, I screamed and fled. Outside the truck, I kept spinning around and cursing.

"That fucking thing sure took a liking to you."

"All right, all right. That was too much. Fucking things! Unreal."

"Been there. You remember, right? Rite of passage, kid."

"Seriously. How do I not do this hellacious shit for the rest of my life? I fucking can't! Fuck this shit." I wiped away the rat and kept swiping at my leg for minutes.

He looked at me intently and never flinched.

"You stay in school, that's what. Do what you can accomplish. Remember this shit, that's what. That's why you're here. You don't want to do this shit for the rest of your life. I had no choice. You do. And you know how fucking miserable it is. Don't ever do it. Don't settle and don't get distracted. That's all. You can do better if you put your mind to it. But, it's going to take giving yourself the best chance with the most options."

I sat on the bumper as Dad finished the barn by himself. We did the rest of the barns without incident. As Dad got the signature from the barn office manager, I sat outside. A guy named Bearly came by. Name was really Lee. They tossed the Bear on top of that. He had an overflowing brown beard and he carried a pellet gun on his shoulder.

"Get many?"

"What?"

"How many you kill, kid?"

"A bunch, I guess."

"I'm going to set that whole pile you saw on fire tonight. Motherfuckers gonna burn."

"Great. That should be a really pleasant smell."

"You don't seem like a killer at all. Not like your old man. You don't seem like you have the stomach for it, pansy."

"I'm not, I guess. But I'm no pansy, hillbilly. Not getting off on burning rat bodies. Sounds exactly how I want to spend my nights."

"No matter, boy. Your old man'll start to weed this shit down and then it won't be fun anymore."

"Killing these things is fun? You're fucking whacked out."

"Better than mucking stalls, that's for shit's sure."

"If you say so, hillbilly Jim."

"I know so, asshole. You see those fuckers living in

there with those things? People living with those damn things, running over em at night."

"No one's living in there anymore, dickhead. Stop the nonsense. They live in dorms."

"You really are crazy. You ask your old man. Not fucking living in there? Dorms you haven't seen? Dumb as shit, you are. Or, just plain ignorant city homo. Ask him. Right in front of your eyes."

"I will. Now get the fuck out of my face."

"How about I rip your face off, punk?"

"I'd like to see you try, man mountain, Mr. Deliverance."

"Wait here, and I'll get my banjo, pretty boy."

Dad came out with two guys and a bottle of water for me.

"Bearly, Bearly. Easy my friend. He's just fucking with you. Got a big mouth."

"Jimmy Bugs, this boy yours needs to learn some manners."

"True that. True that. Don't pay him any mind, he's just shooting his mouth off. Long day. How about a cold one on me?"

"You say so. I'd keep that prick in check, you ask me. He's got attitude."

"Will do. Miller Lite on me at the clubhouse. Be waiting for you. Nice cold one, on me."

Bearly nodded and walked away. He smiled and

saluted me. Then, he gave me the middle finger as he walked back down the row of barns. I returned it.

"What the fuck is wrong with you? He helps us more than anyone here by picking off rats."

"Guy's a shitshow. Inbred, you ask me. Burning rat carcasses for shits and giggles. You kidding me?"

"Well, no one's asking you and it helps. Who gives a crap if he gets his kicks hunting rats? We do it."

"That's because we're exterminators. He's just a freak."

"That may well be, but we're surrounded by castoffs here, my friend."

"What the hell is he talking about, people living in the barns? That doesn't happen anymore."

"Of course they still do, stupid."

"No one lives in this shit. That was years ago when Dee was here. That changed."

"Who said it changed? I'll show you."

"You're kidding me?"

"I'm not kidding you."

We drove over to another barn and Dad pulled over near a man washing a horse. Thoroughbreds were all grouped in the few barns we didn't do today.

We walked through the barn. Rats ran everywhere and there was a scratched white door on the edge of the stalls. Dad tapped on the door with his flashlight. A small Mexican boy opened and Dad said something to him in Spanish. We went in, and I could see holes in the corners and grease trail marks on the corner.

"They're in and out of here all day and he won't say shit because he's afraid of getting deported. Dee was in one of these rooms all those years ago, as you know. Nada has changed. Zilch."

"How do they get away with this shit? I mean, doesn't someone realize this is happening and care?"

"Think these guys are going to say anything? They're getting food and medical. A few bucks to send home. Helluva lot more than most. And the track, bottom line—cheap labor."

"Horses are treated better, if you ask me."

"No one's asking you. This is how it works. And if they say fuck it, they'll be twenty guys to take their spot"

"This is fucked up."

"That's right. Welcome to working in America."

The boy moved awkwardly away from us as Dad went and dropped two bait blocks into the hole in the wall. He reset the triggered snap trap in the corner. The boy's eyes moved around and he cleaned up some porn magazines from the bed and grabbed a few beer cans from the floor and threw them in the trash. He had on ripped jeans and a torn Saratoga sweatshirt. Dad handed him five glue traps as we walked out.

"That kid is around your age. El Salvador."

"What the hell kind of living is that."

"What people have to do. And I can guarantee you that isn't the worst of it. And you think you have it bad helping me out. Talk about hellacious shit. He's been living with those damn things. Won't say shit about it, even if they bit him."

"All right. Maybe our work isn't as bad as that, but it's pretty bad."

"Maybe it's not as bad? You've got to be kidding. This shit pays the bills and we're going home to a house. Remember that as you get yourself ready for college, all right? A lot of people have it far worse off than you do. Think about the crap that kid has to do. Far worse. And he has no freaking guarantees. Could be shipped out tomorrow for all he knows."

We got back in the truck and headed out of the track. We'd have to come back in a day or two to see the first baiting results. Something told me there'd be piles of dead rats and they'd burn the bodies as Bearly planned to do. The carpenters would wait for the death toll to rise and then start to repair the stalls and seal up some burrows.

I felt sorry for calling the work hellacious shit as we got back into the truck to head home. But I knew that's what it was. And Dad knew it too. Maybe it wasn't as bad as some jobs, like knowing guys my age had to sleep where the rats ran overhead and underneath. Maybe we were doing something useful. At least it would make things a little better for somebody.

We drove through the gates and headed to the deli for water and Gatorade. Dad and I went in and we ordered meatball heroes to go. My shirt was soaked through, and I was tired, but I was heading home to rest and play video games. It was good to be helping again and better to be leaving as we headed west on the Belt to Flatbush Avenue.

"We talk about how the other half lives sometimes… remember what the people coming into this country have to do. Make you think twice when you daydream of better days, better things."

"That kid make it home, sometime? I mean, once he gets some money together?"

"Possible. But think about how much he'd have to work. Just to get back. And we're talking below minimum wage. Things you see in this work. They should stick with you."

"They will."

"Even if it is hellacious shit."

He smiled, and I gulped down a draft of ice-cold water as I stared at the ocean out towards Rockaway. The traffic snarled its way like a snake along the coast, and the sun was glittering like gold off the water in the empty channel.

Beehive

Dad coughed and lit a Marlboro. The sun was strong and we'd have to wait for it to fade as we headed out to a beehive in a tree in Garden City. The red truck had the ladder atop the cab. The rope was tightened through the gaps in the windows and my left hand rested on the tight line over my head while my right held the ladder in place up top.

I'd been stung twice in my life. Neither one of them on jobs. I stepped in a nest retrieving a Whiffle ball with Paulie and got a random bite near the backyard pool. This tree nest ahead of us was quite large, according to the homeowners, and the family was freaked out.

"I ever tell you about that stupid crap I did on my first bee job in California? Where I put fucking honey on me to attract them away from the nest? Dumb as shit. Even then I only got stung twice. That's it. Knock on wood. Think we're tied there, right?"

"Yep. Two for me. That's it."

"Got something you want to talk about?"

"Not really. Have a lot on my mind."

He took a long pull on his butt and shot a wad of phlegm out the window. He had streaming cobwebs on his hat and smelled as usual like chemicals and sweat.

"Mom said you and Molly breaking up before college."

"Yeah, well, you probably knew that shit was coming."

"Well, maybe. But I know it's hard anyway. Like me and Franny long before your mom."

"I know, I know…the lady you got the panther tattoo for to cover her name up. Can we just skip the details of that one, again?"

"Sorry for the repeats. And I know things have been hard with baseball turning like it did."

"You could say that. I couldn't fucking throw anymore because of my goddamn head. Bouncing throwbacks to the pitcher. Fucking embarrassment. Like I can't stop freaking thinking and just do what I need to do."

I stopped and stared at the airport we were passing. A steady flow of planes lined the sky above us, landing one by one, as we inched along in eastbound Belt traffic.

"Playing varsity baseball is nothing to sneer out. Sure beats anything I ever did."

"Useless anyway. Who the hell cared if I played beyond high school anyway. All stupid pipe dreams. I wasn't going anywhere with it."

"Well, you were good at it. And you enjoyed it."

"I guess so."

"You know so. And you also figured out all those years ago now that banking on the Majors, or anything else for that matter, wasn't the right way to go, right? Certainly weren't the type putting all your eggs in one basket. Never did that, and that's strength and smarts right there."

"Realized that in Hell's Kitchen."

"I was there. I remember that ride home."

"Freaking Manny Ramirez."

In my freshmen year, I played a game with the varsity squad in Hell's Kitchen. I sat on third base, dreaming of Major League glory with the Mets. The opposing team's third base coach started talking. *Third base, third base, pay attention, back up.* I shrugged him off and got in my squat. The coach at George Washington spoke again. *Third base, I'm telling you, wake up and back up!*

I looked through this Dominican man, figured he was trying to get in my head. The next fastball thrown whizzed by me off the bat. I heard it pass me and wouldn't have gotten my hands up if it came at me. *I told you, I told you! Back up.* I nodded and listened and knew something changed. That guy up there was something else, something I didn't have, nor could I get even if I did nothing else.

"That guy could swing the bat, boy."

"I know it. Nothing you can do about that. Could have practiced every moment and nothing was going to change that I wouldn't ever hit like that."

"True, that's why you don't hitch everything to one star. You keep the options open. Get what I'm saying? As you always have been. You've always had a good head on your shoulders, even when things didn't go your way, and you keep open to the idea that not everything is always going to go your way. What makes you interesting, kiddo."

"I just have no clue, really. Just going through the motions. Not sure what the hell I'm doing or where I'm going."

"You'll get there. Just don't run yourself into the ground because of it. Shit's gonna happen. Don't be like me trying to burn the candle at all ends and falling apart about it. Life's too short and people can help you get where you need to go. Just got to ask for help, sometimes."

"Tell me about life being too short."

I pointed to the cigarette smoldering in the ashtray.

"Stop your bullshit. Only thing that keeps me sane."

"Your funeral."

"Yeah, well, we all got to die somewhere, somehow. Might as well figure out what makes you happy and follow it."

"And this is really what makes you happy? Surrounding yourself in smoke?"

"I didn't say that's what made me happy."

"Then, what is it?"

"You'll figure it out sometime. You're smart. Sometimes you shouldn't get so lost in your own head."

"Whatever. I AM lost in my own head. Just not sure what's ahead of me, that's all. Maybe that's normal, but how far can you go from here. And where to. Just a lot to be uncertain about."

"Of course, it's normal. Talk it out. Don't keep all that crap bottled up. Creates a mess. Just don't let it wear you down and out. If this work teaches you anything, it's to respect tenacity that surrounds you. And to realize, there's a lot to bring with you as you search for new things to do."

When we approached the house, I saw the paper wasp nest hanging from the branch of a tree. It was tidy colonial on a tree-lined street. Sun was barely peeking through the tree in the yard and a swarm buzzed around the hive. The owner was at her front screen-door and a German shepherd barked at the front window.

"Thank God! The kids haven't been able to get out at all. I'm terrified even to go to the car! And my husband is allergic. He won't say it, but he's scared shitless too!"

We loosened the rope and Dad waved to her.

"No worries. We got it. Will have it out of here soon enough."

"You're going to take it down today?"

"Absolutely. We'll douse it first and then take it off. Damn thing is quite a work of art, you ask me."

She made the motion of hands in prayer, and I sat underneath the tree staring up.

A perfect hive: huge and symmetrical with a dark hole right in the bottom. From below the hive looked like rock cliffs to be scaled by climbers. Circles upon circles formed with care with a dark recess in its core. Colony must have been vast.

"I'd say close the windows and doors for a bit. Let us give it a good spray, knock them down a bit. I'll give you the sign when it's ok to open up again."

We leaned the ladder against the tree limbs. I went back to the truck and got the two cans of wasp freeze and sprayer.

"That's a thing of beauty, right?"

"It is pretty amazing how they make that thing."

"Kind of a work of art, if you ask me. Shame we have to get rid of it, but it's too big and these people are petrified."

I held the ladder in place and Dad started to pull the rungs up into the tree. We angled the base section and let the fly section rise up to lean against the branches. It was an old elm, a majestic strong tree with massive branches for arms and a trunk that could withstand a truck plowing into it.

"If it goes well, I'll freeze 'em. You can spray the ones that fall down. Use the fan setting for the nozzle. Then maybe we can cut this down and preserve it."

"Works for me. I'll keep a trash bag handy."

He climbed the ladder and I held it in place. Once he got within range, he motioned me away for a minute. I stepped away from the ladder and grabbed the sprayer. I pumped the canister full of air and waited for falling wasps.

Dad aimed and fired a jet of wasp freeze into the nest.

Like rain the wasps fell to the ground in puddles. Many died immediately. Others twisted on the ground below the tree. I came in and sprayed them, covering fallen wasps with fan spray as quickly as I could. A few wasps still buzzed around the hive, around Dad's head above me. He waited and sprayed the wasp freeze again and a slow trickle from the hive dripped out of the black hole to die on the ground below.

We waited a minute or two. Dad used up the can and continued to climb a few more steps on the ladder. I put down the sprayer and went back to my post at the ladder. Dad tossed the empty aerosol down to me and I pitched it on to the lawn for trash. I kept my eyes up for a minute, as the sun's rays moved through the branches. Dad reached into his belt for his Swiss army knife. His arm extended up to the branch holding the hive, and he snipped the branch and held it away from him. Slowly, he put the knife back in his belt.

A few wasps still circled his face. He gave them no mind, just kept his eyes on the hive in his hands. He took a step down the ladder rung and a wasp stung his neck. The hive slipped from his hands and headed down, hitting me in the head. I let go of the ladder, yelling and cursing, and ran. The ladder shifted off the trunk, and Dad was now clinging to a branch. Slowly our ladder slipped through the leaves and came down with a crash on the lawn.

I was running up the street, swatting wasps away. Dad was cursing. And the homeowners came to the door again to watch.

"Everything ok out there, fellas?"

"We're good. Just a little slip of the ladder. Be bagged and out of here soon enough. Jonah, mind giving me a hand up here?"

I came back after a quick jog down the road. Dad was slung over a branch like a cowboy on a horse.

"You all right up there?"

"I'm fine, but I sure wish we had a video of that to share. Jesus, what putzes we must look like."

He laughed from up above me, taking in how we ridiculous we looked.

"Ain't that the truth."

"Now get me out of here."

I got the ladder upright with a wobble and released the rung locks from the fly section and brought it down to the base. The ladder swayed over me, as I moved it slowly below the tree again and used the pulley to get it back up to dad and get the rung locks secured.

I held it tightly as he placed his boots on the first rung. He made his way back down to the ground.

We looked at the nest. It had a small dent from my head, but looked pretty much intact.

"Believe that shit? And that's after hitting a hard noggin like yours."

201

"Hardy har har."

"Let's bag this thing quickly, get the signature, and get the hell out of here."

We gave the nest a final spray and then sealed it up in two plastic Hefty bags. Dad wrote up the job ticket and I placed the equipment and the garbage bag in the back cab of the truck.

I heard Dad laughing as the homeowner opened the door and handed two waters over. She signed the ticket. We gave a receipt and Dad walked back to the truck. He handed me a bottle and bent his over to mine for a tap of cheers. I saw his neck red from the sting.

"Now that was some funny shit. Real professionals, men at work. I'm stuck in a freaking tree and you're running down the block, swatting away at wasps. Keystone Cops."

"Sting ok? I'm really sorry I let go like that. I just…"

"Never had a wasp nest fall on your head, Jonah?" He laughed.

"Well, I should have held on. Sorry."

"I dropped a nest on your head, kid. There's no need to apologize."

He gave me a pat on the shoulder and we packed up the car in silence. We drove out of Garden City towards the Belt Parkway.

"Third sting, huh? You're in the lead."

"Yeah, go figure that shit. Pretty unpredictable, those fuckers…"

He lit a Marlboro and let smoke wash over him like rain.

"Where is America's Funniest Home Videos when you need it? That shit must have been hysterical from across the street. Quite a crew, we are."

"Quite a team. And that was like Keystone Kops out there."

"At least we can take a step back and laugh. And thanks for talking things over with me and helping out. Means a lot to know what's happening."

"Don't worry about it. Happy to help out. Even when you're dropping wasp nests on my freaking head."

"Maybe the hurdles were your event after all. Should've gotten you into steeplechase or something instead of baseball. Who knew?"

"I've got time, right?"

"You certainly do."

We drank our waters and made it home. The paper wasp nest stayed outside in the chemical cabinet for a week. Eventually, the old man brought it down into his tool room and shellacked it for preservation. I gave him a hand with the second coat of lacquer. He kept it on a shelf with models and other curiosities, to keep track of our work and collect dust.

Nursing Home

During my first college summer, I came back to do city routes on my own. Mostly nursing homes. Dad was friends with a guy named Rabbi Weinstein. He was a doctor from Borough Park, and he and his wife and their families owned like fifteen nursing homes. We did all of them. He got a kick out of my dad and enjoyed his politics. Dad enjoyed bragging that he had a college son with an exterminator's license.

Dad told me to check in with the Rabbi out in Whitestone. My crappy blue Toyota plugged along out towards the Whitestone Bridge. I'd be there, then College Point, then Morris Park and University Heights in the Bronx. The next day I'd be out in the Rockaways for the entire day.

I checked in with Lee, head housekeeper. She was always arguing with Dad about politics. She was from Ukraine, spoke in a heavy accent and was always complaining about something. Nice lady, who loved to bust Dad's chops to get the most out of everything, but she knew he did a good job. I was always a little unwelcome there because I certainly wasn't as thorough or smart about jobs as he was.

"Where's the boss today?"

"Staten Island. He sends his best to you and says go easy on me."

"Likely story, young man. They have 4 and 5 cleared

out for you. Think there was a complaint in the log on 5. Give it a check. That lady can be a little trying…"

"Will do. Dad said Rabbi is here today and check in with him."

"Yes, he's around. I'll let him know you're here and can catch up later."

I hated nursing homes. The unmistakable smells filled the hallways of cheap skin lotion and bleach cleansers. The nurses hated your guts. Always a quip or complaint, even with the ones flirting with you as you made the rounds. And everyone claimed to be allergic. I always tried to make friends and smile, and ask if anyone saw anything, but it never quite worked out.

"Hell no! I got allergies. You ain't spraying here today, are you?"

"Yeah, talk to Lee. Doing the floor. That's why they had you move the patients out."

"Well, I'm getting out of here. I ain't sticking around to be poisoned by you. NO WAY, NO HOW."

"No problem. Enjoy some fresh air and have a good day. I'm not spraying nurses' stations, anyway. Just a little dab of gel for the roaches. No smell. See many?"

"See many? You funny. Of course, we see them. They everywhere."

"Well, maybe it's a good idea not to keep food in the drawers. Make it easier to stay on top of it, right?"

"What you saying? We don't keep food nowhere."

This was usually a losing battle. You'd open a drawer and there'd be cookies, crackers, and fruit everywhere.

"Ok, no worries then."

There were 20 rooms per floor. I checked the nurse's log on problem areas. Found a few. I checked a glue board under the nurse's station and placed some roach gel underneath the station. Most of the residents were downstairs in the rec room. I could see one lady walking the halls. She walked the corridors in circuits, one long step, one short, like she was skating an oval at Central Park. She nodded as she passed and continued her circles. Think she did it all day, every day, if they'd let her.

In room 504, I found a porter. He showed me a night table, infested with roaches. The stuff was removed and crackers and cookie crumbs were everywhere. Porter said he found apples and bananas and pound cake in there as well. We sprayed and the roaches came out the back.

"Bad, right?"

"I've seen a lot worse."

"No way."

"Much, much worse. Mucho. I'll tell you."

Of course, I was thinking about this time I was doing an apartment building in Midwood earlier that summer. Dad had it as part of my Rockaway route in the morning. Nice guy, probably in his thirties, was always there to greet me from 3B.

"Man, you see how I keep this place. I clean, I scrub. Do

everything I can. No trash. I even sealed the doorways and pipes fixtures. Got to be the old lady across the hall in 3A. I'm *telling* you."

"I'll pay her a visit. We'll get to the bottom of it."

Now 3A was always a conundrum. I'd knock, and usually the lady said something like *No thank you*. It was time to change that. I let the super know about the complaints. He said he hadn't been in there for a while and came with me to knock on the door. Sergei Roknov was from the former USSR. His family immigrated ten years ago to Brighton Beach and started getting into apartment maintenance and management.

"She always quiet. Nice lady. You see her sitting out front during the spring time in her beach chair. Don't see many family though. Mostly alone, it seems."

"Well, 3B keeps a clean ship, so they got to be coming from somewhere. Worth a look."

"All right, I'll knock with you and let you in if she's not around."

We knocked on 3A and Sergei spoke for us.

"Mrs. Leahy, exterminator. Need to service today."

"No, thank you, dears. I'm fine. Have a blessed day."

"No, we got to come in, ma'am. Got to take look this time."

"Well, this is inconvenient. Please give me a moment."

"Take your time. No rush."

We waited a few minutes in the darkened hallway.

The walls were a sickly beige color. I smelled onions everywhere. Just as I sat on the steps, a roach crawled out from under the door and Sergei bolted.

"What da shit is this."

He knocked again.

"Mrs. Leahy, please. Have to let our man in."

I pumped the sprayer and made sure the tip of the gel injector was clean.

I heard the lady opening the bolts and removing the chain.

"So sorry, dears. What was this about again?"

"The guy for bugs, ma'am."

"Oh, they're no trouble with that here. Maybe elsewhere."

"No, we need a look, please."

"Well, suit yourself."

She opened the door, and I saw them everywhere. On the walls above the kitchen. On the kitchen table. They were climbing above the doorway.

"Holy Christ."

"Well, please don't take the Lord's name in vain, young man. Are you a Catholic?"

"I am, miss."

"Isn't that nice? I go to St. Brendan's every day."

"Baptized there, but I'm over by Good Shepherd now."

"That's lovely. What a nice parish over there."

I made my way into the kitchen. Roaches in every direction. Stove. Fridge. Sink.

"Can I get you a cup of tea, gentlemen?"

I stared at the tea kettle and roaches were on the outside of it. One was just burned by steam arising from the spout.

"No, thank you, ma'am."

I asked Sergei to remove Mrs. Leahy for a minute while I began to spray. Frozen roaches in the freezer, live ones in the fridge itself. The oven was running, as was the broiling pan. I'd never seen anything like this. As I pulled some paper bags away from being wedged next to the oven, a whole wave of German cockroaches came rushing out and spread in all directions. Roaches in cups, on plates. Everywhere you looked.

"Listen, Sergei, I think we need to get her out of here. Is there anyone we can call? We need to fumigate this place, pronto."

I went downstairs and called my dad. He needed to see this. He laughed at the call and said it couldn't be that bad, but he'd come by, anyway.

"Ma'am, is there some place you could stay tonight?"

"Why young man?"

"Well, we've got to fumigate. You see these roaches, we need to get rid of them, right away."

"I don't see what the problem is, I just say, no and I shoo them away. That's all. Get, get, I say."

"Right, well, we can do better than that. You don't need these things around you."

"I could call my daughter and see the grandkids tonight."

"That's perfect. Let's do that."

"Let me just find the number."

She got some stuff together. I followed her for a moment into the bedroom and crushed on her pillow and sheets were dead roaches, which I guess she slept on.

Dad came in laughing.

"Serge, this boy of mine pulling the panic alarm on you?"

He looked around.

"Holy shit."

"Yeah, Jimmy. Real bad. Lady is a little kooky. Something not right."

We brought out the aerosol cans and set off a bunch. We sprayed after that.

"You weren't kidding. Never seen anything quite like that."

"She slept on them for God's sake. They were everywhere."

"I can say this much for sure, boy. That shit ain't happening to me. No way I'm around for it to get that off kilter."

"Stop. You have no idea what later in life brings."

"The hell I do. I ain't living that long. That much I know."

"Stop the crap, all right?"

"No crap here. Just the truth. Not losing my mind and drifting off into madness like that lady. And no goddamn nursing homes. You can find the gun and end it, if it comes to that."

As I retold the story to the porter, I felt the same as Dad. We cleared out some drawers and dumped crumbs into waste baskets, and I sprayed things down and talked about keeping things cleaned up.

Down the hallway, I walked into a room with a man in a wheelchair. His name was Giuseppe. He stared out the window at the Whitestone Bridge and the trees. He never spoke. I wondered who came to see him and whether they cared. He never wanted to leave the room, they told me. Every time I came in, he stared out at the sky, regardless of the season. Sometimes people cried when I came in. Spoke to me about their kids. Or asked if I knew when lunch was coming in. Some people screamed out in agony. This man only stared out the windows. I wondered what he saw and what he thought, day after day, looking out as the blue turned to bright oranges and reds, before fading into darkness.

Dad said it would never be him and I believed him. No way he'd be sitting in a chair in a room. There wouldn't be that time to grow old.

I put gel around the heating units and the bathroom. Giuseppe never looked at me.

"Have a good day, sir."

He nodded his head and continued to watch the trees and sky. A fresh breeze swept through the windows.

The next room seemed empty when I walked in. I started to spray and dab the corners, give a quick check of the night tables for infestations. Then I heard a lady's voice. She came out of the bathroom, naked.

"Oh, Lord, ma'am."

"Jesus? Is that you?"

"Ma'am, not Jesus, I can tell you that much."

"I've got lots of questions, Lord. Can you sit and pray with me?"

"Not right now. Maybe next time."

I backed up as fast as I could and jogged through the doorway. The naked lady followed into the hallway, and I pointed her out to the nurses.

"Oh, she up here talking Jesus again."

"Yep, well, she thought I was the Lord coming to visit."

"She think it of everybody. Marie, you get your clothes on, girl, and get back downstairs."

I waited at the nurses' station and Rabbi Weinstein came from the elevator.

"How we doing up here?"

"Well, fine, besides that lady thinking I was Jesus."

"We've got plenty of sightings of him, on this floor in particular."

"That we do."

"When you finish, pop in to the office. Need to chat about something."

I went back to work and started worrying. Didn't sound like him. And I couldn't be the one to lose an account. I went back over all that I'd been doing there. Things were in pretty decent shape. Some of the nurses hated me, but that's ok. Lee thought I wasn't as careful as dad.

Shit, this wouldn't be good. I thought about losing all of the Rabbi's work in a chain reaction. The old man would have a shit fit.

Goddamn it. I walked through the rooms, trying to be extra careful with all of my sprays and dabs. I double-checked with the porter before I went to the elevator. Outside, I stowed the gear in the trunk and wrote out a ticket. I saw Lee and gave her a quick update.

"You tell your father we like to see him. Ok? No offense, but no one gets nervous when he's around and the state comes in to look."

"No offense taken. He's always got things under control. I'm trying. I pay attention, but he's the man at this."

"You're a college boy. Your father's got big things in his head for you."

"Trying not to disappoint."

"You won't. He always says the best things about

what you can do with yourself. A poet, he says."

"Well, maybe, but poets don't make money."

I said goodbye to Lee and headed to the Rabbi's office. His secretary asked me to take a seat. I could hear him in there with dietary. Some kind of issue with a patient's family. The director stormed out.

Rabbi Weinstein summoned me in. He had a large window, looking out to the Whitestone Bridge in the distance. His desk was stacked with papers and pictures of his family.

"Jonah, coffee? Anything?"

I felt a sudden surge of guilt, like we'd get the axe and I'd be the one to relay the message.

"I'm good, rabbi. Everything all right?"

"It's your dad. Worried about him."

"Well, he's pretty thick."

"Thick as shit he is."

"Right. Yeah, it's his great virtue in some ways."

"And his curse, as well. Listen, I think he's got to start taking his health seriously. The smoking. The chemicals. The years of the ironworking before that. All of it. He's got to get himself a real physical. Right away, I think."

"You're right, but he doesn't listen to anyone about that. Like he's going to run himself into the ground."

"Your father is hardest on himself. And he wants you and your sister to have the best of everything. Unfortunately, young man, that means he ignores a lot of things."

"We don't need a lot, believe me. But we would like to have him around."

"He's never forgiven himself about some of the things that happened years ago. Like he feels he deserves to suffer."

"You've heard about some of that?"

"Not the details, believe me. He's too proud to delve into that. But, I know it wasn't good and know how he got his act together."

"It wasn't good but it's past us now. Water under the bridge."

"Well, he's got to stop punishing himself, if you ask me. You can tell me to shut up, but he's a good man. A mensch, if you ask me. And, regardless of what he says and what happened with that putz partner of his, he's a good businessman. Honest. Trustworthy. He's just too hard on himself."

"Like he works himself to death."

"That's right, and you know what I tell him all the time?"

"What?"

"If it can be fixed with money, then it's really not all that important when it comes to fixing."

"I hear you. Solid advice."

"You need to get him to try to make peace with himself. Let those demons go. It's the only thing he can't do on his own."

"I'll try."

"You'll do it, son. He has so much faith and pride in you. He beams every time he comes in to talk about you. Like he sees all these things he never gave himself a chance to have. Help him to let go of all that's happened. It will mean the world. Talk to him sometime. And get him to see a doctor, for goodness sake."

"It's a tall order…he thinks they're all quacks"

"I know he thinks that, but it can be done. I always told him he should have pushed you to be a doctor. None of this decide your own path silliness…poetry…"

"I don't know if that would have worked, Rabbi."

"A little blood, guts, and death too much? Please, we all know we have to die someday. The question is how we choose to accept it. The one thing you don't want to have is regrets."

"No, I don't."

"Trust me, I live with nothing but regret for my father. What I should have said, how I should have thanked him. All those things. And he never even made it here to see what we could do. It's not where you want to be."

"I'll talk to him."

"Good. It will make a difference. Now how's this place holding up?"

"We're keeping it together. Even though these patients keep me on my toes."

"Tell me about it. They'll drive you crazy.

Meshuggeneh. That's what you call it. But necessary."

"I appreciate the concern with my dad. Take care, Rabbi. Thank you."

"Take care of that man. He loves you, even though he can't possibly say it. Irish are thick."

I left Rabbi Weinstein and headed to College Point. Dad was still on the road, somewhere. And as I drove the blue Toyota out of the lot, I thought about Rabbi's advice. There was more to talk about than work. I didn't turn on the radio to my other stops or the way home, and I thought through silence.

Drilling and Patching Holes

Termite work was brutal in summer. Dad needed tests, so I was helping McFadden out on the rig. He was a brutal pain in the ass and yet Dad got a kick out of him and kept him around. McFade, as I called him, was an ex-cop. His girlfriend was the secretary in the old office near Coney Island when we shuttered it. She was sitting at the desk and answering phones as my dad's partner, Teddy, ran up thousands in gambling debts, hookers, and helicopter rides to Atlantic City.

She didn't say shit. No one did because it was payday, easy street at Dad's expense. No one said a word as Teddy robbed him blind. The office was closed and McFade got drunk and threatened to come to Marine Park and shoot my dad in the head for costing his girlfriend a job. From what Mom said, he did come one night, drunk out of his gourd, and Dad told him to put a bullet in his head and end his misery. McFade was full of shit and got back in the truck and went back to his hole in the wall bar in Gerritsen Beach. He ended the threats and went back to working his routes.

Dad looked the other way, mostly. Maybe he was scared, more likely he was grateful that guys like McFade and Dee stuck by him and kept the business afloat. I was meeting McFade out in Bay Ridge for a termite job today. This meant I was doing a termite job and he'd drink coffee and read the New York Post.

He was out in front, leaning on the truck, when I arrived.

"Joanie, what took you so long?"

"Traffic. I had a stop out in Rockaways first."

"Old man said he'd be over here later. Need to dig the trench in front and start drilling the holes, so I can start pumping this shit. All right? Need something? Beer? Soda, or something?

"I'll just take a water. Didn't get a chance to stop beforehand."

"All right. I'll be back. Make sure you get deep enough with that front yard trench, there's roots in there, looks like. Get your back into it."

"Right. Back into it..."

McFade gave me his fade. He'd go to a local Bay Ridge cop bar, I was sure. He'd be back stinking of booze in an hour or two, sounding off on perps and what it was like on the job and how much cash he just won on the ponies. He seemed to have a watering hole scoped out in every part of New York City.

I tuned out his bluster and bullshit and pulled the shovel out and started in on the front yard. First, you had to trench the yard and then drill holes along the perimeter. Then clean the concrete dust up, wait for the chemical to be pumped and then patch the holes.

Sun baked down on me. Somewhere along the street I could hear easy listening. A lady in a rocking chair stared at me from across the street. I dug the shovel into the dirt behind the two bushes before the front windows. Roots were deep and tangled. I clawed the shovel in between the house and hedges and started trenching. Every shovelful unearthed more gravel and rocks and bits of discarded concrete. Sometimes you'd hit a piece of foundation and dig around it. Process was slow-going and exhausting.

It was brutal. Scoop after scoop of dirt pushed away, until I reached a decent depth for the chemical to soak the perimeter. I was dying of thirst. McFade wouldn't be back and I was sweating and filthy already. I knocked on the door and a young mother came to the door.

"Can I help you?"

"I'm sorry. I need to plug in the drill. Mind pointing me in the direction of an outlet?"

"Of course. There's one out there by the garden light switch in the yard. Could you use a water?"

"That would be great."

"Where's the other guy? The guy with the truck and chemical?"

"He'll be back. He disappears sometimes for a bit."

"A lot of work for one, no?"

"We'll be fine. And he'll be back sometime soon."

She got me a plastic Solo cup of ice water. I downed

it in three gulps and found the backyard outlet by their pool. I ran the electrical cord extension and plugged it into my drill, making sure to twine the cord around the end so it didn't pop out immediately.

Drilling was never-ending. Around the whole house you drilled holes for the termiticide. Goal was to get to the soil so it seeped in for the termites, eating away at the house innards. I set the drill bit for the job. I'd start on the neighbor's side, since they weren't home, make my way across the backyard, and finish up heading up the driveway.

My jackhammer was heavy and clumsy. I never understood what drill to use for what ground. I just used the one attached until it looked worn to the ground. I knew how to turn it on and how big a gap to leave between drill holes. One foot plus between my drills. Sometimes I misfired and chewed up a little concrete. Today I was hoping for an easy quick drill session.

The first four holes were easy. Aim downward and straight through to dirt. As you drilled down, there was tact to pulling the drill out. One smooth, continual stroke down and right out. In a few minutes, my arms and back ached and I needed a break. I took a few minutes. A young boy stared at me through his dining room window. He was probably curious when this strange guy would be done, when he could go back outside to play ball. I'd probably stare at me too if I was him.

The fifth hole stopped dead. I'd pull the trigger and nada. Down, I pushed until finally it stopped seizing up. I cursed into the sky, wrung out my arms, and worked the drill until it released. Then there were a few easy holes. Two seconds and you'd see the brown dirt at the end of the bit, before falling to the gravelly driveway. Every few holes, and you'd get a full stop again. By now, I was dripping sweat in the heat with no relief in sight.

I was about halfway around the house, when Dad came strolling down the driveway.

"Hey, brought lunch. Where the hell is McFadden?"

"McFaded. I'd guess he's at the bar having a few before gracing me with his magnificent pumping ability."

"He's good for pumping a lot of bullshit. But, he's loyal. Stood by us through thick and thin."

"I know, I know. He's just decided to start retirement from work early."

"Quite a character that guy. Talks a good game, but pretty much full of shit."

"I've been saying that for years."

"Brought you a ham and cheese, lettuce, tomato, mustard on hero. Gatorade in the bag as well."

"Sounds great. Thanks. Bring something for yourself?"

"Wasn't feeling too hungry."

"Half of mine?"

"I'm good kiddo. Take a break."

I pulled the hero apart and took a large bite. Fruit punch Gatorade was icy cold and I took a large mouthful before digging back into my lunch. The mustard was a perfect spicy brown. The ham and cheese melted in the hot sun with every bite. And the bread was fresh and crusty on top.

Dad picked up the drill and with short, sweeping drills, he knocked off 10 holes in the amount of time I'd done 3. I finished a half and then grabbed my dustpan and brush. I went over and began cleaning the debris from Dad's holes as we chatted.

"So, I've got more tests, doc says. Blood work. Scans. Pet. Cat. You name it, I'm getting it. I, um, have to see an oncologist, it seems."

"They're thinking cancer?"

"Who knows what they're thinking…these people are bloodsuckers."

"You shouldn't be drilling. Let me do that."

"I'm not freaking dead, Jonah."

"I didn't say that, but you never know when to go easy on yourself. Don't push so hard."

"You sound like the damn doctor. This shit is all I've known. Been working since I was ten years old, full-time nonetheless. Don't really know much else, nor will I."

"Rabbi Weinstein told me to get on you about taking care of yourself."

"Or I'd wind up in one of his nursing homes. God knows that ain't happening."

"I know, but still…you don't have to push so hard, all the time."

"He's a good man, but he's had it a lot different. Lot different than me."

"Just looking out for you. That's all."

"I know he is. Know you are. Appreciate it."

"Just give it a rest awhile. Cut back on the work and the smokes. Sort shit out."

"I'm trying, but it's funny. Never thought this work would be all I'd do, you know? Thought there would be something after it."

"That could happen. Got time"

"Let's not kid ourselves, Jonah. This is what I got. And as far as I've been concerned, I've been on borrowed time since I was 18 years old."

"Come on, none of this death wish crap."

"No death wish. Just really thought I wouldn't have much to be proud of, and I mean that. Growing up, my old man treated us like shit. I thought I'd disappear into nowhere, until I met your mom. And I know a made of a ton of stupid, bonehead mistakes. We all know that. But, I'm proud of this and giving you guys a chance to do a little better."

"I appreciate it, but we'd like to have you around, if it's all the same. You're a pain in the ass, don't get me wrong, but your heart's in the right place and you owned the shit that happened. Many wouldn't have done that."

"Thanks, Jonah. I don't know how much I can scale it back, work's made me tick for all these years, but I'll try not to drive myself into the ground."

"Deal."

"Want a hand cleaning up the holes? I can get word to McFadden to get his ass back over here to pump."

"I got it. I actually like sweeping the dust away from the holes. Cathartic."

"Cathartic, eh? Always love the vocabulary. Keeps me on my toes."

Dad walked up the driveway to his truck to make a call, and I continued my drill hole sweeping. Keep the strokes swift and don't let the concrete dust spread too far. Make sure the debris doesn't get wet. I bent over and whisked away the concrete and dirt from every hole, a steady line up and down the house, ready to be filled with treatment.

Five minutes later, I heard McFade's laugh and Dad's voice. I went around to the front and they were chopping it up. McFade was smoking, so was Dad. And they were filling my trench with chemical and Dad had the shovel, ready to pat down the upturned dirt when it was time. McFade was in a storytelling mode.

"So, you know how it's like. This kid came into the bar last week. Real fucking wise ass. And he's shoving around, getting fresh with Lynn, thinking he freaking owns the place. With ME there. You kidding? No way, pal. Take a seat. Well, he didn't like that very much, and well, let's just say he became acquainted with my favorite law enforcement tools."

He held up his fists, and Dad just laughed. It was a crock, but that was McFade. Somewhere in his head he was out chasing down perps or standing up for the honor of a two-bit hole in the wall.

I dumped my bucket of drill dust in the trash and went for my patch materials. McFade already started in on the holes. I followed him. Dad was talking to him about some issue with the track in between heroics at the bar and some old crap from the precinct. I tuned out his nonsense and focused on getting my things together.

Here's where I got to exercise some exterminating artistry. This was my specialty. In my bucket, I had various sizes of corks, a roll of heavy-duty paper towel, a screwdriver, and a bottle of Quikrete. The final part was patching. Here you pushed the cork down a bit, but not too far. You needed it to catch, so it didn't get sucked down into the hole and disappear. If the drill hole was precise, it was easy. Small cork, pressed with the screwdriver, and then a careful topping of instant concrete. Dad said I had a knack for this. I had the patience for it, and there was nothing worse than a bad driveway or basement patch. If the drill went awry, the hole could be larger and the corks wouldn't stick. Then you had to get creative. Try a larger size cork, fill the rest of the hole with a sizeable bit of paper towel, and give it a shot. Nothing looked worse than when you just couldn't fill the hole and you'd have to grab the trowel and smear a bit over the whole thing. I avoided this anytime I could.

Dad watched as I made my way around the perimeter.

"Got to hand it to the kid, he's got the knack for patching the holes. Neat and trim."

McFadden nodded. "Drills down. Cleans up. Patches up well. Kid has got it covered."

Dad handed me a bottle of water from the truck.

"Hydrate. I'll see you home. Good work."

I finished patching, walked the entire perimeter with an old grey rag to touch up any last off-kilter dabs, or instant concrete drifts. I rubbed a drip away from a hole along the backyard and rechecked my father's pat job along the front trench. I stowed away the gear, and McFade gave me an extra twenty we received as tip.

"Thanks."

"You're not still doing any of that tagging shit, are you, kid?"

"No, gave that up long ago. Why?"

"Well, I'd have to knock some sense into ya."

"Really?"

"That stuff only leads to worse things, believe me."

"You sound like my old man from years past."

"They got squads out for that, now. My day we'd just grab you, beat the crap out of you, and spray your fucking hands."

"Seems like a great way to make the city a safer place."

"That quality-of-life stuff matters."

"How about cops taking matters into their own hands. Not a problem, right? Just part of justice?"

"Listen, if you resist, you know what's happening. How it works."

"McFade, roughing up a guy already in cuffs isn't normal, and it's not right."

"Sometimes you got to keep people in line, show them who's boss."

"Right. By breaking the law and committing assault in the process on someone who's already in custody and defenseless."

"Your pops said there was a lurking liberal in you. Just don't let all that bleeding-heart shit cloud your brain."

"And don't let all those war stories cloud yours, old man. Three packs a day and pushing 60 isn't keeping you a spring chicken."

"Wise guy, eh? If I got a hold of you, you'd rethink your wise mouth, kid."

"See, that's it, Johnny. You wouldn't get a hold of me. I could run circles around you and you'd be panting in two minutes."

I danced around McFade, doing my best interpretation of float like a butterfly, sting like a bee.

McFade threw a half-hearted hook at me as I ran

around him, feigning jabs and crosses. He stopped swinging and I kept laughing.

"You're a riot, kid. Catch up next week. Take care of your pops."

"Will do. See you next time."

I started the car and let the AC run at full blast. My patch jobs were hardening, and I hoped none of them collapsed or needed touch-ups. I drove the car down to Shore Road, towards the Belt entrance. I stared at the Verrazano, buzzing with late afternoon traffic and remembered my uncle Jack who worked on it. He was the guy eating a sandwich in *Lunchtime Atop a Skyscraper*. Wondered if Dad would ever retire, get the chance to.

I drove under the bridge and watched the summer sky shine beams down into the waters off Coney Island. I sped along the highway, thinking of Dad and working jobs. The sun flickered off the sea and the tankers waited at bay for deliveries. I wondered how many jobs Dad and I would see together anymore as I shifted lanes into the middle of the road and made my way back home.

TRAP AND RELEASE

Professor Peterson was breaking us down, as he said. No more bullshit. We were starting with the basics after our lousy first efforts at short stories. I hated college right now. Bunch of kids in white hats and Birkenstock sandals with socks, and I was working twenty hours a week in the copy center underground.

Creative writing was what I wanted. Short stories. Novellas. Poems. Now, I was back to writing cause and effect, definition, argumentation…all to get our writing muscles exercised for future projects. The walk over to Harkin was bitterly cold today for and eight a.m. seminar. Today, we're getting back workshop drafts on a process piece. Process? I don't know how to do anything. Peterson said that's bullshit; everyone knows how to do something. I disagreed with him.

As I walk up the stairs to the third floor, I'm thinking how he'd take my sarcastic creamy peanut butter and raspberry jelly on seedless rye. My gut says it's not going to be good. I'm wearing a dirty white Pirate hat to fit in and I'm sitting in the back today. I'm still wearing my construction boots.

Class files in, and heat slowly hisses from the old hall pipes. I can see the trees of the front lawn, swaying in a slight autumn breeze. The tall blonde girl next to me is in a massive brace and crutches. She's a soccer player who fell down the steps in my dorm during a party two weeks ago. Peterson loves her. He points to her as our model of classroom dedication, as giving yourself to something greater than ourselves. The devil in me wants nothing more than for her to blurt out that she slipped down the stairs and tore her ACL all on her own.

Peterson usually wears his tweed jacket with patches. He's tall, salt and pepper beard. Today, he's just in cords and a white button-down shirt, sleeves rolled up, and a solid check tie. Means business. Immediately starts thumbing through the drafts and looking for comments. I readjust in my seat and wait for bad news.

"All right, so a lot of crap here to wade through. Gagliardi, terrible grammar but thanks for the info on oil changes. Thomas, lifeguard, eh, not much happening, even though I appreciate the inner-city spin. Boylan, now here's where we see effort, folks. How to rehab a torn ACL. Brings be back to my days in Amherst, working through a pretty similar patch of injuries, when I was playing tailback. Really like how much of you is in here."

Under my breath, I whispered to Boylan, "*Should have been how to do a keg stand, play beer pong, and not get injured at a kegger.*"

"Fennell, something we all need to hear?"

"No, sir."

"Well, coming from a man with an ironic PBJ paper,

I don't think you should be saying much."

"It comes out pretty well, sir."

The class giggles for a moment, but Peterson isn't amused.

"Ah, wise guy. Brooklyn, right? Wise guys seem to grow on trees down there."

He circles around the front of the class.

"So, this paper has absolutely nothing unique about you. Nothing. That was my charge, as you recall. Something you know, perhaps only you in this room know how to do, and make it be personal, precise, come to life. Correct?"

"Yeah. It's just, I'm drawing a blank, really."

"Well, I want to see one of those from you, on Wednesday. To be read in front of the group. *Capische*?"

"Another how-to?"

"Exactly."

I rolled my eyes and he caught me doing it.

"Problem with that, Mr. Fennell?"

"No, I'll give it more thought this time. Figure something out."

"Good. Next class. Let's turn our attention to the article assigned for today's discussion."

I looked out the window and didn't say a word today. College sucked. I had no clue what this guy wanted and what I'd spend the next two damn days writing about.

When it was over, I strolled over to the library and walked through the stacks. I found a quiet cubicle and folded my arms to rest my head. Peterson's office was across the way, in a tiny closet-like office. I waited for him to come back for office hours in an hour.

Other kids had something they could do. I didn't have a clue where to go. I wasn't a chef, mechanic, real video-gamer or tinkerer. I played baseball in high school, but nothing seemed original about that.

Peterson arrived like clockwork, with a striped scarf on and an English cap.

"Jonah, what can I do for you?"

"Dr. Peterson, any assist on ideas for this process piece? I'm not being a jerk, just drawing a blank on ideas."

"You do any work before you got to college? Play sports?"

"Both. Just having a tough time with the 'saying something about you' part."

"Listen, I didn't mean to bust your chops today, but I knew you could do better, stronger. Something else, maybe only you can do. Know what I'm saying? Processes don't have to be pedantic, ironic, or perfunctory. Try to make it unique. And I can't tell you how to do that. Dig down into things you've done that others haven't. Know what I'm saying."

"Think so. I'll get a draft going tonight. I did have

some odd jobs in the past, I guess."

"If you're going to be a good writer, I think you first have to dig down and see what matters early on, what you've already experienced."

"Makes sense. I'll do some real thinking on it."

I went to work for two hours making copies. Load the machine. Check for jams. Take jobs at the counter with the correct ticket info: duplex, 2-1, stapled and collated, booklets. Maybe this was it. But probably not. Seemed like a crap, work-study job that no one cared less about than me. I sat at my work station for a minute, tried to brainstorm ideas and had to listen to Sherry, the office worker, rattle on about the shows she was going to over the next six months: Def Leppard, Van Halen, Poison, ZZ Top, BonJovi… an endless stream of heavy rock, hair bands. I gave up.

I clocked out early and headed back. Needed to clear my head and get set on this. I walked across the lawn to the Grotto. Right before the chapel, an Eastern grey squirrel was being fed from the hand of one of the priests. He had dozens around him. Some climbed on him. He whistled and they descended from the trees, right there before the grotto and chapel. For a few minutes, I did nothing but marvel at Father Doctor Doolittle, feeding his squirrels with nuts and calling them by name. I walked back to the dorm to call my dad, thinking oddly about squirrels.

"Jonah, what's happening, buddy? How's college treating you?"

"It's all right. How you feeling?"

"Hanging in there. Not dead yet."

"Dad! Come on. You got to stay positive."

"I know. Those sessions take a lot out of you."

"I know. I'll be there to help pretty soon."

"You keep plugging at what you're doing. Don't worry about me."

"I do need your help with something, though."

"You need cash? I can send you a check for a few bucks if you need it. Girls? Being careful, right?"

"Dad! Just need your help with an essay."

"My help? You need my help with college work?"

"I do. I need help with a process topic."

"What the hell is that?"

"Describing how to do something."

"Oh… and you want to write about something I know? Really? *Exterminating*?"

"I am an exterminator's son. Was thinking it's kinda the only thing besides getting abused in a lumberyard that I know how to do. Peterson played baseball and football. Those seem like dead ends, done before. Maybe this would be different. Something he hasn't seen, you know? My first effort was a dud. Let's just say he didn't appreciate irony."

"Probably not wise trying to be a smart ass."

"Nope. Mind helping me fill in the details of a job?"

"Whoa, this is kinda cool. I mean, me helping you with college work. And writing nonetheless?"

"Don't get too crazy. Only one assignment, all right?"

"My pleasure to help. What're you thinking here?"

"What do you think works? There's a lot. Right? Too much, I think. I'd have to narrow it down a lot."

"Rats? Done plenty of those. How about when we bombed the lady's apartment when the roaches were in the teapot? Hahaha."

"Both too gross. I don't want to freak anyone out. I may have to read it aloud."

"You good with that?"

"I am, I think. Write about what you know. Right?"

"Heard that's how they do it."

"I'd thought a little about termite work."

"Not bad. Lot of steps and variables there."

"Or squirrel trapping? Crazy priest here talks to them and they walk all over him. Made it come to mind."

"A Pied Piper for squirrels."

"Wild, right? Dude could make you some money."

"You know, I think trapping could work. Contained. Clear steps. Let's just make sure we get precise with how it works—all the ins and outs, dos and don'ts."

"Sounds good to me."

"I've got all this shit downstairs. Will pull some of the brochures from the files and then we can break it down."

He went down to the office and I grabbed a notepad and Bic pen for an outline.

Dad consulted trap brochures and dug around in the file cabinets for all he had on our materials. We always used Havahart traps, which had tips on trap and release. Atop the brochure was a company slogan: **Havahart**. *For pests and predators. The trap that cages them as it catches them.* It admonished homeowners to feed families, not furry friends. The system was built to cage the wild creatures moving in to crawl spaces, attics, barns, garages, basements and barns.

It was made from galvanized wire mesh, resistant to rust and corrosion. It was ready for immediate use. You just had to select the model for the type of intruder. The 1020 with its gravity-action doors on both ends gave extra confidence for timid mice, voles and shrews. The 1025 had a spring-loaded door at both ends, perfect for rats, weasels, and flying squirrels. The 1077 was for squirrels and chipmunks. Skunks and rabbits usually got the 1078. A 1079 was useful for feral cats, raccoons, and woodchucks. And finally, the 1081 was the right choice if you were caging a bobcat, nutria, or small dog. A right cage for every size pest and predator.

We broke things down in the first steps: choosing equipment wisely and tips for identifying the trapped animal. Then, on to trap-baiting, cage-removing, and animal-releasing.

Instead of the exotic trapping of a rabbit with some vegetables or bread, I stuck with the common gray squirrels. Bacon and meats were good for minks and ferret. Raccoons, opossum and porcupine, you might go with some smoked fish or bacon. Muskrats liked parsnips, apples, and carrots. For the standard squirrel, we often just used a blob of chunky peanut butter. Sometimes, it was grains or seeds to go along with it. An occasional can of cat food went in the trap, mostly for raccoons. We set traps out on runways, in passageways or holes used often by the creature. Placement, like with rat traps, was crucial, in order to best lure the target pest in the correct runway.

The trapper's job was then to set the springs and wait. After a successful catch, your job was to remove the cage. You had to wear gloves and carry the cage by the handle. The real interesting trick was what you did when you left the attic. The trapper had to take the cage five miles away to release the squirrel. Anything less than that and the squirrel returned to its space, drawn back with its instinctual homing device. Squirrels worked their way back to their attic nests with speed and precision. Five miles away, in a park or nature preserve, the trapper stopped the vehicle and brought the cage out of the truck. The squirrel cage was set down, with the trigger door aimed for the trees, or the interior of a park. The trapper then pushed in the safety lever and pulled the door up, and out zoomed the squirrel, sometimes after a moment or two of hesitation. Sometimes, the squirrel needed some coaxing, some assurance that life wasn't about to end with a lever crushing down upon its head.

Often, you'd see the squirrel wait a few seconds. Its panting, heaving breast surging up and down. The tail cocked and ready for anything. Alarm sounds escaping from its mouth. The door to freedom was open. The squirrel bolted. Most times, the squirrel darted through the grass and pounced on the first waiting tree. It looked back from the base of the tree trunk, and continued its climb into the high reaches of the branches, where the leaves disguised its movements. Sometimes, they stopped and looked back. They spied the trapper letting go of the open trap door and picking up the empty cage. Wild releases always felt good, capturing the beast and removing it from someone's house. Mission accomplished. It was now free to roam, run the tops of trees, or settle down into the nook of an old tree trunk. Then, it would gather its acorns and rummage through garbage and avoid the dogs on park walks. I liked the ones who looked back with a gleam in their eye. At one moment, life was sealed shut and existence was waiting for the flood or the pain of the door being slammed down, forcefully on one's head. The next moment, a portal was lifted, and there was hyperventilation, until nerves sent it scurrying through the doorway and out into freedom. Every now and then, a squirrel looked back and was grateful for a second chance and another tree, another park.

I jotted it all down. Equipment. Baiting. Placement. Setting the trap. Removing the trap. Releasing the squirrel. All there.

"So, how about if we include an example from your past, my boy, of what *not* to do? A little comic relief?"

"Oh man, I forgot all about that."

"Well, let me refresh your memory."

So, he did and here's how it went. A squirrel was in the back of the truck. We forgot about it, honestly. One time we did that and the poor thing froze to death in the truck. This frantic guy had waited hours. We took him out of a house in Five Towns, worked all day, and were headed home. Right before we pulled up, I remembered him, so we turned around and went back to Marine Park.

Squirrel's nose was torn from his assaults on the cage. He'd dug red tracks through his fur and skin from the back-and-forth assaults on the metal bars. Frantically, he knocked the cage from side to side. Guttural sounds emanated from the back of the truck. He was pissed and scared.

We pulled up to Marine Park. Dad was beat and checking his messages. He motioned for me with his head to do the release. I went to the back and took the cage out gingerly. Squirrel banged the cage furiously and

I nearly dropped it twice. This guy meant business. I saw the terrified look in its eyes. He rattled the cage, but I held the top handle tight in my trembling, gloved fingers. His stomach heaved and he made intense alarm calls. I saw his heart beating through his fur with every lunge at the metal cage.

Dad always grabbed the cage bars freely with his calloused hands—he never worried about a scratch or a bite. His knuckles were nicked and his hands were hardened by forty years of work. The grunts stopped as I swung the cage forward. The heaving breaths of his lungs grew wilder. His heart must have been beating faster than ever before. I'm certain he sensed the end—a painful, trapped, creaturely death.

I placed the cage on the sidewalk, pushed the safety and opened the lever, then jumped back in anticipation. In my haste, I'd totally forgotten to aim the cage towards the park as I was supposed to do. Instead, the open door was turned toward the street and the houses across from the park. Squirrel was out and running; he ran across the road and went up the steps of a brick house. The now released squirrel stopped for a moment before some grocery bags that were propping open a screen door. He darted right in the front entrance to the home.

In pure, stunned amazement, Dad and I both stood there, staring.

Dad motioned me back to the truck. "In the car, now. Now!"

"Oh my god, what an idiot I am! Should we go back and leave a card?"

"I think you need to stay in school, son, because trap and release is not your strong suit."

We laughed as we drove off, but he was so right.

Dad and I ran through my outline with all the relevant details, including my comic misstep, one more time.

"Once you get it down, sleep on it and then read it again to yourself. Make sure you didn't leave anything out. Glad to listen, once you've got it on paper."

"Thanks. I can't tell you how much I appreciate it. I'll save you a copy."

"I'd like that. The fellas will get a kick out of that."

"You'll get a footnote as my information source and fact-checker."

"Good luck with it. Keep me posted."

I propped up my outline notes and started my draft on my Brother Word processor, a computer monitor with blinking yellow type, where you had to print one page at a time like an old typewriter.

Two days later, after some slight tweaks and revisions, it was on Peterson's desk when he walked into class on Wednesday.

Without a word, he picked it up and gave it a quick read. He still was eyeballing it during attendance.

"Mr. Fennell, this is most interesting and impressive. You did this kind of work?"

"Yeah, my father's company. I'm still a New York State Exterminator."

"No shit?"

The class laughed. And with that, he began to read "Trap and Release of Eastern Grey Squirrels." I sat frozen and nervous. I didn't want this read. Not to the class. Not out loud. Maybe it was the work, maybe a little class embarrassment. I don't know. Maybe I was pretending, hiding being an exterminator's son for as long as I could. I looked around and students were listening. Boylan in the brace nodded. When we reached my comic interlude, they laughed and I threw up my hands.

"Always room for comedy, right? Even in process pieces?"

"That's funny, Mr. Fennell. Should have left your business card."

"Exactly. I think I said that to the old man on the way home."

"Now, this is one I'm keeping. Straightforward. Gutsy. And with a sense of humor, mixed in-between. Well done there, Mr. Fennell."

"Come on, Professor, you're taking it home just in case those squirrels come back to the attic."

"Maybe that too."

We went on in class and I stayed back as Peterson packed up.

"You didn't seem like you wanted me to read that at first. How come?"

"I don't know. Kinda reveals that I've had to do shit work for a living. Seems like a lot of these kids haven't, to be honest."

"But that's a good thing."

"I don't know if it feels that way from where I'm sitting. Sometimes you'd like to forget some of that stuff and find some new directions in life."

"New directions are helpful. But don't feel regret or shame about where you came from and what you did to get here. No need to hide any of that. And if people look down on you because of it, that's about them, not you."

"I guess so, Professor. It's just sometimes you'd just like to walk away from having to kill things for a living, knowing your father had to do that to get us anywhere. Sometimes it just feels better to forget it."

"I hear you. Sure, there are plenty of things writers would like to forget about. Escape is a powerful tool. Not to be underestimated. Sometimes, though, by looking at what really happened, that's where we find the things we need to set straight, in order to get into anything else. Know what I'm saying?"

"Somewhat. It's heavy, like figuring out where you were, so you can get where you want to be."

"That about sums it up. Ever read Hemingway? Did my dissertation on him."

"Sure, we read *Old Man, Farewell to Arms, Sun Also Rises,* and a bunch of short stories. Some great stuff there: "Indian Camp"; "Big Two Hearted River"; "A Clean Well-Lighted Place"; "Soldier's Home"; "Hills Like White Elephants." Father Taylor, my junior-year high-school teacher, was a big fan. So was my dad, frankly."

"Both fathers have good tastes. Read *A Moveable Feast* sometime. Would be good for you. Hem said he decided to write one story about each thing he knew about. Always stuck with me. Think it's pretty damn good advice."

"Write about each thing you know. Course he was also walking around Paris and hanging in the cafes when he said that though, right? Not the worst place to stroll around, if you ask me."

"Not too bad at all. And worth a visit sometime in your future."

"Dad said that. Said there's some place kids pushed boats to each other. I don't know. He said he'd never get there."

"Perhaps you will, Mr. Fennell. That makes a difference."

"I guess you're right, Professor."

"Have a good day, Mr. Fennell."

"You too. And, um, Professor?"

"Yes?"

"Mind if I get your comments and grade on the paper? I got an A, right?"

"You got an A."

"The old man exterminator would really love to see what you thought in ink. He hasn't been exactly doing great lately."

"Sorry to hear that. My pleasure to share my thoughts with you and your father. He'll be proud of what you wrote. See you on Friday with my comments."

"Thank you, Professor. Appreciate the push and the extra chance."

"My pleasure."

I walked out to the hall. I had classes to go to and work to do. But I was thinking of Dad, working in Brooklyn, thinking about that phone call later on, when he'd hear about how our trap and release work went over in my college writing class. I thought about mailing my paper home so Dad could see our work together.

Routes and Masks, Ledges and Ladders

Winter break was not what any of us expected. The tree was decorated, but we barely lit the colored lights. The star on the tree was crooked and no one bothered to get on the ladder to fix it. Dad's treatments were once a week, and I took him to the chemo sessions down in Sheepshead Bay. We prodded him to go to Sloan, go back to a hospital he serviced for years. He thundered his refusal every time we asked, saying he'd never step foot back in there again. *Over my dead body* were his exact words. He lost weight, lost his hair. His gaunt face had slight stubble across it, and he stopped wearing his work shirts and jeans. His work boots hardened under the coffee table, a table now scattered with pill bottles and Solo cups of Ensure. He was never in the mood to eat. Never.

Dad stopped being able to go down the steps to the basement. Took too much out of him. Mom set him up on the couch upstairs first. By Christmas, we decided to get a hospital bed in there and rearrange the furniture.

A few days after Christmas, I took him to a treatment consultation. He'd been going for a few months while I was away. We talked on the phone then a couple of days a week. Small talk on school, sports, girls, work. Today, we drove down Ocean Avenue towards the bay. Mom's birthday was the next day. New Year's was three days ahead.

"The guys are strapped out there, Jonah. You wouldn't mind catching up on some of my missed routes for a bit, would you?"

"Of course. I'm here. In fact, been thinking about coming back permanently. I've got plenty of places to transfer to around the city. CUNY, Fordham…Got options."

"You stay where you're at. Don't give up on all that scholarship money. Doing well, and it will bring you places. Need to stick to your guns, kid."

"My *guns* are telling me to be around here more to make sure things stick together."

"Listen, everything is together. I don't want to get sucked into this shit. You'll regret it, and so will I. Pitching in like you do is great. Helps a lot. But you're not screwing things up there to get involved down here."

We drove past the rows of apartment houses leading to the bay. The ships were docked for the winter.

"Maybe we take one of the boats out of Sheepshead this spring? We never did that."

"I can't even get down the stairs, Jonah. Think I'm going fishing? I can barely get to the toilet without taking a break halfway. Way it is."

"It'll turn around. You just have to keep positive. Put a goal in front of you. Like fishing out of Sheepshead.

Catching a game at Shea. Heading upstate. Finish the 1954. Shit like that. Keep it simple, but positive."

"I feel like shit, kid. This crap they're filling me up with is like Drain-O. I feel like I'm being hollowed out inside."

"We can turn it around. See what he says today. Maybe there's another option besides them hooking you up to that damn drip."

"We'll see. Anything is better than this shit."

I parked in front. Dad had on a Giants sweatshirt and some grey sweats. His white sneakers looked strange to me, like he was a man out of costume. He carried today's *Daily News* under his arm. We checked in and he started reading about the Giants' NFL playoff chances and a couple of Hot Stove rumors for the Mets.

Dr. Seshadari called us in fifteen minutes after our scheduled time. He had on a brown suit and paisley tie. A green facemask was slung around his neck. He pulled it off over his head and tossed it on the desk.

"Doc, my son, Jonah. He's away at college. Come down to lug me around a bit and give a hand with the company while I'm going through treatment."

"Hello, young man. Please, both of you, take a seat."

We sat in the brown leather seats. Dr. Seshadari looked around his desk. "Please excuse me for just a moment. Water?"

"We're good, doc. Thanks."

He left. The office was clean and sterile like the other rooms in the clinic. On one of the file cabinets, I saw pictures of the doctor with two children. His diploma hung behind his desk, but I couldn't make out what colleges or medical schools he attended. There was one green plant in the corner, soaking in some winter light. I pointed to it. "Reminds me of that Brother Cyp story that Owen used to tell us, about plants and parent-teacher conferences?"

"*Madam, your son is a vegetable. I sit him by the window and water him twice a day.*"

"That guy was hilarious. He used to send me to the corner deli every week in high school, just to figure out what soups they had. *Mr. Fennell, run down to the deli and ask them what's special that they have for me.* I'd go back and forth three times for that guy before he'd make a decision."

"Always sounded like a character. Like when Owen said he was at the talk at St. John's. Trying to tape the speech by the ambassador of China on some old tape recorder and out comes blaring Barbra Streisand with 'I'm wearing second-hand clothes, second hand-clothes...' and he starts pounding the thing into the ground like he's in some Marx Brothers movie."

"Priceless. He was Mr. Mixed Metaphor. Like when he told Owen, *You don't change horses in the middle of the canoe.*"

"Right. Right. He, um, died right outside of Bishop Ford last year, right?"

"Yeah, he was putting up the Christmas crèche. He and someone else were halfway done, and he just sat down in a chair, went to sleep, and that was it."

"Not a bad way to go, actually. Peaceful. Doing something you like."

"I guess so. He did that every year, early in December. Just went to sleep right there besides the manger."

"Fitting."

Dr. Seshadari came in with a bulging folder of materials. I saw scan pictures and lots of other insurance materials. He put them on the desk and grabbed his desk phone to check a message. He called the front desk after that.

"Yes, reschedule tomorrow. Whatever my calendar suggests. Just confirm the reservation this evening."

The doctor adjusted his glasses.

"Ok, Jimmy. Well, we got the last blood work and scans back as I told you last week. You're a brave man. Tough. And a good man. A fighter. But, it looks like it's time to give up."

"What??"

"Whoa, so it got worse, doc?"

"I'm afraid so. Much worse."

"Are you fucking kidding me?"

"Jonah, ease up."

"Who the fuck says something like that?"

"I understand you're upset…"

"Upset? You just told him to give up? Who does that?"

"There are times when you realize that there isn't more that can be done."

"Then, you tell him what the options look like and offer shots at a Hail Mary. Come on, man, no one says give up. What's wrong with you?"

"Jonah, relax there. He can't change things."

"I'm not relaxing anything. That was fucked up."

"I'm sorry this is such difficult news. I understand how hard it is on you and your father and the family."

"You have to forgive him, doc. It's just a lot to put your head around, you know? I know it wasn't going good, but…"

"I'm sorry, Jimmy. I am. We tried what we could. Doesn't seem to be options left."

"Options left? What kind of bedside manner is this? It's like Mr. Roboto in here and you're just reading some data points and checking him out on the next flight."

"Jonah, back off here. Take it easy. You're not making anything here any better."

"I'm suggesting that we consider hospice alternatives. The cancer moved a lot more aggressively than we imagined. I'm sorry."

"Just sorry, here's some hospice and fuck off?"

Dad grabbed my shirt as I stood up and pushed me

towards the door. I cursed under my breath, ran my fingers through my hair and spun around in a circle.

"Go wait outside. I need to hear what he has to say about what's next without this bullshit from you."

"I'm truly sorry, young man. There is no easy way to handle any of this. But we need to be realistic about where we are."

"Next time you're doing research, Dr. Seshadari, how about looking to find bedside manner or anything resembling how a human being acts in these situations."

"You're upset, but…"

"Goddamn right!"

I walked into the hallway, crying. I wanted to pounce on Dr. Seshadari and beat him up and down the hall of his clinic. I listened at the doorway, leaning against the wall, as he gave Dad a packet of information about hospice nurses at home and hospices, in general. The scans showed a progression straight across Dad's chest. His scans were lit like a Christmas tree.

Dad walked out of the office and pointed to the exit.

"That's it? We walk out? Thanks for playing…"

"I need you to shut up, calm down, and let's get out of here."

We drove silently. I turned off the sports radio and listened to the tires on the road, the sound of the engine accelerating. Everything was blurred.

"You're not ape-shit pissed at what happened back there?"

"I'm shocked. Naturally. His matter-of-fact *give up* wasn't expected. No, it wasn't. But what is that going to do to change things? It is what it is and we have to face facts."

"We get a second opinion. We try something else, another doctor, that's what. Don't just listen to this shmuck."

"What do you think they're going to say? That they're going to experiment on me and make me a pin cushion for every drug on the planet? Come on, Jonah. If you'd kept your head on your shoulders, you would've seen the scans. It's spread across my chest. We'll talk to someone else, but it's pretty far gone, kid. They tried."

"Fucking bullshit. We should have just gone to Sloan in the first place instead of this crap hole in no man's land."

"Let's take it down a bit when we get back home. This anger isn't going to help your mom or Merry handle this. Hear me?"

"I'm sorry, but none of this is right. Isn't fair."

"Whoever said life is fair, kid. Come on, you know that. Sometimes it's just a crap sandwich and you got to deal with what you've been given. This is what we got."

"I hate all this fatalism. Like you've been on borrowed time since age fifteen. Drives me crazy! Just bullshit. You want to give up."

"If I wanted to give up, I would've checked out long time ago."

We drove for a minute. Dad looked out the window. I tried to focus on the road.

"You know what I could go for?"

"What?"

"Roll N Roaster."

"Really? You're hungry?"

"Surprisingly, yes."

"You got it. I'm buying."

We drove to the lot in Sheepshead Bay and I hopped out.

"Usual?"

"Roast Beef. Cheese Fries. Make it a shake as well."

"Split some onion rings?"

"Works for me, kid. Let's split the cheese fries too, if you don't mind. I'll never eat all that. Eyes are bigger than my stomach, you know."

I went inside the fast food place and people were happy. Two kids ran around with orange, brown and yellow balloons. One of the workers spun a wheel for free food, celebrating a birthday. She won a free sandwich. The waitresses ran behind the counter in super-short dresses and brown stockings. Even the older ones were eye candy. Place looked the same from the 1970s when Mom and Dad went on dates after meeting at a block party. I knew they came here after the movies, talking about life ahead, flirting, making crazy plans for the future. And now we were here.

I placed the order and went back to sit at a table and wait, instead of checking out waitresses. I rested my arms on the yellow Formica table and stared up at the frosted, yellow bulbs above the dining area, the grooved, up-and-down beams to the right of me. Families were here, first dates, friends catching up about work and sports. A retiree ahead of me stirred his lemonade. A kid at the other table squirted large mounds of ketchup on the plate in circular motions to make a mountain, until his dad told him to cut it out and put the bottle down. One guy in a leather jacket flicked his receipt in his fingers repeatedly as he paced, waiting for his order. He looked around and stared at his watch, like he had to be somewhere, anywhere but here.

I thought of years of family journeys here. A short night out to avoid our kitchen: roast beefs, cheese fries, onion rings, mozzarella sticks, chicken tenders, cheeseburgers, iced teas, and lemonades. How many times I took those times for granted. I stared out to the parking lot and Dad was staring back inside at me. We caught eyes. And I waved back with the receipt. He nodded his head, gave me a short salute, and they called my number.

I collected the food from the waitress in the short skirt and headed to the car.

"Think we should bring something back for everyone?"

"I think the plan was to get pizza for everyone when we got back. They probably ordered it already."

"Yeah, we messed up that one. Let's just drive down the bay and eat the sandwiches over by the boats. You can blame me for screwing up dinner."

"On you."

"Those waitress outfits never get old, huh? Been like that since I started dating your Mom. Comforting to know some things stay the same."

"That's the truth. So, it's brown jumpers. White shirts. Brown stockings. That's what you were thinking about?"

"Well, I'm not dead, Jonah. *Yet*."

We laughed as we drove down Emmons Avenue and parked near the fishing tackle shop and the old clam bar. The fishing boats sat idle, docked to the piers and bobbing slightly in the tides. A couple of fishermen sat with their poles, bucket, and tackle boxes on the concrete benches. A steady stroll of foot traffic worked its way down the marina. A kid held the hands of his parent as they both counted down, 3, 2, 1 before they launched him up into the sky, higher and higher, down the avenue, until the parents said it was enough, and the kid began to pout and whine.

Dad and I put the sandwiches on the dashboard. He sipped his vanilla milk shake and we put the onion rings and cheese fries on the console between us to share.

"You know what I remember? The boat we built."

"Loved that thing. Still out there behind the shed."

"Surprised the wisteria hasn't eaten it."

"It tried. Still tries. I won't let it. Saving that thing for my son. Hopefully it still floats until then."

"It'll float. We did a good job on that thing. Not like that damn raccoon cage I had you help me with."

"Rocky ate right through that thing."

"Grapes and cat food on paper plates. Can't believe I fed that thing with a bottle once."

"And walked around with him around your neck."

"Friends got a kick out of that. Exterminator with a pet raccoon."

"You didn't drown him. Isn't that what they wanted you to do?"

"Yeah, that lady was a cuckoo. Drowning baby raccoons. Nuts."

"We gave him a shot. He was just too damn big for the cage."

"He hung around for a while. You'd see him on the garage, waiting for a handout. Sure he finally made it down to the creek."

"So, you're really going to hang on to that boat? Give it to your kid?"

"I am. He or she should see I was able to build something. I mean, I may be a crappy carpenter, but that thing was seaworthy."

"You painted it over?"

"Yes, I got rid of the tags. Just blue and green now. My colors. Merry's Anchors and Whale. Other things I find cool. A rat even made it on there, believe it or not."

"Of all things. Merry did those for you."

"She did. She can paint. I mean, really well. I, of course, can't draw a stick figure. But I can do bubble letters in spray paint…"

"That crap. At least you're done with that garbage."

"I know you disapproved. Probably why I did it."

"To get back at me. Maybe I deserved it. Guess it could have been worse."

"I never got caught. Just something I had to do. Can't explain it."

"You don't have to explain. I know rebellion, believe me. Could have hightailed to the coast, I guess. You stuck around. Could count on you. I appreciate it."

"Lot of good happened. Certainly more good than not."

"Thanks for the second chance. That night, you know, that just wasn't me…that's why I needed to make amends, set it straight."

"I get it Dad. AA and such. Really helped there."

"I probably should have stuck with it fully. Such a thing as a dry drunk and that could be me, sometimes. I know it. Grumpy bastard."

"We never saw a repeat of that night. Just took awhile to see past it, you know?"

"I get it. My old man blamed me for burning down the house. I never forgave him for that. Never. You know, I saw him again, years later?"

"I didn't know that."

"Yeah, tracked him down. He wound up a wino on the Bowery. Dropped out of everything. Hobo. I guess I just needed to find him, look him in the eye."

"How come?"

"Maybe just to tell him I wasn't going to be him. Maybe came close though. Almost fucked it all up. All of it."

"What did he say when you saw him? What was it like?"

"It was nothing much. I gave him a few bucks. Told him I got married and was buying a company, having a kid, you. And I'd never be him. And, he just smiled. Turned his back and went away, really, with a shopping cart of crap. Most of him was gone anyway. Bottles of Ripple, rot gut."

"Never heard when and how he died?"

"Nah. Guess I didn't care. No one did. Assuming it must have been Potter's Field out on Hart Island. Dregs. Where they bury the indigent."

"Sad story. Give up on life. Die alone. Toting your stuff in a stolen shopping cart. Pretty tragic."

"True, kid. He drank himself down the drain. Now, I made plenty of mistakes, but I always kept people around me. Made sure I fixed all those things I broke. No matter how long it took. Only route to take in life, only way to live, if you ask me."

"Fix the things you break. Own up to it. Way to move forward."

"Sometimes you just have to take off the mask and own up to your shit. Sooner you can do that, the better."

We finished our food. The remnants I collected and tossed in the trash by the water.

"Thanks for the sandwich. Rats and gulls get a treat from me tonight. I can't remember what's it like to finish food anymore."

"And we have pizza waiting for us."

"That's right. And telling everybody the freaking great news. That should be a treat."

"We'll ease them into it. We've got a lot to figure out together."

"You just promise me one thing. Regardless of what happens with me, you stick to your own path, kid. Write, explore. Don't get stuck thinking you've got to do this, have to do that. That'll handcuff you forever. Do what you want to do, need to do. Do that, and you'll never work a day in your life."

"Rabbi always used to say, *If it can be fixed with money, it really isn't broken.*"

"Wish he banged that into my head years ago, I'm afraid."

"You fixed the things that mattered."

"I certainly tried."

We pulled up to the green house. Merry was there at the door. Dad walked slowly out of the car and toward her. He hugged her as she came to embrace him on the way in.

"How'd it go?" she asked. "Showing some signs it's taking?"

"Let's go in and sit down with everybody."

They were all there. Mom, Aunt Theresa, Uncle Owen, Merry, Dad and me. Dad caught his breath and sat on the edge of his hospital bed. Everyone came in with coffee cups. They offered us some, so I took a mug of black Colombian. As Dad spoke, he had copies of his scans in hand. He had results from his blood tests.

After the news, we made calls. Some prayed. Some looked up options. I carried the scans and test results to an oncologist, who agreed with the assessment and said he was sorry. I made phone calls across the country for an answer. We all did much of the same. Mom said novenas and sprinkled holy water on Dad. Dad said it burned. Merry painted things Dad liked and made sure his prescriptions were picked up.

We carried Dad to the toilet. Brought him nutrition shakes he couldn't swallow anymore. New Year's faded into memory, followed by a bleak, hard, cold January.

Dad didn't look good. The hospice nurse came by and

explained how it worked. The coffee table looked like a pharmacy counter, peppered with red Solo cups with nutrition shakes. Occasionally, I'd get Dad a little weed to ease the pain. He smoked it with his Marlboros.

Dad's gear was there, still, at the door. I used what I needed: a sprayer, a few empty traps, and his mask. I brought the stuff in every night when it wasn't in use and it sat there below the *Lunchtime Atop a Skyscraper* figures on the ledge of the stained-glass window.

In the stained-glass window box above the television were eleven statues of working men from *Lunchtime.* The stained-glass window had a yellow flower petal in the center, like a spiral seashell. The bulb petals were green on the bottom, red on the top. A smoky white glass allowed light to pour into the darker living area. The sandstone statues were collecting dust. They hadn't been moved or noticed in years. Mom and Dad had started collecting them years ago. Merry and I found the rest in the brightly lit stalls of the Union Square holiday market and in a New York collectible shop.

The statues were in shadow in a late afternoon sun, aligned precisely like the men in the famous photo— my great-uncle, one of them. The man in the middle, shirtless, eating a sandwich. Grandma needled him for years about being bare-chested in a cap for a picture. I thought it was perfect, just right for us.

Dad was now on a hospital bed staring ahead at the

TV and the figures on the ledge. His work days were over. We watched the Giants win a game in brutal subzero cold. We talked about their chances in the Super Bowl. And he grew worse by the day.

Two days later, I came downstairs in my South Brooklyn Exterminating shirt with the Coney Island Light on it.

"Need anything?"

"Sure could use a hand to the bathroom if you can manage it."

"No problem."

"Where you off to today?"

"Give Dee a hand at the track. Check in with McFade. Then, I'm doing the Rockaway stops."

"I even forget where I used to be out there."

I grabbed Dad by the arm. He was too weak to walk, or even shuffle his feet. I brought over the walker and propped him on it. I wheeled him through the dining room to the bathroom, grabbed him around the chest, feeling how slight his frame was now. He gasped for breath, like a fish on a shore. I lifted him and placed him on the seat. Gingerly, I helped pull his pants and diaper down. I gave him some privacy. He called out when he was done, and I brought in the wipes.

"Fucking unbelievable. To think that this is where it ends up. Diapers and your kid wiping your ass."

"You did as much for me, at one point."

"I just never imagined that this would be me. Ever."

I pulled up his sweats and, with his arm around my neck, lifted him up the walker and wheeled him back.

"Want the TV on?"

"Nah, I'm sick of that shit. And the good old movies come on later on Turner."

"Just so much sports analyses you can take, right?"

"Play the game already. Stop talking about it. I don't need stats on how the punter performs on Sundays during leap years for Christ's sake."

"Need anything before I head out?"

"Water. You're off to Rockaway later?"

"I am. Track first. Nursing homes. Rehab Center. Then back."

"Good."

He pointed to the men on the ledge. "It's funny. Ever since, I've been laid up in here, been actually looking at those guys on the beam. Seems like eons ago I was up there. That was some courage. Those Newfies, Indian guys working up there without safety nets. Look at the stuff they did."

"Maybe a little bit of crazy as well."

"You know it. A good dose of it. But they got shit done. Building stuff up there in thin air where jets fly. Crazy when you think about it, and how fast they got stuff done."

"Nanny never stopped teasing Uncle Will for being shirtless."

"Ragtag exiled Irishman, sent off to Newfoundland. Drinking whisky and bourbon up there. Talking in thick dialects. Tiptoeing across narrow beams of steel. No safety nets, nada. Just trusting the guy next to you to keep you safe, get the job done."

"I don't think you ever lost that sense. It stuck with you on many a ledge."

"I tried to keep it with me. Wanted to remember what they did was harder than what I'd do. Mattered. You were in something together up there. Was a long way down, but it was reaching for something better."

"Like remembering that kid you helped out in the barns."

"You remember that?"

"I don't forget."

"Makes me happy to know you held on to that. Keep it with you. Always someone who's on a worse ledge than you are."

"Dad, I've got tell you something.'

He is all attention, not a shade of drowsiness, not a hint of pain coming from his weathered face. His grizzly, stubble of a beard turns toward me. I'm worrying about breaking down right before him in a well of tears.

"I just have to tell you something. Been trying to say this for a long time. Just couldn't. Remember when we had that talk at the track awhile ago, about me wearing shorts and you kind of bailed me out, that time when the rats were all over the place?"

"Of course, that was hilarious."

The day crystallizes in his mind. I know he recounted it to friends numerous times, as he explained to his pals the reasons driving his son's white-collar college pursuits from a blue-collar beginning.

"Remember when I said to you... *What the hell do I have to do to* not *do this hellacious shit for a living?* And you told me to stay in school and do what I love? I am so sorry I ever said that. I can't tell you how much I appreciate the sacrifices you made for me and Mom and Merry. I never told you how much I admired you and your hard work. And there is no one I respect more. You kept going, even when it was impossible. Helped people as best you could. Strongest person I've ever known. And I am going to freaking miss you so much, man. I am. You never gave yourself enough credit for any of the things you did, what you overcame. But I know it now. I know the work, know the sacrifices. I know life isn't easy, isn't fair. Sometimes it's vicious and can cage you in if you let it. But you never gave in to it. You carried your weight, walked the ledge. Fought those demons of the past and made amends. Made it right. And I thank you, from the bottom of my heart."

Tears welled in his eyes, and he reached for my hand. He squeezed his fist tightly. Power tingled through those fingertips.

"You said a few times: *I don't know where the hell*

these kids came from, certainly not from me! Remember that? You were wrong about that Dad. I am who I am because I learned from you. I learned to never quit. I learned to work hard and make sacrifices for the things I believed in. I learned to never hide from my past. I am here today because of the things I learned from you. And I am grateful. I may not have always shown it, but I am *so* eternally grateful. I will never forget all that you did for me. Forget the writing, dreams of better things. I learned what I needed from you. I learned not to look down on anybody and to work with my hands. I learned how to handle adversity, and in a sea of troubles, never back down, never quit. I learned that an underdog needs courage, a strong will and relentless determination to succeed. You can't learn that from any book or any school. You may read it—but you need to live it to learn it. Words can't express how much I appreciate all that you did for us. All the good that happened around you, wasn't just some accident. It wasn't just some bit of luck that things worked out. It was because of you, your determination, your will to fight against the odds and never quit. This family fed off of you. We always will. I'm here today because of the lessons I learned from you. And I just needed to tell you that."

He is crying for the first time in my presence. Mom said he cried at my high-school graduation, as I walked awkwardly across St. Patrick's Cathedral in a tuxedo. I was the first Fennell to graduate from high school, first to go to college. Now he wiped his tears and re-gripped my hand. He patted my hands through clasped fists.

"Thank you, Dad. From the bottom of my heart. You never gave yourself enough credit. You were my hero in life. And I mean that. We may be different in some ways—

He laughed at this.

"But at our core, we are exactly the same. We come from the same place. We fixed things, patched things up when we needed to. I love you, man. Always will. And I will never forget what you did for me. I'm here, holding the ladder, always."

His lips quivered a moment. The strength in his fists returned. His hands were cupped together. The words welled up in his throat a minute. His head nodded repeatedly and then he said, "Thank you, Jonah. Thank you. For everything. You held it together for me. You even tidied up the mess I made. Always. This mean the world to me. Love you, pal. I'm really blessed to have people like you and Mer and your Mom. Blessed."

I wiped away my tears, as he did the same.

"Maybe I'll stay around today. Hang around a bit, to keep you company."

He stared at me intently. "Got to go to work, Jonah. Gotta go to work, pal. You got things to do."

"I can stay, do the route tomorrow. Can always play catch-up."

"Got to go to work, pal. I need you to go to work."

I looked at him, understanding that this meant something. The end. And I had to go to do Dad's work and find my way.

"OK. You sure?"

"Sure, son. Got to get to work."

I said my goodbyes to the family and returned to give Dad a hug and shake his hand and look at him intently, one last time. "Love you."

"I love you too, boy."

"Goodbye, Dad. God bless."

"Goodbye, pal. Already has."

I did the track in a haze and drove the usual route to Rockaway, turning down before the golf course on to Flatbush, past Floyd Bennett Field, and out over the Gil Hodges Marine Parkway Bridge. The old mask was next to me on the passenger's side. I glanced at it and thought about Dad wearing one like this on an airplane many years before. Stops were done mechanically. I don't remember anything. I drove under the elevated train near Arverne, when I got the urge to stop. I parked along a deserted street and went to the beach. It was abandoned. In the distance, I saw a man walking his dog and throwing a stick in the sand.

The waves roared on the shore. The skies were grey, and a steady stream of jets was in a landing pattern over Rockaway. I thought about Dad, about travel, about airport visits. I thought about the mask in my car, the ones we wore all our lives to keep out the toxic fumes and to keep our vision clear. A lot of haze was around us, always. I listened to the sea and said a prayer for Dad's soul.

I got back to work. And I knew already what happened when Merry called me to say things had gotten worse and come back. I knew all of this, as I made my way back to Brooklyn, slowly, giving the old man the time he needed.

I stopped at the parking lot in Floyd Bennett and walked across Flatbush to visit Horseshoe Bay, where Dad took me as a kid years ago. The glass shined even in the overcast skies. The papers from decades ago swayed in the compacted layers of years of landfill. Perfume jars and broken pottery. Broken graffitied boats lay moored on the water's edge, some of it mine. The cordgrass waved in the winds coming off the sea. In the distance I watched the cars on Gil Hodges Bridge. One boat lay anchored under the bridge, seeking some type of fish, and I knew my dad was gone.

I prayed for him, looking at years and years of detritus, washing up on the shores of time, and I felt peace. Tears came and I watched the waves intently, thinking about the little gems to be salvaged by pilgrims for years to come. I watched a boy and his father down the beach, the father telling the boy not to get cut by the broken glass and pointing out fascinating juts of glass, worn down by the sea water. They passed me with a nod and went on their way.

I went back through the reeds to the car. It was time to go back, time to mourn, and time to get to work. I drove home to my family, remembering days of being an exterminator's son, and ready to get to work at reliving and retelling what it was like.

Before the house, in the front garden patch, I saw Mom and Merry waiting for me. Under the flight path of the airport, the smell of jet fuel filled the air. It was everywhere. The cold winter air was brisk. There were other places to go, and the sky was filled with pink and grey shadows as the sun descended over the private houses of Marine Park, not so far away from ours. Dad was sixty years old. He died looking at the men on the ledge. His gear was at the door with his mask on top. A ladder sat idle in the backyard near his garden.

Merry's Eulogy

We sat in Good Shepherd Church with snow falling outside. Light still streamed through the stained-glass windows. Merry and I wrote the eulogy and I proofed it. I knew I wouldn't be able to read it, so she did. I wandered the church before we began and said prayers to St. Francis. Dad liked him. Thought he was a rebel. Mom carried her rosary and holy water from Lourdes. Dad would be buried in Greenwood, and I'd visit him there. Merry ascended to the pulpit and I recorded what she said:

"Jimmy 'Bugs' Fennell was not a church guy, but Good Shepherd holds special memories for him. He was married here thirty-five years ago. This is where my brother and I received the sacraments. It's where we were doused with holy water, ate the bread of life, and received the fire of the Holy Spirit.

"I think many of you could get up here and speak about my Dad. Each of you would have a different story to tell. But I do think we'd all start by saying the exact same thing about his integrity, honesty, generosity, intelligence, courage, his knowledge of all things bug, his dedication to his family.

"My Dad loved his work. And he loved to dream. I think he would have done the job for free. He built and rebuilt South Brooklyn Exterminating. He could name any insect and figure out how to bait anything. He'd climb a four-story ladder at any angle. He was fearless: crawled under houses, went out at all hours to pick up squirrels to save them from freezing to death, built a baby raccoon a shelter with my brother and raised it. He was a man of many contradictions. He quoted Emerson and said, "A foolish consistency is the hobgoblin of little minds." He wanted my brother and me to pursue something we loved to do. He said if we loved our work we'd never work a day in our lives. He didn't want us to exterminate, but he got a kick out of it when we did. I think he liked having painter-and-writer kids who also knew about rat-baiting, mosquito-dunks, and squirrel-trapping.

"My Dad said that our mom raised us, that the smartest thing he ever did was to have her stay home with us. She did everything, according to him. What he didn't realize was that we learned so much from his example. We learned the value of real, hard work. We learned about decency, fairness, and honesty. We learned about sacrifice and its rewards.

"My Dad was a character. He had a flair for colorful language. He wasn't perfect. He had his share of demons, like so many others, but he fought them and beat them. And when they got the better of him, he owned up to it, fixed it, and made amends for it.

"My Dad was smarter than he let on. He knew a lot about

so many things. He read far and wide, from archaeology to myth to history to baseball. He was always opinionated. He loved poems, movies, Egyptology, gardens and smoking cigarettes. He loved driving long country roads with good music on the radio. He loved model planes and collecting 1954 Topps cards with my brother.

"He loved his family. My Dad was tough and he told people the truth. He had the most expressive eyebrows. He preferred cash to credit and believed wholeheartedly in something his friend Rabbi Weinstein said often: If it can be fixed with money, it's not really worth worrying about.

"My Dad had no regrets and no real enemies. He had thirty pairs of blue jeans, two belts, and sixty South Brooklyn work shirts with Coney Island lighthouses on them, because Mom collected lighthouse. It's true.

"My Dad was strong. He cried once in my presence, when my brother graduated from high school in St. Patrick's Cathedral. I'm sure there were other times, but he did a good job shielding me from them. He shielded me from a lot of things.

"I don't know how one measures the value of a man's life. I suppose it's different for each of us. But I do know that my dad had a family who loved and believed in him, a successful business, and a dedication to hard work and dreaming big. I think that is quite a testament to the value of his life."

Safari

Rat College happened every year. I just finished graduate school when selected. I even forgot I entered to go. Maybe a lark, for old times' sake. Every year, the Department of Health ran workshops for professionals on rat control. This year, I was going. Not that I was working in the field anymore. More of a tourist, so to speak, with past connections. Besides, exterminators weren't exterminators anymore. Now the politically correct title was pest management professionals. Whatever that was. Dad would have laughed his ass off at this. No more mention of exterminating, or killing anything, God forbid. Just managing pests.

Dr. Coughlin led the seminars. He had a PhD in rodentology from Purdue and was a national expert. The lecture hall was packed: exterminators, parks department, sanitation. And me, a graduate in creative writing with a NYS Pest Control license.

Rat College was in downtown Manhattan. After the first break, I stayed back and wrote in my journal. Most of the guys went out for smokes. I had a copy of Whitman on my desk. Dr. Coughlin walked by and picked up my copy.

"Something tells me you may be a bit different from a few of our other participants. What's your story?"

"Great seminar, doc. I guess you could say that I'm coming from a different perspective. Still have my license, obviously, but I finished my MFA in fiction and poetry. Always wanted to come to this, though. My Dad came years ago and loved it. Said it was the best class experiences in the field he's ever had."

"No kidding. MFA, huh? I love writing. Poems especially. Been doing that since I got to Purdue. Who's your dad?"

"Jimmy Fennell. He was a past president of the association years ago. Passed a few years ago, unfortunately."

"What a character. Sorry to hear that. I remember him well. Smart fella, but a little rough around the edges, you'd say."

"Certainly could say that. He thought banning DDT was a federal crime. He had a lot of different sides."

"I remember him railing on about that. He paid attention, though. That he did. I actually remember him talking about you and your sister way back when. She's a painter, right?"

"Yeah, Merry. Photo realist."

"Pretty specific. Not interested in abstraction, I assume."

"Only marginally. We get a kick out of some of the lunacy of the current art scene."

It was a few days of seminar, including field trips

out into the urban laboratory of downtown Manhattan. We traced through alleyways of nineteenth-century New York. The rats were still there. We tracked them to burrows in parks, saw how they fed on our waste. We made notes on overflowing trash receptacles and saw trail marks right into buildings.

One day, we made our way as a group to the federal courthouse near Five Points. Dr. C had on his MTA security gear. He carried a backpack, had a notebook in his hand for field notes, and a flashlight. Outside the court there were dozens of burrows on the plaza. Parks Department workers, probably tipped off to our visit, were conveniently sliding granular bait down the holes with long plastic tubes.

Dr. C laughed at them. "So, what's wrong with this picture?"

"Overflowing cans. Plenty of food options. These animals are too smart for this. They'll just ignore the foreign bait in the hole and keep feeding until they shut down the fresh food supply."

Rat grease marks ran along the edge of the building and right into the service entrance to the court.

"Quite a remark on our criminal justice system, I'd say. Can't keep the rats out."

We finished the three-day seminar. Got a 96 on my final exam. And I stayed in touch with Dr. C. A few times, he asked me to count burrows in Brooklyn parks like Cadman Plaza and report back to him for the Department of Health. I pitched an idea about writing a magazine piece, sometime.

One day I got a call from him.

"Interested in going on safari?"

"Of course. Where to?"

"We'll meet up near South Street Seaport. Check on a few sites and then go to midtown. Maybe grab a beer afterward and catch up."

We met that night near South Street. The park was fenced off and going through a major renovation. Rats loved demolitions. Trash sites where people tossed their garbage over the fence. We sat there, watching them run at dusk. Trashcans overflowed and people still tossed trash on top.

We watched a lady balance a burger box and cold fries on top of a teetering tower of trash. It fell down the side and Dr. C walked over to talk.

"Ma'am why did you throw that there, when you see it's overflowing and probably going to wind up on the ground?"

"You need to mind your business, sir. I tossed it with the garbage. That's all."

"This is my business. I'm with the city, studying these health conditions."

"What health conditions? You giving out tickets?"

"No, ma'am, I'm just curious about how people act

when it comes to rats. Part of public health."

"Well, I'm minding my own business, and I don't know nothing about rats. They nasty."

"That's true, especially when we're feeding them."

"Not my problem. I just work around here. Not feeding them. There are nuts that do just that, like the pigeons."

"Right, but you see what you just did…"

"Not me, always clean up after myself. They need to keep on this trash."

He threw up his hands and we walked away.

"I'm telling you… I was watching this spot in Harlem a week ago. Couldn't figure it out. There's a school on the block. Out of the blue someone just starts throwing the trash mid-block. No rhyme, no reason. Sanitation doesn't pick it up because it's not where the usual pick up is, and lo and behold in a week, more people are doing it. I stopped one guy and asked him why he's tossing his kitchen scraps there all of a sudden. Really had no clue, but he said everyone else was doing it, so… "

"Makes no sense."

"Precisely. That's people, in general. No one had any clue why they were tossing trash there. Rats loved it. This thing grew to four feet high in two days. Not kidding, I took pictures. Makes you think we're the dumb ones after a while."

We made our way along the Battery and then headed

up to the African Burial Ground on Duane Street.

"President mentioned that he'd like to visit and we have this."

"Rat burrows in sacred ground?"

"That's right. And no one wants to take control to get rid of them. City issue. National parks. State. A mess of finger-pointing and voila—rats burrowing in sacred space and no one knows who should handle it."

As we approached rats ran from the mounds and along the memorial. They saw us coming and darted back to their holes. Dr. C spoke briefly with a ranger there, looked like he gave him some clean-up advice.

"You see why they're the third most successful mammal. It's because we don't think through what we do. Someone else will do it. Reason why they thrive down here and always have."

"That's pretty much a disgrace."

"And we're going to have the President visit with that happening? Come on!"

"What got you into these things? I mean, there are so many creatures to study. Why rats?"

"Because they're smart. They're survivors. And they take advantage of our laziness. Pretty incredible when you think of it."

"Smart creatures."

"With incredible instincts. They know when something's not right. You've got to outsmart them and too often, we're just playing right into their wheelhouse, making them thrive."

We left downtown and walked up to Bowling Green for an uptown train.

"Now, unfortunately, you can't really write about specifics when it comes to the MTA. Only vagaries. How it works. Where we're headed might be a little intense. These things don't get to you, do they?"

"Nah, I've been doing this work since I was like five years old. Tracks. Nursing homes. All of it."

"Ok, because we're going to be in some tight quarters and I want to try something out."

"No worries here."

"I'm thinking that this colony changes its eating habits, depending on the time the trash flows through. I've been keeping an eye on it for a couple of weeks. Think they've shifted habits, based on when the garbage train rolls through. Pretty incredible."

It was hot. I took out my notebook to jot down a few thoughts about where we were headed. We walked through a quiet station. Commuters rolled through hours ago, and we headed to the off-limits area just twenty feet from the platform. I saw them there. The rats running like a steady stream under the door. It's a trash room and they feasted on whatever's been left behind for pickup. As we approached, I heard them, through the door. Squeaks. A few skirmishes and squeals.

Dr. C banged on the door and pushed it in. There had to be over a hundred rats in this tiny room. They scattered in seconds, some out the very doorway were standing in, right by our feet. Some through cracks in the wall. Some were still in the garbage, moving the bags around, hoping we'll just forget they're there.

"Step in. Let's try something out."

"What are we trying?"

"Infrared camera. Cool piece of equipment I picked up."

I already felt the sweat building as the door shuts.

"Stay close. Stand super still. Not sure if they'll figure out if we're here. Let's see if they do."

He shut the light and we stood by the edge of the wall. In a minute, garbage began to rustle not more than six feet away. I heard scurrying overhead. I heard paws climbing up the side of the trash bin. The smell was awful... gag inducing. I saw Dr. C slowly bring the camera into infrared focus and rats started coming back. Sounds escalated. All kinds of trills and aggressive squeaks. More and more rats piled into the trash. Fights over food escalated. A rat ran right over my foot. They were everywhere. Eating. Fighting. Squealing.

Dr. C nodded his head. He didn't seem bothered a bit by our proximity to over a hundred rats. He just took his time and finished recording. The he tapped on the light with a flick of his flashlight. Once again, the rooms emptied in seconds.

"Amazing creatures."

I moved out of the door, sweat pouring down my face and my spine, shaking involuntarily.

"That was intense."

"You could say that. Really didn't pick up we were there. Interesting, huh?"

"A little terrifying."

"Let's grab a pint. Go back on safari another day."

"Welcome news."

We popped into an old Irish pub and ordered pints of Guinness a few blocks from the station.

"So, what are you writing about?"

"Thinking maybe a book about working with the old man."

"How long ago did he pass?"

"Couple of years ago. Cancer. He would have gotten quite a kick out of safari. I can tell you that much."

"What's the stickiest situation you guys were in?"

"I'd say days at the track. Time when they stopped paying for barns."

"Brilliant idea there."

"It was running, and I was a real genius those days. So, I worked shorts out to do the initial baiting. Was not my wisest choice or best day on the job. Said some dumb things to the old man I regretted."

"Like what?"

"Asked him how not to do this hellacious shit. Made me feel awful."

"Sure he didn't mind. He wanted you guys doing something different."

"He did. But I still shouldn't have said it."

"Cheers to Jimmy Fennell. Quite a character."

"Cheers."

"I lived with damn rats in a barn during my dissertation work. Only got nipped once, and that was crawling from underground. Put my hand on one on a ladder rung. Never saw it. In my opinion, nothing quite compares to the bites of divorce."

"That bad, huh?"

"Ever read Billy Collins's poem on it?"

"Can't say that I have."

"Once, two spoons in bed, now tined forks/ across a granite table and the knives they have hired."

"Powerful visuals there. When was your divorce?

"Four years ago. Brutal one. I kept the farm, though. Wasn't giving that up."

"Always thought that's how my folks would wind up. They didn't, but sure seemed like that would have been the way to go, all those years ago."

"I'm sure your pop was a hard guy to be married to. He was a tough character, with soft spots every now and then from what I saw. Like how he'd talk about you guys. You and your sister."

"He loved to harp on saying he had no clue where we came from."

"An Exterminator's Son. Sounds a lot better than a Son of a Pest Control Professional. PCP. Kind of loses the ring there, even though I'm all for these guys looking more professional, more Integrated Pest Management. It just loses a little something in the translation as a writer."

"*Exterminators* has a flare to it. Makes for a lot better stories in the long run."

"Sounds like it. Melville had his whale, right? Poe's raven. Maybe someday it'll be the rat. These things have stories to tell."

"Dad said the same and you're probably right. The Norway Rat, that isn't from Norway."

"Think your Dad would be taken aback that you're thinking about writing something about him?"

"Think so. Last thing he said to me was, got to go to work. I did and he died while I was doing his route that day."

"Like he knew."

I nodded. "Like he knew. Freaky."

"He'd be proud of you. He'd also enjoy the fact you're returning to your roots. Shows character. Something many are lacking these days."

"For a while after his death, I tried to set a lot straight… finish things we set off to do. Also finished a card collection we started… 1954 Topps. And, last year, I made a trip to Paris."

"Great city. Why there?"

"Dad mentioned this place years back. Said kids pushed boats back and forth to each other, across this little fountain. He said I should see that. See, we used to build and paint models together. Somehow, I knew I had to see that soon after he passed."

"How was it?"

"I went for a conference. It was just about one of the most moving things I've done. Hell, he told me about that when I was kid, exterminating the New York Yacht Club. Felt good to get there and see that. Something special. Can't put it fully to words."

"Something to write about. For sure."

"Definitely. And while I was there, I went to La Place de La Concorde. Used that title on a bad, sentimental piece I did years ago. My professor, guy named Peterson, ripped me for it. *No foreign titles. No foreign titles.* Well, I thought I had to visit."

"What'd you see? Pretty bloody history there."

"I know. I felt something would happen there and it kinda did. Was walking around the edge, and this guy in an Egyptian suit, like King Tut or something, was standing on a box. I didn't see him at first. When I got closer, he pointed at me and shook his head up and done. Dad loved Egyptian stuff. Collected all kinds of trinkets. First date he and my mom had—they went to the Egyptian collection at the Brooklyn Museum.

Seemed like Dad was giving me the nod or something. Hard to describe."

"Sounds like you had quite the eye-opening journey. An American Exterminator's Son in Paris."

"Doesn't have quite the Gershwin ring, but I'll take it. South Brooklyn Exterminating takes on the world."

"And lots of exterminating stories from the city to mull around."

"Well, I can't write about rats in subway stations, according to our friends running the trains. Maybe it'll be good to relate what it was like to do the job here."

"And someday, safari. Believe me, it has potential. Lots of stories with these animals. Just look around and you'll find them."

"Epic story of chasing down and outsmarting rats."

"Or protecting and feeding them, like some of our neighbors like to do."

"Just don't mention any of this happening in the subway."

"That's right."

We clinked glasses and laughed. Dr. C and I said our goodbyes, and I headed back to Brooklyn. As I waited for the train, I watched a rat come out from a garbage container in the middle of the platform and then slink back underneath the bin as the train pulled into the station. The man next to me shivered.

"Nasty things. They everywhere. Never get rid of them."

"That they are and you're probably right."

I was on a B train back to Marine Park. We'd go express to Kings Highway. I watched the downtown city lights as we came out of the tunnel at Grand Street. Brooklyn Bridge was off to the right. The harbor was empty, except for the Staten Island Ferry in the distance. A helicopter lifted off from its downtown pad. Cars rolled along the BQE. Bikers rolled on back to Brooklyn and people strolled the bridges. I had my notebook out and started jotting down story.

I thought back about what I'd left behind with Dad. Years in and out of places, handling bees, ants, termites, roaches, mice, rats, squirrels, raccoons, opossums, and even snakes. The train rolled on over the Manhattan Bridge towards Coney Island and I didn't feel a pang of regret for growing up an exterminator's son. What I learned to do and how to survive... Dad's sacrifices along my journeys.

I wrote my first description of him in that notebook in the tunnels beyond Atlantic Avenue:

Jimmy Bugs Fennell worked from the car, driving across New York with route cards on his passenger's seat and a storehouse of deadly chemicals in his trunk. Jimmy Fennell, licensed exterminator, killed pests for a living. He wore a dark blue work shirt, buttoned to the top, only the collar opened up for air. He had a pack of Marlboros in his breast pocket and a Parker pen next to it. A white t-shirt protruded from his chest. He had dark blue jeans, bought from Sears Roebuck, and construction boots laced to the top of his ankle. Men always wore belts on their pants. His belt was worn and brown, and he had a flashlight holster looped around the end of it. He always wore a baseball cap atop his jet-black hair and his glasses were steel-rimmed wire ones. His glasses dug trenches into the bridge of his nose, and when he took them off, they left a blood imprint behind them. His hazel eyes told stories of endless struggle and sorrow, and yet his face was often gentle and grizzled. A moustache formed the top part of his lip, and he worked in the world with a light shadow beard, which waited until the weekend for the razor.

His dark skin was leathery in spots. His hands were caked with dirt. His palms were worn and cracked from hard labor. His daily scrubbings with a nail brush and Lava soap did little to chip away at the grime embedded under his fingernails. He was a black Irishman. He passed for an Arab or Hispanic. His hat usually had cobwebs hanging from the brim or the filament hung across the back of his head like a drape. The threads blew during windstorms and made his head look as if ghosts clung to the back of his mind for dear life.

Jim Fennell was a hard man with soft edges, who wore many masks. Every night he carried his silver canister of poison into our home to avoid it's being stolen or frozen out in the cold. The handle dug trenches into his palm and made them callous. Broken blood vessels popped in his hands and blackened spots appeared under his fingertips. His jeans and work shirts were spotted with sweat. He peeled off his clothes only to sleep. When he rose in the morning, it was a new South Brooklyn Exterminating work shirt and jeans. He donned a pair of wool socks and laced up his muddy boots.

Outside the green house, he was a driven man with a ferocious temper. He worked as if the devil himself was at his heels stoking the fires of his engine. He drove the streets of New York enraged and edgy. His route card took him on a daily spin around the five boroughs of the city. His car was filled with paper bridge receipts and dirty soiled map books. Everything was stained with chemicals and soaked in the smoke of tobacco. Ashes drifted across the car mats and into the console crevices. The canisters of compressed aerosol spray rattled in the brown boxes in the trunk. Snap traps were loose on the floor of the backseat and a squirrel cage rested behind the driver's seat. Buckets of rat bricks were stored in the trunk. There were packets of poison pellets in individual bags and plastic jugs of liquid insecticide lined the back trunk of the vehicle. The entire car was a hazardous condition in constant motion. Combustible liquids shimmied in their containers and traps and cages shifted and squeaked in the stop-and-go traffic. To outside eyes, the car was a deathtrap on wheels. Cigarette butts burned holes in the carpet floors of the car and fast food *wrappers lay folded like a forest of paper under the seats. A porno magazine or two were rolled and squeezed into the spaces near the seat buckles, and quarters and dimes and pennies were tossed along the bottom well of the car for the daily toll baskets across and under city rivers.*

I closed my notebook and exited the train at Kings Highway, and walked past the old Dutch farmhouse, and past James Madison High School, all the way back into Marine Park. I kept going, right to the edge of Gerritsen Creek on Avenue U and stared at the Gil Hodges Bridge, flickering its lights to Rockaway in the distance. Jets passed overhead on the approach to Kennedy. A solitary boat anchored out in the distance with its searchlights on. Cars sped by going east and west on the avenue. A raccoon went to the water's edge of the creek to look for food. Ducks slept in the coves of the shore. A rowboat was hidden there out in the reeds, waiting for refinishing, I was sure of it. So were some stories. I turned around and walked through the soft lights of the park. Time to go back home and get to work.

Acknowledgments

So many people encouraged and guided me in getting this book into the world.

Thank you to the writers who made suggestions along the way, namely Vinnie Wilhelm, Rene Steinke, Andrew Cotto, Tobias Carroll, Robert Lopez, Johnny Evison, Ron Currie, and Charles Bock.

Thanks to my writing students and colleagues at St. Francis College, especially Allen Burdowski, Esther Klein, Tim Houlihan, Theo Gangi, Greg Tague, Lisa Paolucci, Scott Weiss, and especially Caroline Hagood, who pointed me in the right direction when I needed it.

Special thanks to the members of the Carroll Street Collective, particularly Mitch Levenberg and Jason Dubow.

I'm grateful to my friends and colleagues at the Brooklyn Book Festival, Whitman Initiative, Vol. 1 Brooklyn, and NewLiterary Project, and notably the mentorship of NewLit's Joseph Di Prisco, who kept pushing me upward and onward with this story.

Thank you to my agent, Liz Trupin-Pulli from JET Literary Associates, for her guidance and vision.

Much appreciation to my childhood friend, Paul Marciano, for living through some of the story with me.

I owe a huge debt to my best friend and literary traveler Frank Gaughan for his patience, wit, and wisdom.

And last, but not least, thank you to my family: Janet Briggs and the Long, Marney, McGrath, McPartlin, Fennell, and Maloney families; Bill and Kathy Gradante, Danielle and Manuel Sattig and the entire Sattig clan in Vienna and Munich; Paul O'Beirne, Ned O'Beirne, and my sister Jen Maloney, my aunt Eileen Sadlier, and my children, Dan, Charlotte, and James Maloney. And a special thank you to my uncle, Brother Owen Sadlier, OSF, who taught me that learning and writing were the keys while I was learning to walk.

Finally, much love to my wife, Lauren Maloney, who made so much of this possible with her quiet grace, heartfelt care, and unwavering support.

IAN S. MALONEY grew up in Marine Park, Brooklyn, where he worked as a NYS Pest Control Technician. He is currently Professor of Literature, Writing, and Publishing at St. Francis College, Director of the Jack Hazard Fellowship for the New Literary Project, and Contributor at *Vol. 1 Brooklyn*. Ian serves on the Literary Council for the Brooklyn Book Festival and on the Board for the Walt Whitman Initiative. He holds a PhD in English and Certificate in American Studies from the City University of New York Gradute Center.

.

Made in the USA
Middletown, DE
30 April 2024

53648344R00177